"This is a book for the offended, t _____ ͟o ͞ ͞͞
exposes the consequences of evil and the power of love and
forgiveness in Christ. It's a book for the moment!"
—*Pastor Tunde Cole, Nigeria*

"This book is as if it is downloaded from Heaven. The characters
became valued friends. Read it and ascend to new heights of love,
forgiveness and hope."
—*Sharon Johnson Gilbert, USA*

"Jealously, eny, resentment, betrayal, corrupted thoughts and
deeds...no cut card whatsoever. What happens when someone close
to home, living under your roof, displays such despicable, cavalier
and callous behavior? Just what do you do? What do you do when
you witness someone...whom you love so deeply, whom you would
sacrifice so much for, even your life...morally and ethically
deteriorate, right before your eyes?

'Love First to Forgive' provides the reader a front row seat for
witnessing the journey of sacrifice, victory, God's Power of
redemption, and unwavering forgiveness, and love. "Love First to
Forgive" reinforces the saying, 'it ain't over 'til God says it's over! A
powerful must read for all ages and cultures!"
—*Media and Management Strategist and*
Chairman of the Raymone K. Bain Companies, LLC,
Raymone K. Bain, USA

Love FIRST TO FORGIVE

Love FIRST TO FORGIVE

Only the Holy Spirit Can Change the Heart of a Sinner

SABRINA MARIA EVANS

Published by Passion for Purpose, LLC
Gaithersburg, Maryland
www.passionforpurpose.vip
hello@passionforpurpose.vip

For worldwide distribution.

Printed in the United States of America.

ISBN: 978-0-9962051-4-6

All Scripture verses taken from the Holy Bible, New King James Version.

Cover design by Sabrina Maria Evans.

Dedication

To God, our Awesome Father, whom I worship and love with all that
I am. To Jesus Christ, You reign over my heart. You're my
everything. And, to the Holy Spirit, my Helper, my Instructor,
my Love, and my one True Friend. I love You so much.
All of the credit for this book goes to You, Holy Spirit. I could not
have written one word without You. Thank you for the privilege,
Holy Spirit, to work with You on this project.

Acknowledgement

My sincere thanks and gratitude to my beautiful children I adore and am so grateful for having. I love you more than you know. To my spiritual mom, the Honorable Alexis M. Herman for all you do in my life and for being a mother to me. I love you so much. To my spiritual dad, the late Dr. Charles L. Franklin, for believing in me and supporting me. I miss you, Dad. To my biological Dad, Herman D. Evans, for being a precious Dad to me, I love you. To my biological mother, Margo H. Briggs and step-dad, Fernal J. Briggs, thank you for the roles you've played in my life, I honor you and love you. To Congressman Sanford D. Bishop for making time during your campaign to add the finishing touch, a meaning forward. I am forever grateful. To the cast members of the video trailer for this book: Kaelan Laurence (narrator), Margaret M. Gray (Nana), Chioma Jacleen Iwouha (Amelia), Dr. Vanessa Weaver (Margaret), Diane Yates (Mable), Joe Coleman, former lead singer of the Platters (Uncle Joe and narrator), Donald Tillman (Bruce), Phyllis T. Yates (Faith), Pastor Sylvester Bland (Mr. Smith, the Principal), Deione Hill-Briggs (Cheryl), Karina Helsel (cast member), and Lori Hendricks (cast member), I can't express enough gratitude for helping to make the trailer possible that serves the purpose of this book which is to share with families the message of GOD'S redemptive love through Christ for hope in HIM when its been lost through tragedies. To Caryliss Weaver for reviewing final edits in the last hour; I'm so grateful. To Raymone K. Bain for graciously writing the press release. To Prophet Peter Smith Onoriobe for endless prayers, fasting, and belief in this book. To Vincent Noble for all of your invaluable advise, counsel and encouragement. To Aubrey Anderson for input in the development one of the male characters. To Donald Tillman for editorial help and encouragement during the critical stages of finalization. To Gino Isaac, Ida Jallow, Stacy McGann, Prophet Michael Shakespear,

Apostle Patricia Slaughter, Pastor Rick Walker, and Pastor Kenneth Williams for your encouragement. To Monique Beidleman and the team members of Amazon's Create Space for editorial support. To Pastor Tunde Cole, Prophet Divine Angel Patimo and Sharon D. Gilbert Johnson for your devotion, love and appreciation for the amazing message in this book from GOD and your help to market and distribute it. I deeply love and appreciate each of you. Pastor Tunde and Sister Sharon, thank you for your endless help during edits. You have no idea how grateful I am. Sister Sharon, thank you for the collaboration in writing the description and my bio for this book. I appreciate your help more than you know. And lastly, to the mother and grandmother figures whose lives and stories always inspire me, especially my maternal grandmother, Hattie Edelen, Margaret Pitt Dozier, and the Godmother of the Civil Rights Movement in America, Dr. Dorothy I. Height.

Foreword

by US Congressman, Sanford D. Bishop

Forgiving others is an act of courage and a demonstration of a humble spirit. It takes humility to say I'm sorry and truly mean it. It takes courage to let go of past hurts, anger, and abuse. But, Sabrina Evans' book, "Love First to Forgive" is a powerful reminder that courage and humility are under girded first by love. Not "love" in the worldly, romantic sense, but real "love" that flows from the Presence of God in our hearts and in our lives. A love that says, "I can do all things through Jesus Christ, who strengthens me."

This is a book for individuals, for families, for anyone who has experienced or witnessed jealousy, lies, manipulation, and deceit. This is also a book of laughter and teachable moments that will inspire anyone who holds God's love in their hearts.

Amelia, could be anyone's daughter today, who's self-centered and willful spirit blinds her to the loving and spiritual foundation that her mother, Margaret, tried so hard to lay for her. Anyone of us, who has been blessed to have a strong, caring, and praying grandmother, would wish that the witty and joyful spirit of Amelia's grandmother, Nana, were ever present today in the lives of all of our children.

Sabrina Evans, a gifted, spiritual, and prophetic writer has once again opened the door to God's Word. This time, she has done it by letting us experience the power of a loving heart in Lynn, Amelia's archrival. She reveals how understanding and supportive families can lift us up and encourage us not to lose hope, despite the difficulty. Finally, she reminds us that God is ever present, especially in the midst of tragedy. I hope that you will enjoy reading, "Love First to Forgive" and be renewed in God's love as I was.

Introduction

A Message from the Honorable Alexis M. Herman

Dear reader, "Love First to Forgive" is a book that is truly written for these end times in which we are living. This is a book that will cause each of us to search our hearts for hidden sins, be it jealousy, greed or a multitude of others and, to ask the question are we Rapture ready? Are we ready to enter God's Kingdom with a joyful and clear heart and hear the words "well done, my good and faithful servant, well done." "Love First to Forgive" is a must read for the entire family. It teaches us that we have generational responsibility, not only to demonstrate real love for God, which is foundational, but it is real love that is required for salvation.

Prologue

Hi, I'm Nana, Amelia's grandmother...some people in this world don't stop pushing for personal gain until tragedy happens. The story of that game is about lies, manipulation, and deception. Only one person can change the heart of a sinner...the Holy Spirit, not any wisdom from man or power by man's might, no matter how much we may try. The changing of someone's heart only happens when they let the Holy Spirit in. We do as the Lord says, *"in all our ways acknowledge Him, and He shall direct our paths."*

This is a story about a young woman's changed heart, and the power of God's love and forgiveness—sometimes narrated by me.

—Nana

Chapter One

"Mable, is that you?" Nana's looking over her shoulder toward the sliding glass door that connects the back porch to the family room. It's Mable, Nana's twin sister, coming through the door. She uses her own set of keys to come in the house.

"Well, who else could it be?"

"Oh...Mable..." Nana looks. " You aren't the only one who has a set of keys to my house, dear."

"You're right about that! But, you know Margaret isn't coming over here at seven thirty in the morning, unless it's an emergency. Joe doesn't even use his keys, and Charlie..."

"Don't even say it." Nana stops her, putting her hand up.

They both laugh. Nana has three children: Joe, the oldest; Margaret, in the middle; and Charlie, the youngest, who's never around.

With her forehead slightly squeezed and a look of inquisitiveness on her face, Mable slowly walks toward the sofa, looking at Nana curiously. Holding a box of Nana's favorite Krispy Kreme doughnuts in one hand and a Starbucks mocha coffee in the other, Mable's standing for a few seconds suspicious of something she's wondering about. Nana's smiling, looking out at the array of blue colors gleaming from the bright sun in the beautiful morning skyline. Her house sits on several acres of land.

"*Sissssy!* Did you give Samuel a set of your house keys?"

Nana and Samuel have been courting one another for a year now. The children know him, but *not* that their relationship is getting more serious.

"I never said I did." Nana's still smiling.

"*Sissy!* You gave Samuel a set of house keys?"

"I don't know what you're talking about, Mable. But, inquiring minds would want to know?" Nana's chuckling a little.

"Oh my goodness! Well, as long as he's sent by the Good Lord and *not* the devil, that's *fine* by me!"

"Honey, let me tell you something, *right now.* If Samuel *was* sent by the devil, I'd have to *beat* him down myself and *pray* for forgiveness later! I agreed to be with the wrong man once in my life…Stanley. I'm not trying to do *that* again." Nana's been married twice. Stanley, her first husband, emotionally and verbally abused her for years. Frank, her second husband, was a good man. He truly loved her, but passed away ten years ago.

"Well, if that's the case, then I'd join you and we'd have to repent later!"

They laugh, because they've had their share of bad relationships in life and understand how painful they can be. Now, in their early seventies, they're looking forward to peace and joy, not drama.

"Now, can you *imagine* that?" Nana's laughing, looking over at Mable. "Two old ladies beatin' down an *old* man!" Nana's seventy-one, and Samuel's seventy-three.

"I know...right!" Mable laughs. "Can you imagine...trying to get up off the floor! 'Cause we'd probably *fall out* after trying to beat him down!"

Nana chuckles again, looking back out across the horizon, over the expanse of land in back of her house. "Huummm, life *certainly* is interesting. We have plans for the way *we think* things should turn out, only to find out sometimes, life ends up totally different than what we thought."

"That's why we have to make sure we're in the *Will of God* and not *ours!*" Mable looks at Nana.

"*Exactly*, Mable!"

Putting the box of glazed doughnuts and coffee on the table, Mable nestles back in the pillows of Nana's comfortable oversized sofa. Sighing, they both look at the bright-blue sky, forgetting about everything for a moment.

After a couple of minutes, Mable picks up her reading glasses on the end of a pretty, handcrafted sterling silver chain hanging around her neck and places them on top of her salt-and-pepper colored hair.

"So what are you doing out back this early, Sissy?"

"Oooh nothing. Just been sittin' out here all morning long, thinking and sipping on spearmint tea. You know I love my spearmint tea." Spearmint grows wild in Nana's backyard, so she brews a fresh pot just about every morning.

"'Bout what?"

Even though they laughed a moment ago, Mable senses that something is wrong.

"How this world is such a *different* place now. Nothin' like when we were children, Mable."

Breathing in Georgia's sweet spring air, Nana leans her head back, rocking in her favorite chair passed down from her great-grandmother, reminiscing about her childhood days. Somehow rocking in this chair always calms her spirit when she's the most upset.

"You can say that again, Sissy. It's different and *crazy* out here now days! Who would have ever thought we'd hear a Russian president say, 'the only things that interest me in the United States are Tupac Shakur, Allen Ginsberg, and Jackson Pollock!' *And*, that he doesn't need a *visa* to access their work!"

"See, you making my point, Mable! That's *exactly* the kind of thing I'm talkin' about!" Nana's picking up her tea to take another sip.

Mable laughs. "I don't know the other two guys, but I know Tupac. And, I just can't see a Russian president listening to Tupac!" Laughing again, Mable's trying to imagine this in her mind.

"Well, there's a whole lot we could say about that statement, you know! But, I will say this…the *good ol' days*, the way *we* knew them, are gone!" Nana's nodding her head, rocking back and forth in the rocking chair with her hands crossed over her lap.

"Sissy, you ain't *never* lied!"

"And, I ain't gonna start either! The truth is the truth!"

Sitting her purse on the floor, Mable's shaking her head. "It's so sad thinking about just how *much* times have changed. Between more natural disasters, terrorist attacks, wars, bombings, and hijackings, it's almost *frightening* going anywhere, traveling or otherwise. Look at the plane from Malaysia that went down. Two hundred and thirty-nine passengers and crew on board—missing! It's so sad, Sissy, so many young people on board!"

Exhaling, Mable looks off into Nana's beautiful, picturesque garden, forgetting for a moment about the hot doughnuts that just came out of the oven at Krispy Kreme. Nana's garden is beautifully landscaped and enclosed with tall privacy trees. It also includes a pond, a wrought-iron bench, rock works, bonsai-shaped trees, stone pillars, columbine flowers, orchids, and an assortment of pavilions. Flagstone and lights line the pathway leading from the house to her gorgeous garden. It's perfect for reflecting and enjoying peaceful moments. And, it's just the right kind of place one needs to escape from the world.

"Yup! See what I mean, Mable? Somebody probably hijacked *that* plane!"

Quickly coming back to reality, Mable grabs one of the doughnuts out of the box, forgetting to offer one to Nana.

"Sissy, I just *feel* for this younger generation coming up today!"

"The *younger* generation? You mean *our* generation! I feel for us! What can we do if "crazy" holds up Walgreens? I mean, don't get me wrong, I know Kung Fu, but the old gray mare ain't what she used to be!"

Bursting in laughter, Mable remembers when they were young, how Uncle Walter used to teach them martial arts techniques in the backyard after school. In those days, martial arts classes were unheard of. But, because Uncle Walter got his black belt when he lived in Japan for a year, he taught them how to defend themselves. However, their bodies are obviously not in the same condition they were then.

"I used to wonder what Momma meant; she said that all the time! I remember looking at her singing that song when we were in our early twenties, trying to understand what she meant. 'The old gray mare ain't what she used to be.' Then, after we turned forty-five, I *knew* what she meant!"

"Who you telling! If I don't get enough rest, I'm on the highway *to mess*, honey!"

Slapping their legs and laughing hard, they both sing together:

The old gray mare, she ain't what she used to be!

Ain't what she used to be!

Ain't what she used to be!

The old gray mare,

She ain't what she used to be!

Many long years ago!

Many long years ago!

Many long years ago!

The old gray mare,

She ain't what she used to be!

Many long years ago!

"Wheeeew! Boy, oh boy! That's so funny, Mable! Our bodies really do change over time!"

"Yup! From decade to decade, it's *always* something new going on and something else we have to adjust our minds to! I just wish Momma had told us what to expect in our later years!"

Momma wasn't much of a talker or a joker. She was serious by nature. She had lots of responsibilities, from working for Mrs. Willis in the next town over to caring for our own house; from cooking, cleaning, and overseeing homework to managing the financial affairs for our dad's family cotton business. Some Saturdays she'd even pick cotton herself. Time she hardly had, let alone enough to do extracurricular activities with us, except on holidays, but she worked just as hard those days too.

"Ooooh! How I *love* singing that song now!" Mable smiles. "It reminds me of Momma."

Nana smiles back at her.

Settling back down from laughing and singing, Nana wraps the large, colorful shawl a friend from Kenya gave her over her shoulders and takes a sip of tea. Nana loves big scarfs.

It's slightly nippy this morning, but nevertheless the cool breeze coming in through the screen door is pleasant. Nana so enjoys sitting on her back porch. After she retired, she refurbished it, having a custom-made porch built along with the Japanese-style garden, for days when she just wanted to come out back and relax.

"Let me have one of those doughnuts, Mable, before you eat 'em all up! Been watching my weight and sugar level, but with the way I feel right now, I could eat that *whole* box!"

Mable laughs. "Oh! Forgive me! I sure did forget to give you one, Sissy, and bought them for me and you! Here, go ta town! Help yourself!" Mable holds the box over toward Nana, grabbing a second one real quick first. "Here, take this napkin too."

"You know, Mable, the world is no crazier than some of the things going on in families right now, *including* ours! It's just new times, but same tricks! That 'old dragon' just been busy disguising himself in all of these different kinds of ways. I'm going to tell you something, Mable. It's one thing to know Jesus; it's another to be spiritually one with Him and baptized in the Holy Ghost! People need the Holy Ghost to truly live as Christians!"

Shaking her head in agreement, Mable uses the other hand to pull her shoes off, so she can prop her legs up on the sofa. Then, she gives Nana a serious look. "You got that right! 'Cause the only way to overcome the devil is by the Blood of Jesus and the *Power* of the *Holy Ghost!*"

"Amen! Amen!" Nana agrees. "There are Three that bear witness on earth! The Bible says, "and these Three agree as one.""

"Preach it up in here, Sissy! Come on, now!"

Mable throws her hand up in the air, starting to get excited, holding the doughnut in the other hand.

Nana and Mable are Spirit-filled women who've "been around," so to speak, and have witnessed the manifestation of the God's Power in their lives.

Moved in the Spirit, Nana points her index finger up toward the sky. "The Spirit!"

Mable slants her head to the right side. "The Water!"

Nana follows with, "And, the Blood!"

Mable puts the doughnut back in the box quickly, spreading her arms out, bowing her head, and praising God. "Yes! Yes! Yes! Thank You, God! We praise, You!"

Nana throws both arms up in the air, holding her doughnut in one hand with the napkin dangling under it. "We worship, You, and adore You, God! Thank You for the protection of the *Blood* and for giving us Your Spirit!"

They're both overcome in their love for the Lord.

Mable's lifting her head up to the ceiling. "Wheeeeeew! Yes, Lord! Thank You, Father!"

Mable knows, like Nana, the Holy Spirit helps us, and that He is our only True Friend.

Deep in her heart, Nana experiences an intimate moment of praise. "Amen! Amen! Amen! Just talking about Jesus and the Holy Ghost *moves* me! Because, I *love* the Lord!"

One thing about Nana…even though she loves to joke, she loves the Lord.

"Sissy, when I think about people out here today who don't have the Holy Spirit, it just saddens my heart."

"Mable, mine too. They have ears, but don't hear the Holy Spirit. They hear what they want to hear; that's the problem. They have eyes, but can't see or even understand the spiritual things of God, so that they can live the God kind of life we can only have in

Jesus. They're carnal minded, Mable, not spiritual. They don't think about spiritual things. They're always moved by their emotions and not the Holy Spirit. They don't know to pray or speak into someone's life, let alone their own. But, they know how to gossip and think about themselves. It's sad. In fact, many 'church folk' today don't live Christian lives like they say they do. They think they know the truth. But, the "truth" they think is true is a lie! That 'old devil', Satan, got 'em fooled sending false teachers, prophets, and pastors in churches. Then, you got those that turned away from the faith, if they didn't you wouldn't be hearing about so many scandals. You here 'em preaching inspirational messages directed by board members just to get a rise out of people, not spirit-led messages from the Holy Ghost! Who do they think they foolin'! Most of them just want your money! That's all. Instead of being led by the Holy Ghost, they're led by greediness!"

"That's *so* true! Isn't it such a shame? You don't experience the ministration of the Holy Spirit in many of these churches today. Yet, they say they know Jesus. What makes it even worse is that they don't really believe or practice what they're preachin' themselves!"

Still excited, Nana takes a quick bite of the doughnut. It makes her so upset.

"I know! People walk in with wheelchairs and diseases, and leave with them! It's really sad out here now. Some pastors just don't have the Holy Ghost. I wish they did and pray that they will. They send people back home and tell them to pray on their own…which they should be able truly…or, they tell them to go to the 'prayer warriors' in the church for prayer. It's just sad. And, the people…it's just so upsetting…most of them don't know how much they're lacking in the knowledge of God's Word."

"Yes, you're right. It's just so sad now, Sissy."

"See, Mable, what people need to do is seek their own personal relationship with the Holy Ghost, 'cause that's where the *Power* of God comes from through our union with Jesus. But, many don't. It's good to have people around you who you know can pray against the devil's works, but people need to know how to pray for themselves! And they don't, because it takes having understanding of who we are in the Lord, boldness to use the authority Jesus gives us in His Name and faith they say they have, but really don't. They're lost in the ways of the world and think like the world which is all about what they want, the flesh! Look at Amelia, my own grandbaby, for instance. Hate to say it, but she can't..."

Mable joins her in completing the sentence, looking with her eyebrows raised, knowing it's the truth.

"...see the *forest* for the trees!"

They just chuckle. Mable drinks some of her mocha coffee and picks her doughnut back up.

Nana looks upward. "Lord Jesus, *help* my grandbaby, Amelia. She is so lost, Lord!"

"But Sissy, it's true. Faith told me..." Mable pauses to reach for a sofa pillow to rest on her lap. Faith is Mable's granddaughter, Amelia's cousin. "...when Amelia used to go to church with her, she acted just like most of them church folk, claiming they know Jesus, hoopin' and hollerin', paying tithes just to please their conscience, but still acting like heathens!"

"I *know*, Mable. It pains me to agree, but it's true." Just talking about Amelia begins to upset Nana all over again. "All this stuff with Amelia has just been bothering me."

"Sissy, I *didn't* want to tell you what Faith told me last week about this older man Amelia's seeing now, but I *had* to, because she's your grandbaby. Faith says, he not only sells drugs, but organizes a ring of dealers and is abusing her on top of it all. I just feel so *bad* for Margaret, but we *have* to tell her."

Margaret is Amelia's mother.

"Mable, Amelia's heart just *isn't* in the right place and nobody can fix it, *but* Jesus. Lately, she's been raising Margaret's blood pressure up like never before!"

"Sissy, you know what old folk say, 'you can bring a horse to the water, but you *can't* make him drink it.'"

"Mable, I try to tell Amelia that all the time. But, she acts so double-minded. It's real simple, if we draw close to God, He'll draw close to us. She needs His help."

"But we have to *want* Jesus first, Sissy, and you know what Grandma Pitt used to say, 'some people just don't *want* Jesus.'"

"That's right. I remember. That's part of the reason why I'm worried about Amelia."

Mable's getting a little angry now, seeing the affect Amelia's having on Nana. So, she tries as much as she can to conceal her feelings for her sister's sake. But, she couldn't hold onto what both of them know is true.

"Sissy, I know you're upset, but we both know there's something deeper going on with Amelia. She's got issues!"

Hesitating, Nana sighs deeply and takes another sip of tea. All of a sudden, great distress comes over her face.

"I know. You're right. Amelia seems to have this 'hunger' to be approved in *everything* she does, because it fulfills this lack of adequacy in her. But, *now* it's out of control. You know, Mable, I *wish* instead of her turning to negative things, she would turn to Jesus."

"I agree. A mind and a heart like Amelia's is playground for the devil. It's no telling what's going to happen. I don't want to say this, but I have to, Sissy."

Mable pauses, looking at Nana seriously again.

"This situation with Amelia doesn't look good. I know she's your grandbaby. Heck, she's my great-niece. But, the *truth* is the *truth*. Amelia is just *too* manipulative and she tells *too* many lies."

"I know, Mable, that's why I've been out here all morning thinking and praying. You know, our 'will to choose' is such a *powerful* gift, 'cause it can help raise us up or bring us down. Unfortunately, Amelia chooses to force her opinions on people; be the center of attention; and consume conversations. It all has to stop or else she could end up in a place she'll regret forever."

Turning her head back toward the garden, Mable nods in total agreement. "Yes, and that place is *hell*."

Taking a deep breath, trying not to get too upset, Mable turns to watch the leaves on the trees blow a little in the soft wind as she squeezes the sofa pillow closer to her body.

"Sissy, just thinking about Amelia wears me out now, and I know it's the same for Faith. They were *so* close growing up. Po' baby, Faith, has *so* much love in her heart. She really wants the best for Amelia. It's so stressful for her. This is her first year at Spelman. She's trying to get adjusted to college life, but she's worried about Amelia at the same time."

"What you talkin' 'bout, Mable? For Faith? You mean for *all* of us! It's stressful for *all* of us! We're a close-knit family. When something's wrong with one of us, something is wrong with all of us!"

"That's true. That's true. It's just that I don't like to see Faith so fixated on Amelia's issues when she has papers to do and midterms to prepare for."

"I hear you. I'm concerned about Faith too. You know Amelia just stirs up so much strife and confusion for no reason, Mable. And, this older man you're talking about is fifteen years her senior. I'm glad Faith told me about him too. Did she tell you his name is Blake? He plays with her mind like a fiddle, trying to control her."

"Sissy, you know he's up to no good!"

"Absolutely! A man his age! With a girl her age! Of course!"

"A wolf in sheep's clothing is what he is!" Mable looks disgusted.

Still rocking in the chair with the large shawl wrapped around her shoulders and her hands crossed, Nana looks over at Mable with one eyebrow raised and a smirk on her face. "You know what men like him call girls like Amelia?"

"I sure do! Tenderonies! That's what they call 'em!"

"That's right! To him, Amelia's nothing, but a *"tenderony!"* I mean, just look at the girl! She's physically gorgeous! Pretty long hair! Beautiful skin! Has a body like a twenty-three-year-old woman! She's built like…as they used to say back in our day…a "brick house!" Why wouldn't he chase after a pretty young 'thang' like that? She looks just like her grandmomma!"

Nana chuckles a little. But, she's still serious about the situation. Mable chuckles with her, understanding she's just trying to find a little humor to break the severity of her concern. She can see the worried look in Nana's eyes.

"Your right Sissy, but she has a mind like a twelve-year-old!"

"True that! As the younger generation says!"

Stopping the rocking chair, Nana takes another sip of tea. Far off in the distance, she sees a family of deer walking near the edge of the property.

"You know, Mable, I'm really concerned for Amelia. I've been abused before. Been there, done that with Stanley. I know how emotional and verbal abuse tears the spirit *down*. It's just Satan, *himself*, raping someone spiritually through another person that allows themselves to be used by him."

Reaching for her cup of mocha coffee again, Mable takes her reading glasses off the top of her head to lay them on the table.

"Yeeees, Sissy, the devil sure can mentally and also physically bring someone down, *if* they let him. I worry about Margaret, because she doesn't know the half of what's going on with Amelia."

"I do too, Mable. It's a shame how we as parents think we know what's going on in our children's lives, yet sometimes can be absolutely clueless!"

"Yup! All in the Kool-Aid and *don't* know the flavor! That's why I thank God for Faith. She's been a wonderful granddaughter. She is so loving and kind, always trying to help others. And, I'm just so glad she can trust me."

"Yes, Mable, you are *indeed* blessed! Because, all I can say about my granddaughter, right now, is Lord *Jesus*, help her! You know, sometimes we can be our *own* worst enemy. It's just too much, Mable! Do you know…" Nana pauses fixing the pillow in the rocking chair behind her. "…my neighbor even saw Amelia in that man's car the other day? It was about two o'clock in the afternoon. He said they were driving down Linden Park Street over by Starbucks."

"What?" Mable's eyes get big as saucers. She's shocked. She knew Amelia was "off the chain," so to speak, but now she's convinced. "Sissy, high school doesn't let out 'til two-thirty!"

"I know! She skipped school!"

Mable can see anger really building up on Nana's face now. "She's been doing *so* well! On the honor roll and all! Mable, I just don't know how Margaret is going to *handle* all of this when she finds out!"

"You're right, Sissy! So, when are you going to tell her?"

Nana's just shaking her head.

"I haven't figured it all out yet. I'm trying to digest it myself, because I'm disgusted with it all. But, I tell you what I am going to do! I'm going to keep *praying* like I have been about it! Besides, I value Faith's trust in me too. I don't want her to feel like she can't confide in me as her great-aunt, but at the same time my granddaughter's life is hanging in the balance! So, I don't know yet, Mable. Margaret's got a *whole* lot on her plate! She's always at school for one issue or another. Just seems like Amelia enjoys starting trouble. You know how it is, Mable, at family gatherings. Somebody's always complaining about Amelia, either for something she said or did."

"You're right. I understand, but I believe in God for a solution."

"Exactly! Me too. That's why I'm going to keep praying about it 'cause she *truly* needs Jesus! I'm trusting that God is going to make a way for this girl somehow, someway. It's in His Word. He can make a way out of no way. He's a faithful God."

Mable nods in full agreement.

"Amen, Sissy! He sure can and He will!"

"Hm!" Nana glances over at Mable with a look of certainty on her face. "Did Faith also mention to you the situation with this girl at Amelia's school? According to Faith, Amelia evidently hates her." Suddenly, Nana draws a blank in her mind trying to remember the girl's name. Leaning her head back on the chair, she thinks out loud to herself, "*what* is that child's name?"

"Lynn?! You mean, Lynn." Mable looks at her.

"Yes! Yes! That's her name! Lynn! Lynn reminds me of Lia. Remember Lia, Mable? My best friend in high school?"

"Ah, excuse me? How many years ago was that?" Mable chuckles, leaning forward to drink the last bit of coffee left in her cup.

"Twenty-five! Why, thank you!" Nana's slanting her head to the side, with a big smile on her face and her hands on her hips under the shawl.

"You mean more like forty-nine...ma'am!" Mable laughs.

Nana laughs, rocking back and forth. "You wish! If Depends underwear couldn't verify my age range, you wouldn't know the difference!"

Mable's laughing hard now, because she just decided the other day to start using Depends once in a while, but hadn't told Nana yet. They usually talk about everything, but missed this one. Life has been so busy with family for both of them.

"Sissy! You too? I just started wearing them when I have to go out of the house for long periods of time!"

Nana's laughing. "Listen! It just got to the point where when I gotta go, I gotta go!"

"Sissy, I know what you mean! I got tired of trickling! Sorry to have to say that, but it's true! But, let's look at it this way: at least we're getting good exercise now, running back and forth to the bathroom!"

"Yes, honey, but thank God for whoever created Depends 'cause they sure do come in handy!"

Mable's laughing harder.

"Too bad Momma didn't tell us about this one either! Talk about singing the 'old gray mare'!"

"Hm! Somebody better tell these women in their forties to start doing those internal exercises we didn't know to do!"

"Yeah, Sissy, 'cause it's too late for us now! The old gray mares are just *that*—old...gray...mares!" She laughs.

Nana and Mable are laughing really hard now. It's so funny to them. They never thought they'd see the day where they would even consider wearing something like Depends.

Now, by the looks of Nana and Mable, one can't tell they're in their early seventies. They look about ten or more years younger.

Calming down, they both smile, thinking about how fast time has flown by.

"Wheeew! Lord, keep us!" Mable shakes her head.

Nana fixes her shawl that fell down while they were laughing.

"Yes, Lord! We need You!"

"Now, getting back to Lynn and Lia." Nana looks back at Mable. "Lynn reminds me so much of Lia. They're a lot alike. Outgoing, smart, friendly, athletic, and in the Lord. Just sweet people! I can't even say I don't understand this 'thing' Amelia has for Lynn, because I do. Amelia's competitiveness is all about fulfilling the feeling of insufficiency that's driving her crazy. I tell you, ever since Faith told me about this situation with Amelia and Lynn, I feel like something bad is about to happen. *Real* bad!"

"Yea! Me too! I don't know what, but it's not good." Mable's shaking her head no. "Ever since Faith told me a few days ago, I haven't been able to get it out my spirit, Sissy."

Moving the pillow from her lap, Mable's repositioning herself on the sofa, crossing her legs.

"Sissy, what do you think it's going to take for Amelia to *get* it?"

"I don't know, Mable. But, I feel like it might be something tragic, unfortunately."

Nana's worried look makes Mable's eyes get big again.

"Wooow! You know, Sissy, the last time you said that, it happened!"

"I know! That's why I'm so concerned about Amelia. We have to pray and fast *together* on this one, Mable!"

"Yeeees indeed! We most definitely do, Sissy!"

Crossing her arms over the shawl, Nana's rocking back and forth slowly. "It just vexes my spirit to see my child agonize over her own child. It's *so* embarrassing for Margaret. She feels like she can only talk to me and Joe. I just thank God she's close to me like Faith is to you, even though Faith is your granddaughter." Nana pauses. "Hey, do you remember what Grandma Pitt used to tell us growing up about a *gracious* spirit?"

Mable looks at her and they both say it together out loud.

"It's like honey! Good for the body, but better for the soul!"

"Ooooooh, how I miss Grandma Pitt!" Mable smiles thinking about the times when she was alive.

"Yes, Mable, me too! She was always *so* gracious in her ways. I just pray God gives me a gracious spirit like Grandma Pitt to deal with Amelia, in the *right* way! Because, my flesh wants to *slap her* upside the head one way and down the other!"

Mable laughs. "Grandma Pitt sure was a *wise* old woman! Remember she used to tell us, 'it's easier to do something for God that we don't want to do when you fear Him, than to do it for ourselves'? When somebody made Grandma Pitt mad, she didn't let it get to her. She was the *epitome* of grace. With most folk, they're downright mad, there's none to be found."

"Yea," Nana says, "you're wondering and thinking...but, I thought you said you love Jesus?"

They both laugh, just having a little fun.

"Seriously, that's why it takes a *willing* heart to be led by the Holy Ghost!"

"Amen to that, Sissy!"

"You know, Mable, it's a good thing Amelia's my grandbaby and that I love her. 'Cause I tell you what. If she were my *daughter* I'd might have to say, 'don't let the door hitcha where the Good Lord splitcha! My children know me.'"

Nana has that certain look in her eye when she lets you know she's not dealing with any mess.

"Mable, you *know* I don't do mess! And at *our* age, I'm not letting nobody 'stress me up,' as Grandma Pitt used to say!"

Grandma Pitt was African, and even though she became "Americanized living in the States for a while," she maintained her way of handling things in order to keep peace around her. She knew how to keep her distance and what to allow in her space, and what not to allow. Grandma Pitt didn't let anybody bring her stress. Grandma Pitt was very strict about certain things.

Mable's still laughing remembering Grandma Pitt. "Sissy, it's funny, but it ain't funny!"

"Mable, we've lived *long* enough to know that a *wise* woman can either *build* her house up or *tear* it down just like the Bible says!"

Mable looks straight at her. "And, by her *own* madness!"

Nana has a look of disgust on her face thinking about all of the things Amelia's doing. "Amelia's only seventeen years old and look at what she's doing already! I believe it's her Daddy! She got them evil ways from her Daddy, Joel! I believe it's a generational *curse* from his family! That's where it comes from!"

Looking at Nana with both of her eyebrows up, Mable's making a smirk on her face. "Ya know! You just might be right."

Nana's shaking her head slowly. "'Cause something just isn't *right*, Mable! Margaret told me Joel had a lot of problems with his

Daddy growing up too. I knew *something* was wrong the first day
Margaret started dating him. I tried to tell her to pray and ask God if
he was the right man for her. Seven years later, she ended up at my
doorstep with the kids *crying*. He left her for his secretary; a pretty
young thang! Margaret didn't trust her from the day he hired her.
But, that's all hindsight now!"

"Sure is! Glad you know!"

"That's why we have to *listen* to the Holy Ghost, Mable!"

"You right about that, Sissy! Though these days, some folk
make you wonder whose voice they really *do* hear!"

"It took Margaret seven years to heal behind that **fool**! We
were all devastated. She was, the kids were, and I most definitely
was, because they were in my house for a *long* time!"

"I was so upset when you told me he left them, Sissy."

"To think a man could vanish in thin air the way Joel did! My
goodness!"

Mad for Margaret, Mable releases her anger with disgust. "It
was abandonment!"

"It sure was! And, those kids never heard from him again!
Bruce was only six and a half and Amelia was five. Bruce managed
with the help of Joe, but Amelia got worse over the years."

"Joel's absence sure did a number on Amelia. Ever since he's
been gone, she's been looking for love in all the wrong places."

At this point, Nana's clutching her lips together, shaking her
head.

"And, in all the *wrong* ways!" Mable agrees. "It's amazing the
effect we can have on our children."

"Yeeees, honey! It's the truth! That's why I thank Jesus for Joe. He really helps Margaret a lot. When they left my house to go back home for the first time, Joe had just won his first of many BET Awards for 'Best Male Gospel Singer' of the year and was in the middle of recording his fifth CD. But, for Margaret and the kids, he put his career on hold for six months to live with them. That Joe, he's been more like a daddy than an uncle to them kids."

"You know, Sissy, Joe's always had good morals and values. I've always loved that about him."

"Well, where do you think he gets them from?"

Nana laughs.

"The Good Lord!" Mable chuckles and smiles.

Nana leans her head back on the chair. "OK, OK! You got me on that one! But, you're right. Joe's always been like that, because he puts Jesus first in his life."

"And, thank God for it!" Mable agrees, looking into the yard.

"Now Charlie, he's a different story!"

"You can say that again!"

"He acts like a runaway slave! Can't pull him away from Wall Street for nothing! Being a stockbroker, he makes good money, buys a new car every year and has a beautiful condo. But, he stopped going to church, keeping up with family and friends, and only comes home once a year for Christmas. What's it worth to gain the world and lose your soul?" Nana sighs. "It doesn't matter what's going on! Charlie ain't leavin' that Wall Street for nothing, honey! We can't count on him at all! The only person who can count on Charlie is himself!"

Mable looks at Nana, pointing her finger.

"See! That's what I'm talking about with people in this *crazy* world! People are just out for themselves now!"

Nana leans up in the chair. "It's just too bad Amelia doesn't realize how caught up she is in her own cords of sin, trying to please herself rather than God, kind of like Charlie."

"I know. This thing she's trying to do to Lynn is downright *mean*, Sissy!"

"Being a fool is all she's being, Mable! It's like Proverbs 10:18! She's hiding her hatred for Lynn and to top it off…she's slandering her! Just pure foolishness and wickedness!"

"Sissy, if something doesn't give…" Mable takes a deep sigh.

"And, soon!" Nana interrupts, looking at her.

Then, they both say together, "It's going to be a disaster!"

The weight of thinking about it all again is starting to take a toll on Nana. She's beginning to feel real bad for Amelia and Margaret. Though they've been joking off and on about the situation, in her heart she loves Amelia so much; that's her only granddaughter. Putting her hands together, Nana's closing her eyes and starting to pray. Mable looks at her and bows her head.

"*Father, in the Name of Jesus, we worship You and honor You. Great is Your Faithfulness!*"

"*Yes, Lord!*" Mable agrees, slightly moving her head back and forth.

"*Thank You for Your Love! Thank You, for Your kindness!*" Nana shouts, looking upward.

"Yeeees, Father!" Mable shouts.

"We magnify Your Holy Name, God! We adore, You!"

"Yeeees, God!"

"You're exalted above all! Thank You, Father! We love, You!"

"We love You, God!"

    "Thank You, God. We worship, You. We worship, You. Thank You for Your grace that keeps us day by day. Your love fills our hearts. We adore, You, God. There's none like You. "

    "Yes, God! The whole earth is Yours and all that is in it. Your Name will be glorified always, God."

Pausing a moment, Nana's moving in the spirit, connecting with God in her heart, nodding her head a little.

    "God, my grandbaby, Amelia, has so much confusion and hatred in her heart. But, I know with You all things are possible. Thank You, God, for the Name Jesus and the Power in it. We have authority through the Name, Jesus. We have authority through Jesus to rule over demons and all power of darkness. Lord, You said where two or three are gathered, You are in their midst. Thank You, Lord, for being with us, right now. We pray that the feelings in Amelia's heart be replaced with love, kindness and confidence in You. We break the influence of devils over her life by the Power of the Holy Ghost, in the Name of Jesus Christ! We break the stronghold over her mind, in the Name of the Lord Jesus Christ! We cancel the plans of the devil against, Amelia, in the Name of Jesus Christ! We declare, the devil has no influence over her mind again, in the Name of the Lord Jesus Christ! Every plan to use Amelia for evil, we cancel, in the Name of Jesus Christ! No weapon fastened against Amelia shall prosper, in the Name of Jesus Christ!

    Lead her to the cross, Lord! Use her disadvantages for Your Good! We declare love, forgiveness, and righteousness shall reign in Amelia's heart to the Glory of Your Holy Name, Lord! We break the chains of destruction in Ameila's life, in Jesus Christ's Name!"

"Yeeeees, Lord! Yes, Lord!" Mable's swaying from side to side, praying in the Holy Ghost.

"Teach Amelia Your ways, O Lord! And show her Your path! Pardon her iniquities and cause her to fear You!"

"Yes, Lord! Yes!"

"Oooooh yes, Lord! Thank You for confirming Your Word! Yes, Lord! Thank You for creating a new heart in Amelia! All glory and honor are Yours! It is done! It is done, in Jesus Christ's Name!"

Then, they both say together, *"Alleluuuuia! Alleluuuuuia! Ameeeen!"*

Nana starts rocking her body back and forth in the chair, holding her arms over her chest, praying in the Holy Ghost.

"Wheeeew, I got chills all over my body! Thank You, Jesus! Wheeew! They're all over me! Thank You, Jesus! Thank You, Lord for the confirmation!"

"Praise the Lord!" Mable's still swaying side to side, praying in the Holy Spirit.

Nana takes a deep sigh of relief.

"Thank You, Jesus."

Rubbing her arms now, Nana looks over at Mable, "hatred stirs strife, but *love* covers sins."

Chapter Two

Lately, Amelia's been talking to Blake on the phone a lot. She met him about two months ago at Starbucks after basketball practice. It was cold a day. Amelia had a taste for her usual…vanilla Frappuccino and lemon pound cake. There he stood at the condiment bar, picking up a straw when she walked through the door. He saw her, but she didn't see him. After paying the cashier, Amelia walked over to the same station to get some napkins. He called her all the time and surprised her with little gifts after school. The rest is history…she started"falling in love."

"Heeey, baby." Amelia lies back on the pillows in her bed, smiling, talking in a tender voice. "I *miss* you."

"You too, baby," Blake whispers, looking over his shoulder.

Suddenly her face changes as she senses something different in his tone.

"Baby, why are you whispering?"

"I just woke up. You know how my voice is when I first wake up."

Not so convinced, she tries to bury her curiosity, quickly changing the subject. She didn't want to believe anything negative about him.

"Baby, let's Skype!"

"Good morning, honey," says a woman's voice, out of nowhere, in a very sensual way. Sitting up, Amelia's holding the cell phone with one hand to her ear while she's placing other on her hip.

"Who is that?"

"What are you *talking* about?"

"I heard a woman's voice just now!" Amelia's looking stunned.

"Are you *crazy*? What's wrong with you 'numbskull'? Haven't I told you that I keep the TV on at night sometimes?" Blake raises his voice, but still with a whisper.

"Why are you *yelling* at me, Blake? I *know* what I heard!"

"Here you go again, acting like a kindergartener! You think I'm stupid?" Blake whispers loudly in a degrading tone.

"I told you before that I don't like you calling me a kindergartener!"

"Then stop *acting* like one! *Look*, you're pissing me off now, I gotta go!" Blake's tone is really bad. He knows what he's doing. He knows an argument is a creative way to get off the phone with her. And, Amelia falls into the trap.

"OK, OK, calm down! I was only *asking*. It sounded like there was *a woman* right next to you." She doesn't want to make Blake any more upset than he obviously is, so she tries to quickly bring peace back to the conversation, but it's not working with Blake who has his own agenda.

"*Look*, I'm a thirty-five-year-old man. I don't have *time* to play games. I'll talk to you later." Click. Blake hangs the phone up on her.

Amelia is shocked. She holds the phone looking at it as if to say, "what in the world just happened?"

Dropping her cell phone next to her on the bed, Amelia falls back on the pillows in utter amazement thinking out loud, "what just happened?" She's experienced Blake's temper a few times before, but not like this.

The phone rings.

Sitting up as quick as she can, Amelia grabs the phone thinking it's Blake calling to apologize. "Baby, what's going...?"

"'Baby'? Who are you talking to at eight o'clock on a Saturday calling 'Baby'?"

It's Faith, her cousin. For the past seven months since Faith started college, she's faithfully called Amelia every Saturday morning to check in with her.

"Faith?" Amelia's looking surprised, but she's disturbed it's not Blake.

"Yes. That would be my name."

"Oh, I didn't know it was you. Thought you were someone else." Rolling her eyes, Amelia plops back on the pillows again. She's so disappointed it's not Blake.

Really curious now, Faith stops in the middle of what she's doing. She woke up early this morning to get a head start with everything, cleaning up her room and washing clothes before studying.

"Well, that's obvious. The question though is…who did you *think* I was?"

Putting one hand over her forehead, Amelia shakes her head. She's really agitated, because she hates when Blake treats her that way. He only started speaking to her like that as of recent.

"Nobody, OK?"

"OK, here we go. Amelia, you must think I'm *stupid*. Please don't play me like you do everyone else. You know, *I know* you. Now, who were you calling 'Baby'?"

Standing in the middle of her dorm room, Faith's holding clothes she gathered to wash, waiting for Amelia's response.

"I said *nobody*, OK?" Turning over, Amelia punches the pillow hard. She doesn't want Faith to know she's upset.

"Oh my goodness! It's *Blake*, isn't it? You're still talking to that man! I can't believe you!"

"No! I'm not! OK!"

Dropping her clothes in the laundry basket at her feet, Faith puts one hand on her hip, slants her head, and sighs with a look of surprise and disgust on her face at the same time. She doesn't like Blake for all the reasons she told Nana and her grandmother Mable.

"Amelia, you're *lying*. I hear it in your voice. I can *always* tell when you're lying. You just don't get it, do you? You're playing with *fire*! You *told* me you were going to call it off with him!"

"Listen, I *know* what I'm doing. It's all good. I love him and he loves me."

"What? *Love* now? Girl, you're playing in a lion's den and you don't even know it! Amelia, if you don't leave that man alone, you're gonna get your *head* bitten off! Better yet, eaten too! The longer you stay with him, the harder it is to get away!"

Worried about Amelia, Faith's crossing her arms, still standing in the middle of her dorm room, looking at the clock. She has so much to do before she starts studying today.

"Faith, I'm *not* in a lion's den. Like I said, he loves me and I love him. *Everything's* going to be OK." Amelia's sitting up in the bed.

Taking a deep breath, Faith sighs. "In your dreams! See…I knew something was wrong with you! *You* just don't seem to understand. You're *messing* with a dangerous man, Amelia. Listen, I *don't* want to see you get hurt, Amelia. For the last time, *please* leave this man alone!"

"Faith, please! It's not even like what you say. He gives me attention and buys things for me, okay."

Amelia's trying her best to convince her, but Faith knows different; she's not stupid. She's had a little more experience than Amelia dealing with abuse in helping other friends who were caught up in the lies and deception. In fact, more than she wants to admit.

"I *bet* he does, and for one reason only!"

"See? Like I said. You don't get it, Faith! You think he's this *bad* guy, but he's not."

"Amelia, you're fooling yourself if you don't think that one day he's not going to *expect* you to pay up!"

"Faith, you don't know what you're talking about, OK." Feeling so frustrated, Amelia's looking at the ceiling, trying to fight back tears. "I *know* he loves me."

"Wow, Amelia! As tough as you are in school and with other people, you mean to tell me you're falling for this loser?"

Unable to hold back her tears, Amelia's voice drops noticeably from the disappointment. She feels unsettled inside, because a part of her knows deep down that Faith is right. What she's saying is true. But, she doesn't want to admit it. Instead, she chooses to believe otherwise. "Faith, you don't understand."

"Amelia, *listen* to me. I know for a fact, people who know certain people that *know* this man *personally*. He sells drugs, and not *only* sells them, but manages others who sell for him. Girl, he is *not* safe!"

"I already know about what Blake does. He told me."

"Whaaaat? Wow! That's even worse! And, you *still* choose to be with this man?"

Walking across her dorm room, Faith sits at her desk. She can't believe what she's hearing. She's astounded at Amelia's stubbornness and unwillingness to let this man go.

"Look, Faith, he says he's getting out of the business."

"That's what they *all* say to get you hooked! I can't *believe* that *you* actually believe him."

Wiping her eyes, Amelia's lying back down on the bed again.

"Of course I believe him. Why shouldn't I? I have no reason *not* to."

Propping her arm up over the back of the chair, Faith rests her hand on top of her head, looking at the floor, disappointed and amazed.

"Cuz, you *really are* swimming in deep waters. Get out now before something happens. *Please.* Don't let me have to say, 'I told you so.'" Faith sighs, wishing she could get through to her, but Amelia doesn't want to accept the truth.

Looking at the ceiling, Amelia pauses, feeling so bad about how Blake treated her this morning. Deep in her gut she knows he's lying. But, what she knows Faith is saying that's true is overshadowed by what she prefers to believe. She enjoys his gifts and flirtatious ways; they're alluring and make her feel good. But, somehow, deep in her heart, Faith's words ring like a siren.

After a few moments, Amelia quickly snaps out of the trance she was in, thinking about all Faith said. Pretending like everything's alright, she continues talking, ignoring the warning signs.

"After graduation, I'm thinking about moving in with him."

Faith's mouth drops. At first, she felt a little sympathy, but now she's getting really angry.

"Now, I *know* you're crazy! Have you *lost* it?"

Trying to act confident, Amelia changes the look on her face as if everything really is OK with her, defending Blake.

"Listen, Blake has his faults, but we *all* do. He can be *really* sweet to me when he wants to."

Immediately, Faith stands up. "Amelia, will you *listen* to yourself? 'Sometimes'?...'He can be'? First of all, you're supposed to be going to college in September. Second of all, this man is *not* a man of God. Thirdly, he's much older than you! He's thirty-five years old for goodness sake! He sells drugs, has his own drug ring, *and,* he emotionally and verbally abuses you on *top* of all of that!"

"Faith, you know what…you're just *too* judgmental sometimes!"

Throwing one arm up in the air and down again, Faith slaps the side of her leg in disbelief. "Me? Too judgmental? I can't believe you, Amelia!"

Taking a deep breath, Faith's trying to calm back down to explain one more time what she's talking about in further detail.

"Amelia, a man in the world who puts *his own life* in jeopardy is highly likely to put his woman's life in jeopardy *too.* A man who doesn't care about himself, won't care about his woman *either.* But, a man of God, who loves Jesus, Amelia…loves himself and his woman also, because he loves Jesus. He's compelled by love for the Lord to love others and he does, because God's love lives in him. And, you'll experience *that* in that kind of man, Amelia…not emotional abuse. He understands that his body and life aren't his, *but God's.* He adores and worships Jesus, and honors his body as a temple of God. He doesn't sleep around with a bunch of women. And, he makes choices that are in God's Will, not his own. Amelia, a man like that will love you the way you deserve to be loved, Cuz, because Jesus lives in him. He'll cherish you not just with gifts and words, but in how he treats you. He's not won't try to manipulate you; he'll be honest with you. He won't do things intentionally to hurt you, Amelia. He'll *support* you, encourage you, and pray with you. He won't tear you down by degrading you and playing games with your mind and your heart. That's what a controlling spirit does, Amelia. And, he won't put you in danger either like Blake is. Trust me, I know these things through experience. And, I've learned a lot through Bible study classes with

Pastor Dan at church. I don't want to see you hurt, Amelia. I love you. You know I do. So, I care about you what happens to you."

"Blake doesn't play games with my mind! You don't know what you're talking about, Faith, because you don't know him like I do!"

Really frustrated, Faith's throwing her arm back up in the air. She's been talking to Amelia about Blake, it feels like to her, till she's "blue in the face" now. She's realizing now...there's nothing else that she can say.

"OK, OK, OK. I give. I tried."

Shaking her head, Faith's exhausted and drained by the whole situation with Amelia and Blake and the conversation. Scooting her laundry basket over to the door, Faith turns around to walk back toward her desk. Books and papers are all over the place that she needs organize later, along with the rest of her room. And, her bed still needs to be made up before she goes to wash clothes. She makes up her bed everyday.

"Amelia, I just don't know what else to say anymore."

Grabbing her laptop off the desk, Amelia sits back down on the bed, crossing her legs.

"Can we please change the subject?

"Amelia, all I have to say at this point is that I'm gonna *pray* for you." Amelia's attitude is growing now, because Faith's telling her what she doesn't want to hear.

"Thank you! You *do* that! I gotta get ready for ball practice. But, oh! I need to tell you something real quick—wait!"

Slamming her papers down on the desk, Faith sighs. She's so disappointed with Amelia. "*What more* do I need to know, Amelia?"

Faith's thinking out loud under breath, "Either *this girl* really doesn't get it or she just doesn't want to."

"Faith! That's me calling on Skype. Pick up!"

"No! Amel..." Faith really has to go get prepared now for studying later.

Click. Disconnecting the phone call, Amelia's waiting for Faith to answer her call on Skype.

"Bleeep! Bleeep! Bleeep!...That's Amelia's incoming call through Skype on Faith's computer."

Faith sighs again, reaching over to click the "video call" button blinking on the computer screen. Standing at her desk, Amelia's looking at her.

"What's up with you now, Amelia?" Faith's looks back, speaking in a low, agitated voice.

"Listen, our twelfth grade spring dance is in three weeks. Remember, I told you I had a surprise in store for Lynn?"

"Yeah? And?"

"Lynn is going to get the shock of her life!"

"What are you up to now! My goodness!" Faith's looking at her like she's crazy. "You're being ridiculous! What are you trying to do now?"

"Lynn won't have a chance to be nominated Queen." Amelia's looking right back at her, talking low.

"Amelia, you'd stoop *that* low to try to do something to Lynn just so she won't be a nominee for Queen?"

"What do you mean '*low*'? Look, Faith, if we don't *take* what we want in this world, we won't get it! *I* am going to be nominated Queen, and *I* am going to win! Think about it, Faith; *who else* could even come close to being Queen of Lake High? Like I told you before; *Lynn* is my *only* competition."

"I can't believe you, Amelia! You just *don't* stop! When is enough, enough with you! *Girl*, one day this pride in you is gonna catch up with you and you're gonna be sorry. *Why* can't you just be *happy* with yourself for once?"

Staring straight at Amelia, not understanding why she just keeps doing crazy things, Faith just looks at her shaking her head.

Paying no attention to what Faith's saying or at the look of great disappointment on her face, Amelia pulls the laptop closer toward her and looks straight in the camera with an evil look in her eye.

"*I*...will be Queen...of Lake High."

"You *just* don't know when to quit, do you? You're sad, Amelia. You need really help."

"Later for you, *Faith*! I thought you'd be *down* with me!"

Amelia's upset that Faith isn't responding the way she wants her to respond.

"What?? '*Down*' with you, Amelia? I'm *down* with you when you're doing the *right* thing for the *right* reason. I love the Lord, Amelia. I'm not down with trying to *sabotage* an innocent person's life for my own personal gain. I don't do that. There's a thing called integrity, you know."

"Please, Faith!"

"*Listen,* Amelia, you're my cousin. I don't *always* like what you do, but I do *love* you and I have your back, just not the way you want me to, not with things like this."

"You just don't understand me, Faith!"

Shaking her head in total disbelief, Faith's sitting down on her desk chair again for a moment.

"What *more* is there to understand, Amelia? I tell you all the time you have *serious* insecurity issues you need to work on. And, whatever this thing is you're planning for Lynn isn't cool...you need to stop it."

"OK, you know what? It's time to go! 'Cause here you go again! *Always* talking about insecurity issues! Who are you? The family guru on mental health issues?"

Picking up her cell phone, Amelia sits on the side of the bed.

Breathing deeply again, Faith slowly shakes her head. There's no getting through to her.

"Look, Amelia. Like I said, I love you, but this thing with Lynn is wrong. The Bible says, love your neighbor like you love yourself. The question though is...do you really love yourself? If you loved God, you wouldn't even be trying to do whatever this thing is you're trying to do to Lynn."

Steaming with anger, Amelia quickly moves the cursor of the mouse over the red phone symbol on Skype to end the call. She looks at Faith.

"Love you too, Cuz. And *thanks*...a lot...for your support!"

Looking back at her, Faith says, "you need Jesus."

Looking really angry at Faith, Amelia's presses the end button with her finger as hard as she can.

In disbelief, Faith looks shocked. "I can't believe this girl. She's gone off the deep end."

Sitting back in the chair, Faith is frustrated and angry. Moving from behind her back a small purple pillow embroidered with her name on it Grandma Mable gave her as a gift, she holds it up to her chest, squeezing it tightly. She grunts with frustration.

"It doesn't matter *how much* this girl achieves, it's *never* enough! She's been class president and won lots of awards. She's popular in school and in the honor's society. My gosh! College recruits from UCLA, Brown, and Spelman are practically *breathing* down her neck!...offering scholarships to play ball! I don't get it! It's *just* never enough with her! What has to happen in order for her to stop?"

Pulling her legs up to prop her feet on the chair, Faith's quickly reaching for her cell phone on the desk to call Nana before she goes to wash clothes.

"Hello?"

Holding the phone in one hand, Nana's stirring navy beans on the stove that's nearly finished cooking. She just finished slicing turnip to add a little bit to her pot of turnip greens that's cooking along side the navy bean soup.

"Nana!"

"Faith?" Nana says, taking a quick look at the turnip greens while stirring the navy bean soup.

"I need to talk to you really quick, Nana."

"Okay baby. What's wrong? You don't sound so good." Putting the spoon down on the counter top, Nana looks inquisitively, wondering what's going on with Faith.

"It's Amelia. She's gone off the deep end, Nana. You and Grandma Mable are the only two people I can talk to about her."

Shaking her head, Nana agrees.

"Yes, you're correct about that 'cause there's definitely something going on with her. We know she's…what's that you young folk say? 'Off the chain!' That's my grandbaby, but it's the truth!" Nana laughs. "Let me not joke about my grandbaby, Lord, 'cause she really needs Your help." Nana laughs again.

"Nana! This is serious."

"OK, OK, baby, you know Nana loves to laugh. The Bible says, a merry heart is good for your health. I keep stress away as much as possible! Now, tell Nana what's going on with you, honey."

"Well, Amelia and I were just talking on Skype and she hung up on me. I called her this morning to check in like I usually do on Saturdays. We talked a little while. I tried explaining some things to help her, but she refuses to listen. She said some disturbing things. She didn't like what I had to say and hung up. But, what bothered me even more was this evil look I saw in her eyes, Nana."

"Is that the program that lets you see people through the computer screen? Your Uncle Joe's been trying to get me to use it on the iPad he gave me for Christmas. But, you know I don't know about computers."

Faith tilts her head down for a minute.

"Yea, Nana, it is. It's called Skype. Listen, Amelia just doesn't *stop*."

"Yeah well, we know that." Picking up another spoon, Nana's stirs the turnip greens to make sure the seasoning is evenly distributed. The aroma of navy beans and turnip greens smell so good.

"Remember I told you about the vendetta she has with Lynn?"

"Yes, I do. Baby, give me a few seconds. Let me turn off my pot of navy soup before it burns."

Squeezing the pillow tighter, Faith looks at the clock, the laundry basket, and her books and papers. She has a midterm next week and time is flying by, she has to get ready to study. But, she can't hold all of what she's feeling in and study too.

"OK, I'm back, baby. Now, what's this about Lynn?" Nana sits down at the kitchen table to give Faith her undivided attention.

"Amelia's planning something against her the night of Lake High's spring dance."

"What? Has she gone mad? Why is she doing that? This has gone to far."

"She wants to eliminate Lynn as an opponent for nominee of this year's Queen of Lake High. Personally, Nana, I think Amelia's *way* out of control now."

Nana's shaking her head becoming very upset.

"My, my, my…is there anything you can do, Faith? This is crazy!"

"I wish Nana, but I don't know what's up her sleeve. She didn't tell me what she was going to do or how."

"This isn't *nothin'* but the devil himself! That's why, baby, I tell you *all* the time…apply the Blood of Jesus over yourself and *pray*! The Holy Ghost will help you! The Lord is our shield against Satan! Our faith activates God's Power in our lives! This just *burns* me up to hear this!"

Nana doesn't usually get real mad, but she's real mad now.

"*You*, Nana? It burns me up too. I'm so frustrated that I had to stop to call you before I could get going with my day. It's too much!"

"Listen to me, baby. Greater is *He* who is in *you*, than he who is in the world. *Always* remember that! You hear me?"

Releasing some of the frustration now, Faith's starting to calm down from the anger she's feeling inside toward Amelia and what's she doing to her life. A feeling of sadness is coming back over her again as her voice drops. She wants to see Amelia succeed in the right way.

"I hear you, Nana."

"Faith, the Bible says, we don't fight against flesh and blood. You have to realize this. We fight principalities, powers, rulers of darkness, and evil spiritual forces in heavenly realms. So, what we're dealing with around Amelia is spiritual. The devil has been using my granddaughter; plain and simple. Listen, God will grant us wisdom, but *we* have to use it when He gives it to us, baby. We have to keep praying; we can't let up. And, we have to believe when we pray that God hears us and answers. This whole thing with Amelia is upsetting. But, I thank God that our weapons of warfare aren't carnal, Faith. They're not things people in the world use to fight. They're spiritual; strong and mighty in God to pull down strongholds. Jesus already defeated Satan. So, Jesus has already won for Amelia." Nana pauses for a second.

"All we have to do is pray with understanding about authority we have through Jesus, have faith, and watch the Holy Ghost who raised Jesus from the dead…move mightily. There's *power* in the Name Jesus; never forget that. His Name is the *only* name that has power. God gave all power in Heaven, on earth and beneath the earth to His Son. Always remember what Jesus said, '*I saw Satan fall like lightning from Heaven. Behold, I give you authority to trample on serpents and scorpions, and over all the power of the enemy, and nothing shall by any means hurt you.*' The difference between Christians who live for Jesus and Christians who say they do, but don't, Faith, is belief. That's it. It's as simple as that." Nana switches the phone to her other ear.

"Jesus said, when you pray, Faith,…believe what you're praying about and you'll receive it. We believe we have what we pray for in the very moment we pray for something. We don't wait to see what we prayed for to believe it. No…it doesn't work that way with God. That's not the way Jesus teaches us to believe. We have to possess what we pray for in the very moment and watch for the manifestation, the outcome, to come to pass. I know this situation with Amelia is disturbing and hard to watch. Me and your Grandmother are going to fast and pray for Amelia together, and especially for this situation around Lynn. Something just doesn't feel right, Faith. But, I know God *is* going to help. You'll see. God will never forsake us, baby. He'll make a way where and when there seems to be no way. God parted the Red Sea and caused a whole army to be swallowed up by it. He's going to help us, baby. You mark my words."

Listening to Nana, Faith's beginning to regain a little strength. That's part of the reason why she called, because Nana *always* knows the right thing to say that helps.

"Amen, Nana. I'll fast with you and Grandma, then. Just let me know when, 'cause I know it's not today with all of that cookin' I heard you doing."

"Good! I'm glad to hear that! Call Mable and tell her, because we're starting *tomorrow*. You know, Faith, Amelia has no business talking to a man like Blake. And, trying to destroy other people is just plain wickedness; it's evil. Amelia shouldn't be plotting against Lynn just so she can win a title. Titles don't define who we are…Christ in us does. She should be thinking about which college she's going to choose, her purpose for God and her future."

"She is," Faith answers under her breath.

"What's that, baby?"

"Nothing, Nana."

Looking out the kitchen window, Nana's wishes deep in her heart that her granddaughter was different, but she's believing God for the solution in Amelia's life.

Placing her feet on the floor, Faith puts the pillow back behind her in the chair. Its no way she can tell Nana what Amelia said about her thoughts of living with Blake.

"Faith, I know you're worried about Amelia, honey, but she's making her own bed. Remember this sweetie…we have to accept that there are some things *only Jesus* can fix. And, baby,…this is one of 'em."

Looking at the clock again, Faith stands up. "Nana, I've said *everything* I can to Amelia. Its unbelievable how she refuses to hear anything I say."

"That's because you're a woman of God talking to a demon who is in her! Either we're born of the flesh or the Spirit, Faith. We can't be both. It's impossible! Jesus said, *"...unless one is born of water and the Spirit, he cannot enter the Kingdom of God."* Christians must be baptized in the Holy Ghost! That demon in her influences her mind! When people want to do what they want to do, it's hard for them to hear the truth. That demon of darkness was sent by Satan to try to destroy her life; that's what he does. And, that's what you saw in her eyes."

"The devil?"

"*Yes*, honey! The devil! I hate to say it, but a *demon* got in my Amelia. And, be clear about this...it's by her *own* choice. Don't forget, *we all* have free will. There's God's Perfect Will and then, there's free will. After we finish our prayers for Amelia, there's only one thing we can do."

Crossing her arms over her chest, Faith's looking curious. "What's that, Nana?"

"Stand. Just stand, baby. The Bible says, be immovable by Satan's schemes, Faith. We have to stand firm, baby, after we've done everything a crisis demands...fasting, praying with the right heart and boldness in the Spirit, being courageous in the Lord, declaring the works of the Lord, believing in God's Word and having faith in Him. Amen?"

"Amen! Because, with Jesus *all* things are possible! That includes my cousin!"

"*Aaaalleluia*! Now, you're talkin'! That's my Faith!"

Sighing, Faith takes the phone from between her head and shoulder and holds it to her ear with one hand, putting the other in her pocket.

"Wheeew! I feel better now. Thanks, Nana. I *needed* that after talking to Amelia. I can *always* depend on you to lift my spirit."

"Look, baby, *God* is a covenant-keeping God. *God* is faithful to His Word. *God* will take something meant for bad and *use it* for His Glory. Look at what God did for Joseph in the Bible. After his brothers sold him into slavery, *God* was with him. He gave Joseph favor with the king of Egypt, making him second in command. There's *nothing* God isn't capable of doing, honey. The question is…*will* He? And, *how* He does something or *will* do something, no one knows. His Thoughts and Ways are higher than ours. There may be a lesson someone has to go through to learn something God wants them to learn." Nana leans back in the chair.

"Listen, the *only way* we can please God is by faith. Having your *own* personal relationship with the Lord Jesus and the Holy Spirit, doing the Will of God, and praying from your *heart* with love, not just for yourself, but others also, is what causes you to experience a *blessed* successful life in Christ. There's a lot of people still praying today about something they were praying for years ago, because they don't believe when they pray. And, there's a lot of Christians who don't live for Jesus that say they do who say, 'I'm blessed.' Some think all gifts are favor from God, but only good ones come from above. Don't forget the devil has kingdoms he tried to give to Jesus. But, praise God, Jesus told Satan where to go! It's called lust of the eyes and pride of life, baby." Nana's thinking about gifts Blakes gives Amelia.

"The devil gives gifts too; they're just not good gifts. Case in point—Blake's. Those kind of gifts don't come from God. Satan provides the bait and some people take it. The enticement gets them. The enemy's gifts appear good, but that's it, you see?...they *appear* good. The real truth about them is revealed as time goes by. You can't sell your soul, baby. You have to live for Jesus."

"Wooow. Amen, Nana."

"Yes, baby. The Bible says, *'every good gift and every perfect gift is from above, and comes down from the Father of lights, with whom there is no variation or shadow of turning.'* Can't say that about gifts from the devil! The gifts you told me Blake gives Amelia after school sometimes; they're from the devil, *himself!* Listen, if the Holy Spirit led Jesus into the wilderness to be tempted by Satan, what makes you think He won't lead us into "the wilderness situations" to be tested too? The decisions we make everyday determine our *eternity*— Heaven or hell. And, if Satan offered Jesus his kingdoms in the world, what makes you think he won't offer the same to people? The Bible says, *'the devil walks about like a roaring lion seeking whom may devour!'*"

"So true, Nana. So, true." Faith takes one hand through her hair, holding the cell phone with the other. Nana's preaching to her spirit...it's just what she needed.

"See, baby, God will *never* tempt us, but God will test us. Jesus was tested by the Holy Spirit when He led Jesus into the wilderness to be tempted by the devil. Notice the difference though, sweetie. Let's not get it confused. He allowed Jesus to be tempted for a reason. Jesus had a purpose to fulfill. His purpose was to save us, conquer death and be the all-sufficient sacrifice for sins, once and for all, so whoever believes in Him would be saved. Jesus had to re-establish God's Kingdom over the earth that was and still is rebellious against God. Just look at all of the things going on in the world today. But, nevermind that there still are many rebellious people. Some people will be that way 'til the Lord's Second Coming. But, their rebellion isn't the point." Getting up, Nana's walking to the refrigerator to get a ginger brew. Like Margaret and Joe, she loves ginger brew too.

"The point is that Jesus did what God sent Him to do. Praise God! That's how we can do all things through Jesus, because He strengthens us as we live for Him, Faith. God gives us more grace to do things we wouldn't ordinarily be able to do. So, even though, we still see people go against God's Will, doing what they want to do, it doesn't mean Jesus didn't establish God's Kingdom here. He did. Glory to God." Nana pauses to take a sip of ginger brew.

"Faith, we all have to make our own choices to do what is right or not. In the wilderness, Jesus faced the same temptations we face in life. This is why through Him, we're more than conquerors and we can do the unimaginable. When we accept Jesus as Lord over our lives and obey His Commandments, He and God come to live in our hearts. We're compelled by His Love in us to do God's Will, not ours. But, I want you to understand something, baby,…God will not force us to obey Him. No, sweetie, He won't do that. That would be control and manipulation. God's love is neither. God gives us permissive will, the power to choose what we want to do; it's free-will. God is love. So sometimes, God, will allow certain things to happen in our lives that may not feel so good at the time to learn from them as I mentioned before. But, know this…God will always be with us and never, ever give us more than we can bear. His Word says, *'God is faithful, who will not allow you to be tempted beyond what you are able.'* Note, Faith, it doesn't *say*, God will not allow you to not be tempted. It says, *'will not allow you to be tempted beyond what you are able,…'* And, it continues to say, *'with the temptation will also make the way of escape, that you may be able to bear it.'"*

"Amen! Amen! And, Amen! Thank You, Jesus! Thank you, Nana, soooo much!" Faith's feeling much better now. She's ready to start her day, so she can study for her mid-term.

"See, honey, while Jesus was on earth, He was man and deity at the same time. He experienced *everything* a human being does in the flesh, temptation and all. He had to, in order to abolish, put an end to hostility that comes from the nature of a carnal person. Mind you now…we're not talking about a person truly in Christ. 'Cause they're some churchfolk that are still in the flesh. They really haven't met Jesus like they say they have!"

Nana laughs and Faith chuckles, knowing it's true. It's just the way Nana says things sometimes that makes her laugh.

"That flesh is a hostile thing, baby! It *wars*, the Bibles teaches us, against the spirit. So, why did Jesus have to put an end to this "war" that goes on inside of us without Him… that was in Him when He was in the flesh?…to create *peace* in Himself as a new man, to reconcile His spirit and the flesh as one body to God. So, when we join with Him, we become one with Christ spiritually. And, when we become one with the Lord, we become new creatures. Make no mistake…we *are not* the same people in Him. And, the good news is that we don't experience what people in the world do. We experience the Lord's Peace in us and His Love. The Lord becomes our Joy which becomes *strength* to us. So, when trouble comes, we know where to take it…to Jesus!" Nana is strong in the Lord. She loves Him so much. Jesus has helped her through so many things she's faced in life.

Rounding up Nana says, "everyone has a spirit, Faith, that lives in their body which the Bible refers to as "flesh," our physical nature. Okay? Do you understand me?"

"Yes, I do, Nana. I'm following you." Faith says intently listening.

"The Bible teaches us, Faith, that our spirits have desires different from the flesh. This is why when we pray, we must get out of the flesh and go in the spirit. People who love the world, live in the flesh, baby. They're sensual beings; they're not spiritual. They have cravings the Bible calls "works of the flesh" which are things like lustfulness, drunkenness, anger, uncleanness, fornication, sexual desires, envyings, and murders. They cannot...I repeat...they cannot, the Bible says, please God in the flesh. Thank God Jesus overcame the flesh, so guess what?...we can too, but *only* through Him, baby. This is *not* something we can do on our own. Don't even think about it. No, no! We all need Jesus, baby; everyone of us. Amen?"

"Ameeeen!" Faith's listening even more intently as the eyes of her understanding are enlightened.

"Through Jesus, we have access to God, our Father who is a God of Peace. Be at peace, baby! Let God's peace quiet your heart and mind, honey. Don't worry about Amelia. Focus on *Jesus* and your studies. Just keep praying for your cousin and *believe* God for a miracle in her life. He'll do it. *God* is always in control. Remember, *all power* is God's. If people keep choosing to turn against God's Will, to not obey Jesus, they'll block their blessings, honey, just like the Israelites did. God can and will turn His Back, if people repeatedly choose disobedience. After God brought the Israelites out of Egypt, they never enjoyed the chance to live in the promise land; not the older ones anyway. They grumbled and complained a lot, even when Moses was on the mountain receiving the Ten Commandments from God. They wanted Aaron, Moses' brother, to make a god to go before them, because they didn't know what was up with Moses. They had no patience. They couldn't wait for Moses to come back down the mountain before they started turning away from God in their hearts and thoughts. So, you see how people can be, baby? For goodness sakes, God delivered them from the hand of the Egyptians when they were in bondage. How inconsiderate a people. Now, doesn't that sound like a familiar story about some people you know?

"Ye..." Faith can't finish saying "yes" before Nana continues.

"I mean think about it for a minute, Faith. How *crazy* would it be to even *think* you could replace God by making a golden calf to be a god? They witnessed seeing the miraculous with *their own* eyes a sea, the Red Sea, which they walked through, mind you, that God split down the middle with a blow of His Nostrils, manna falling from Heaven for food on the journey, water pouring out a rock and God, Himself, traveling with them in a pillar of cloud by day to lead them and a pillar of fire by night for light! What in the world was wrong with those fools?"

Nana laughs. "Lord, have mercy! Excuse me, Lord!"

Faith chuckles.

"See, some folk are just plain *crazy*, Faith! And, we have to accept that. Make a god to be God?! What?! Just craziness! I'm trying to help you understand, Faith, that we can *only* be enticed by what we can be enticed *with*! Issues start with people, baby, not Satan! The devil just capitalizes from them!—their issues, I mean! They need deliverance, honey! That's what a lot of folk need...deliverance! And, that's why they think the way they do, baby, because they need help! The Word of God teaches us, baby, that life's issues come out of the heart. So, from that we understand that they start within! So, what does that mean?!"

"They need Jesus!" Faith's smiling as she agrees. The one thing she loves and appreciates about Nana,...and, her Grandmother too...is that she knows Nana walks with the Lord.

"You, got that right! Simply put...they need Jesus! But, they have to want Jesus first!"

"See, that's it! God chooses us, but we have to choose Him! Oh my goodness! That helped me so much, Nana! Faith's really relieved understanding many more things now.

"We can only be what we believe we are. If people really have Jesus in their hearts, you won't experience nonsense with them, because they have Jesus! Helloooo?? You understand what I'm saying, Faith?"

"I sure do, Nana. You're sooo right."

"Sure, we're all a work in progress, but to be what we are in Christ when we accept Him as Savior and Lord...*new creatures*, Faith, as the Bible says! Stinking thinking *goes*, baby! Old habits *change* for new ones! Everything about us changes! Faith, I want you to always understand something, baby...with people who really love Jesus...you don't see disregard and the lack of reverence for Him in what they say and do! No, no! A thousand times over, no! It's impossible, because God and Jesus *really* live inside of them, just like the Lord says so in the Good Book. God loves obedience. When we obey Jesus, we express love. People who love God are convicted by the Holy Ghost to live righteous lives, because Jesus is Righteousness. They love people, they don't try hurt 'em. They obey the Lord! They don't betray Him like Judas did! And, they might make mistakes, but it won't be intentional, honey! You can bet your bottom dollar on that!"

"Woooow, Nana. Woooow. I get what you're saying." Faith is really thinking about what Nana's teaching her.

"But, the sad thing is that there are still people in the world, right to this day, that think like those people did after God brought 'em out of Eygpt and do the same things they did. They make all kinds of things their gods now and idolize them. And, they love them to their death! It's ridiculous!"

"So true," Faith says thinking about a friend of hers at college.

"This is why we have to keep on praying, baby."

"I fear the Lord, Nana. If I were one of those people, one of the Israelites, who saw what they saw…I would have been afraid to do anything wrong. I can only imagine what it was like seeing with my own eyes a pillar of cloud and fire in the sky and bread on the ground falling from Heaven." Faith's thinking about what Nana said and how ridiculous and unfaithful people really can be to God who's so good to His people. "Wow. I guess some people don't' fear God and love Him, Nana."

"Faith, God turned *away* from them and gave them over, the Bible says, to worship fake gods made up of the sun, the moon, and the stars, and He'll do the *same* to people who repeatedly choose to turn away from His Wisdom and Understanding, if people don't…"

Walking toward the kitchen sink, Nana raises her voice.

"…*humble* themselves, baby,…they got to *pray*, *seek* God and *turn* away from wickedness! *If* they do, Hallelujah!...God will *hear them* from Heaven, He said, and *forgive* them of their sins, and *heal* their hearts!"

Standing with one arm crossed over her chess and the other propped on it now, Faith's holding the phone up to her ear with tears in her eyes, moved by the Holy Spirit.

"Wow, wow, wow." It's all she can say, realizing more in a deeper way what Christ did for us on the cross and what it means.

"Baby girl! I'm gonna say this last thing, and then I'm going to let you go, because Nana knows you have a lot to do today. Me and your Grandma are concerned about you worrying about Amelia. Listen, *Amelia* is choosing her path, honey, and only *one Person* can get her attention."

"God." Faith speaks up softly.

"That's *right*, baby! So, *don't* be afraid for Amelia *or* yourself. Just simply *believe* in Jesus and keep *loving* Jesus in all everything you do. And, don't forget…*God* lives in you, because you love Him. Our Father is a *Good* God, Faith! He said, '*ask and it shall be given you! Seek and you shall find! Knock and the door will be opened to you!*' He tells us not to be anxious for anything, baby! That includes your cousin. Amen? Just ask God to help her when you pray."

"Ameeeen. I *receive* that, Nana."

"I love you, baby girl. Let's talk later."

Sighing with great relief, Faith puts one arm down and looks at the pile of clothes sitting in the laundry basket.

"I *love* you too, Nana!"

"OK, baby. Bye for now."

"Bye, Nana!" Faith's smiling with tears of joy running down her face.

"Wheeeew!" Nana shakes her head, hanging up the phone.

Then, she prays.

"*Father, You're a faithful God. Thank You, for Your Grace and Your Love and Your Word. You say, You'll never allow us to be tempted beyond what we can bear and that You will make a way of escape. Make a way of escape for my grandbaby, Amelia, God from the situation she's putting herself in, in Jesus Christ's Name. She needs Your help. Only You can help her, God. I love You and trust You, Father. Amen."*

After talking with Nana today, it's clearer to Faith that "winning" for Amelia means everything for the wrong reasons. Her faith and understanding about what God's says in His Word increased. Some things she learned from her Grandmother Mable and Bible class with Pastor Dan; others by listening to Nana today. In fact, the conversation with Nana, helped Faith understand more that even though a person, young or old, is extremely talented, beautiful, intelligent, and savvy—they can still lack wisdom and confidence about who they are in Christ...something *only* the Holy Spirit can give. Faith realizes, now more than she did, that the absence of Christ in Amelia's heart is quickly becoming her downfall. And, that the spirit of pride in Amelia, for the sake of recognition and greed, is producing a detestable reproach. She's very clear about who's behind Amelia's actions; the devil. With this greater insight, Faith gained a deeper appreciation for Proverbs 16:18, a Scripture her Grandmother Mable always recites, *"pride goes before destruction, and a haughty spirit before a fall."*

Chapter Three

Margaret has always worried about the absence of a dad in Amelia's life. She does everything humanly possible to support her every step of the way in school and basketball, but now Amelia's behavior is finally taking its toll.

"Amelia!" Margaret calls from the bottom of the stairs. "It's eight thirty! Time for practice soon! Breakfast will be ready in twenty!"

"OK, Ma!" Amelia's logging into her Twitter account, really quickly. She set up a fake username. Unknowingly some friends from Lake High and the neighborhood are following her, including Lynn. On Thursday, she planned to send Lynn another direct message like the one she previously sent. Rushing to send Lynn the Twitter message she didn't have time to the other day before she gets dressed, Amelia quickly types:

> You slut! I saw you talking to John in the hallway the other day. You think you got everybody fooled, but I know who you are! Talk to him one more time and find out what happens!

Chuckling, Amelia logs out and turns the laptop off. Closing it, she places the laptop back on her desk, thinking out loud, "out with the old, and in with the new."

Taking a quick glance out the window, Amelia jumps up, doing a quick turn-about in the middle of the bedroom with a slight smile on her face before she walks to the door.

The sky is bright this morning, the sun is shining, and there are no clouds in sight. Springtime is finally here. New leaves forming on the trees and flowers budding promise that sunshine and hot days are on the way.

Opening the bedroom door, Amelia hears Bruce singing out loud in the shower down the hallway.

Ba de ya de ya de ya!

Ba ba ba!

Ba de ya de ya de ya!

Do you remember the twenty-first night of September?

Love was changing the minds of pretenders!

While chasing the clouds awaaaay!

Ba ba ba ba de ya de ya de ya!

Standing there for a second with disgust on her face and her hand on the knob, she closes the door, shaking her head. "Not again!"

She hates when Bruce gets to the bathroom first. He always takes a long time in the shower.

All of a sudden, Uncle Joe grabs her shoulder from behind. He walked out of the guest bedroom after Amelia opened her door, but he didn't close his, so Amelia didn't hear him. Besides, she was preoccupied being disgusted by Bruce's singing in the shower again.

"Heeey! How's my baby girl this morning?"

Uncle Joe's on his way downstairs to talk to Margaret in the kitchen before she takes Amelia to basketball practice.

"Oh! Uncle Joe!" Amelia's surprised. "I didn't see you come out of your room."

Before arriving from LA, Uncle Joe talked with Nana and Margaret separately. They each brought him up to speed about things going on with Amelia. From his conversation with Nana, he knows Margaret doesn't know about Blake yet. Although he's deeply disappointed to hear the news, he decides not to say anything directly to Amelia just yet. He wants to play it cool with her first to see if she'll open up to him. Uncle Joe knows Amelia well enough to know that if he pushes her or forces her to talk about things she doesn't want to talk about that she won't talk at all, she'll retreat.

"So, what's going on?"

"Oh, nothing. Just rushing to get dressed for practice."

"You sure about that?" Uncle Joe's smiling, trying not to seem too suspicious.

"Yeah, of course." Amelia's giving him a fake smile.

To play game on Uncle Joe, you have to wake up at the crack of dawn. Uncle Joe is street-smart and can read people very, very well. Amelia's smile isn't fooling him. He knows his niece.

"You won the bet last night!"

"What bet?" She looks puzzled.

"Bruce and I made a bet to see who could stay up the longest. You know we're all night owls." Uncle Joe's laughing.

Amelia loves money, so now her interest is piqued.

"Alright, then, cool. It's time to pay up, Uncle. Come to think of it, I did leave you and Bruce sleeping on the sofa last night."

What Amelia doesn't know is that Uncle Joe never really fell asleep. He pretended, because he wanted to see what she was going to do; that is, if she was going to leave the house or not. After hearing about this older man from Nana, and especially that she played hooky from school, he's livid inside. Trying to be cool, Uncle Joe engages her more in the conversation.

"Pay-up time? OK, tonight at dinner!"

"OK, I'm gonna hold you to it!" Amelia's chuckling and smiling for real this time. She's excited now. Money's coming.

Uncle Joe's devastated inside, knowing the truth. He's nobody's fool and can tell something is up with Amelia. Smiling back at her, removing his hand from her shoulder, Uncle Joe walks toward the stairs. Turning back around he says, "Mel…" That's Amelia's nickname Uncle Joe named her when she was a baby.

"Yes, Uncle?" Amelia started heading to the bathroom, but stops.

"When your brother gets out the shower, will you tell him to meet me in the kitchen, please? While you and your mother go to practice, I'm gonna take him to Cracker Barrel for breakfast and then we'll all do something together later."

"Awwwww! Cracker Barrel? I *love* Cracker Barrel!" Amelia's looking disappointed.

"I know! Me too!" Uncle Joe's placing his hand on the hand rail, smiling. "You know I'm going back to LA tomorrow." Uncle Joe pauses. "So, don't make any plans with your friends tonight, because I've got plans for everybody."

"OK, but why so *soon?*"

Despite her ways, Amelia loves Uncle Joe, and she respects him a lot. He's the only constant, older, male figure in her life.

"Mel, if I could stay, I would, but I've got to get back to the studio, sweetie. We're finishing up a recording for my next CD. But, I promise, as always, I'll be back in a few weeks."

Amelia sighs. "Uncle Joe, you *promised* to take me to LA one day to see you record."

"One day soon, babygirl. One day soon. I'll fly you guys out for a few days. Maybe that will be your graduation gift?"

Amelia's eyes get big. Graduation is around the corner. About a month and a half away. "Really?"

Looking at her, Uncle Joe laughs, concealing his real feelings inside. Before stepping down the stairs, Uncle Joe turns back.

"That boy really can sing." Uncle Joe has heard Bruce several times before, but he's realizing Bruce is getting better and better.

Slanting her head really quickly, Amelia looks disgusted. "Please, Uncle."

Turning back around, Amelia's feeling really excited about the prospect of going to LA so soon. She can't wait — palm trees, beaches, Rodeo Drive!

She's singing, "I'm going to LAAA! I'm going to LAAA! I'm going to LAAA!"

Uncle Joe looks back laughing. "We'll see! We'll see! Better keep those grades up young lady! Your last quarter *still* counts for college!"

Stopping, Amelia's putting one hand on her hip, smiling. "Uncle Joe, don't worry. I got that covered!"

Uncle Joe stops and dances on the step to joke with her. "Alright, now! It's your birthday! It's your birthday! We're gonna party hard like it's your birthday! Go, Amelia! Go, Amelia! Go, Amelia!" Uncle Joe loves to joke around as long as it's good clean fun.

One thing about Uncle Joe and Amelia, he always has a way of cheering her up, making her laugh, and eventually getting her to open up to him usually about things she won't talk to Margaret or Nana about.

Everybody in the family knows Uncle Joe is a comedian. People say he takes after me, his Momma. I suppose they're correct. My momma used to always tell me and Mable, "the only way to find joy in this world is through Jesus." She'd say, "joy is *good* medicine for the soul, but a depressed heart dries *everything* up!" Momma was right.

Banging on the door, Amelia's getting agitated all over again. Bruce is still singing in the shower.

"Bruuuce! Boy, hurry up! I have to get to practice!"

Bruce doesn't answer. Amelia's still banging on the door with her hand. Bruce sings louder.

We all know Bruce *loves* to sing in the shower just as much as he *loves* to annoy Amelia. It makes me chuckle sometimes, because I see some of me in him like I do Joe. The only difference is when he jokes with Amelia, he teases her. And she can't *stand* that. Bruce knows her ways, *very well*. That's why he does it. Claims he's making her stronger. On top of that, he treats her like she's five years old by "babying" her all the time. And she can't stand that either. In *my* opinion, he *can* be a bit overprotective sometimes. I guess he does it, because he feels like when Joe isn't around, he's the man of the house. But ,I'll tell you one thing, acting like the head of this household with Amelia in it has taught him *a few* valuable lessons.

I don't worry about Bruce trying to make babies, *any* time soon. With *Uncle Joe* in his ear, the last thing he wants to do is disappoint him, let alone *God*. Bruce *fears* the Lord, as he should. Besides, his mind is focused on college and work. He goes to Morehouse full time, here in Atlanta, and works part time with Margaret's sales division team. For nineteen-and-a-half years old, almost twenty, Bruce is a pretty *mature* young man and a good-looking one too, if I may say so. I've got to give it to my grandson. He's *very* smart. He's a self-taught computer whiz and a *highly gifted* artist. He never took art classes, yet he draws with *precision*. Just *blessed* by God, is what I say. He's better than Picasso and Da Vinci put together!

And, talk about *gifted*—Bruce is good with discernment too. It's just natural to him. When he was a young boy, he always seemed to stay out of trouble. In my day, that was a good thing. 'Cause if we misbehaved, Pop used to tell us, "go pick out a switch in the backyard. Now!" When we came back, Pop would tear our behinds up. It kept us straight though. It sure did strike fear in us. We respected Pop! In fact, I can think of a few people, right now, that can use a lesson on respect the way Pop taught it. Amelia's one!

But, these days it's different. It's against the law in some states to spank a child. Who ever heard of some nonsense like that? The Bible says, *"he who spares his rod hates his son, but he who loves him disciplines him promptly."* That's why the good ol' folk back in my day used to say all the time, "spare the rod, spoil the child!" We have too many crazy people running around out here now, and running the world for that matter, that probably never got a spanking when they were kids! People talk about giving a child a time-out! What is a time-out? Tell a child to go and sit in a corner for ten or twenty minutes? They even have time-out benches and chairs! What some of these children need today is a serious butt whippin'!

When Mable and I grew up around my cousins, if any one of us acted up, not only would our daddies whip our tails, but Grandpop would, Uncle would, Auntie would, and the next door neighbor would too! That's why I appreciate Bruce. The ol' folk don't say for nothing, "it takes a village to raise a child." In his own way, Bruce feels like he's helping Margaret. And, the truth is...he is. I couldn't imagine Margaret doing *all* she does by herself, over all these years. My hat's off to the single moms of the world who don't have a son like Bruce and a brother like Joe.

"Bruuuuuuuuce! I *know* you hear me!"

Amelia's still standing at the bathroom door. Bruce is still singing "September," by Earth Wind & Fire. The way he listens to oldies-but-goodies, you'd think he was an old man. Frustrated, Amelia kicks the bathroom door twice with her slipper. Just as she raises her hand to bang on the door again, Margaret appears at the top of the stairs. She heard Amelia yelling from downstairs. Calmly, Margaret walks toward her.

"Young lady, *what* are you doing? Haven't we talked about this?"

Folding her arms across her chest, Margaret's looking at Amelia like she's lost her mind, kicking and banging on the bathroom door.

"Talked about what, Ma?" Quickly getting an attitude, Amelia's standing with one hand on her hip.

"*Excuse* me? If you don't watch your *tone*, you won't be going anywhere."

Sighing, Amelia's trying to change the look on her face, so she won't get in trouble.

"Ma, you *know* I need to get to practice. Bruce is acting like he doesn't hear me, *and I know he does!*"

Amelia is the only person who has the ability to take Margaret from "zero to ten" in seconds. Gets me so upset, because I know it raises her pressure. For Margaret, it's a real challenge raising Amelia at this stage of her life. She totally dislikes Amelia's "moods." And, everybody knows, even Amelia, that Margaret *can't stand* disrespect in *any* form from *anybody*. But, for no reason *at all*, sometimes Amelia talks back with an attitude, *knowing* she's wrong. It's not like all of us haven't talked to her about this issue before. It's the *little* things she says, and *how* she says them, that piss Margaret off.

Trying to stay calm, Margaret prevents herself from "going there" so to speak with Amelia this morning. Sometimes, the work she has to do just to check Amelia's attitude is exhausting. Today, she plans to relax at home with the kids and her brother, and have a little fun for a change. She works a lot.

Looking seriously at Amelia, determined to keep control of her emotions, Margaret's taking a deep breath, letting her know she's not joking.

"Amelia, go to my bathroom and get ready. Now. I'll be downstairs waiting in the kitchen with Uncle Joe when you're done."

Margaret's usually calm-natured. Even as a child she was that way. It used to *amaze* me seeing her *so* calm. Don't misunderstand me, though; Margaret *can* get upset, she just doesn't get mad very often. She's slow to anger, but when she gets there...watch out, baby! Trust me; you do not want to find out through experience. Talk about a "whipping." By the time Margaret finishes speaking, you'll be on the "*flo'*" as we used to say. And, the interesting thing is she doesn't scream. In her "collectedness," she has this *uncanny* way of making you feel like a "pea in a pod." She gets this *look* on her face that says it all. Unfortunately though, it doesn't work so well with Amelia.

Amelia's temper brings Margaret out of her comfort zone and makes it hard for her to feel at peace inside. She tests Margaret a lot. All Margaret wants is for everybody to do their part; work together so things will flow harmoniously in the house.

It's too bad though. As of recent, things haven't been flowing so well. It *always* seems like there's so much tension, because of Amelia. It's getting *really* hard to interact with her now. But, for the most part, I have to hand it to Margaret; she's doing the best she can. Given the circumstances, she's dealing with Amelia pretty well. Watching from a far, I smile. She acts just like Momma used to. They both have that look that tells you exactly what's on their mind. If people came at Momma the wrong way, "off the hook" so to speak, she'd have them on the *"flo'"* too, as we say, or as Momma used to say, "under the flo' boards." All it took was just one look from Momma. And, after she'd finish with 'em, she'd say, "Now go pick yourself up and call me afterward."

Me, on the other hand, I'll tell it to ya straight! So, if you don't want advice from me, don't ask! I don't hold my tongue. Forgive me, Lord. I know. Sometimes, that's my downfall. I'm working on it though. It's hard, 'cause sometimes people just act like fools! I've *always* taught my kids that most folk fall into one of two categories: "talkers" or "walkers." Talkers talk the talk. Walkers walk the walk.

Despite Amelia's ugly ways, Margaret's always believed in her heart that Bruce and Amelia are "walkers," "fruit producing" people, because they've both been very successful in school. I must say, I would have to agree with her. She pushes them to their fullest capacity in every area of their lives to succeed, because she sees potential and the drive in them to be their best. But, Amelia's drive to be her "best" hasn't quite turned out to be her "best" even though she's won a lot of awards. She has the wrong motives in her heart to succeed. It doesn't pay to gain the world by selling yourself to lose your soul. Integrity is important. Bruce's drive, on the other hand, is is working in his favor. I think, deep down inside, Margaret knows this. Yet and still, she takes *every* opportunity she can, as a mother and a woman of God, to use certain situations in their lives as teachable moments by applying the Word of God. She's a woman of God who really does love Jesus. She practices what she teaches her children. She's always preaching about faith, righteousness, and obedience to God. I just smile. If Momma were alive today, she'd be so proud of her.

Quickly brushing her teeth, Amelia rushes to get dressed in Margaret's bathroom. Like Margaret, Amelia hates being late; it irritates her to the core. Ever since fourth grade when she was late for receiving an award from the principal, she's been a stickler for time. Sometimes, it drives Margaret crazy. But, this morning Amelia excused herself, because her conversation with Blake didn't go well, *and* she was pressed to send Lynn that direct message on Twitter.

Pulling her hair back into a ponytail, Amelia glances to the right, looking at Margaret's perfume collection on the counter top. Margaret loves collecting perfumes from all over the world. They're all arranged on an elegant glass tray, engraved with her favorite scripture: *2 Timothy 1:7, "for God has not given us a spirit of fear, but of power and of love and of a sound mind."* Delicate, hand-blown flowers enclose the base of the tray that was handmade some years ago by a friend of Margaret's who owns a glass shop in a nearby shopping mall. When Amelia gets older, Margaret plans on passing it down as a family heirloom to her.

Still eyeballing the perfume, Amelia can't resist picking up her personal favorite, First by Van Cleef & Arpels. She knows

Margaret forbids her to use any of her perfumes without asking. Holding the bottle in her hand, she takes a deep breath, visualizing Blake smelling her neck. Quickly coming back to her senses, she nearly drops the bottle, almost breaking the tray.

"Uh oh!" Amelia gets scared for a moment, knowing her mom is very particular about people respecting her things. With some things, she tries her mom; others, she knows better.

All dressed now, Amelia runs out of the bathroom. With her long, black ponytail swinging from side to side over her back, Amelia's rushing through the hallway to drop her clothes off in her bedroom and to pick up her gym bag. Suddenly, Bruce opens the bathroom door.

"*Heeeey*, Melibru!"

Since they've been little kids, Bruce always teases Amelia, making up names that combine both of theirs. He thinks it's so funny. I do too. And, Amelia did too, a long time ago. She used to laugh, but now she doesn't. She gets so upset and that's when the fights start.

One time, Amelia was lying on her bed, talking to girlfriends on a group call with the speaker on. Bruce walked in saying, "Poop-Poop!" real loud. When her girlfriends heard him, they laughed *so* hard and wouldn't let her live it down for months. In between classes in the hallway, they'd say "Poop-Poop!" walking by, teasing her for the fun of it. She was *so* mad at Bruce for a long time. In fact, she called me up crying about it, because she was *so* embarrassed.

Rushing back out of her bedroom, she sees Bruce standing in the hallway. With a hard look in her eye, Amelia brushes pass him, almost skimming the side of his body, as if that's supposed to frighten him. It's her way of controlling the situation. In her mind, by doing things like that, Amelia thinks she's annoying him, but she's not. She's only giving him ammunition to push further without realizing it.

"I know you love me!" Bruce is chuckling, standing there looking at her while brushing his hair.

She drops one of her Nike shoes. Picking it up, she gives him a hard look again. "You're a jerk!"

"Now, *that's* what we call love, folks!" Bruce isn't moved.

Really mad now, because he took such a long time in the shower, Amelia rushes downstairs, purposefully not telling him what Uncle Joe said about going to Cracker Barrel for breakfast.

In the kitchen, Margaret's loading the dishwasher with dishes. She hates a messy kitchen. After talking with Margaret for a little while, Uncle Joe goes to the living room to watch TV while he's waiting for Bruce. Amelia dashes into the kitchen, throws her gym bag down by the island, and and sits down at the table to put on her tennis shoes.

"Are you ready now?"

"Yeah, Ma, let's hurry! Coach is waiting!"

Margaret fixed breakfast and wrapped it up on a plate, so Amelia can eat in the car on the way.

Grabbing the plate off the counter and a bottle of Tropicana orange juice from the refrigerator, Amelia quickly picks up her gym bag, throwing it over her shoulder.

Closing the dishwasher door, Margaret looks at her. She's concerned about her dropping the plate rushing so fast.

"Make sure you're holding that plate carefully and go say goodbye to Uncle Joe. He's in the living room."

Rushing around the corner, Amelia's holding the plate of food with one hand and putting the bottle of orange juice in her pocket with the other. Quickly walking up behind the sofa, Amelia leans over and kisses Uncle Joe on the cheek. "Muuuuah!"

Turning around, Uncle Joe looks up. "OK, baby girl. Give 'em your best as you always do! See you when you get back."

Standing at the garage door, Margaret swings her purse over her shoulder, grabbing the house keys off the hook on the wall.

"OK, Joe! We're leaving! I'm staying at practice with Amelia! We're coming back home afterwards!"

Margaret loves basketball just as much as Amelia. Her dad was a fanatic and loved to play ball himself. Even though Margaret's a working mom, she tries her best not only to attend Amelia's games, but practices also. She has always felt that if Bruce and Amelia had a dad, he would be right there with Amelia at all of her games and practices as well.

Holding the door to the garage open, Margaret's intensely watching Amelia walk fast with the plate of food in her arm. Seeing that look on her mom's face, Amelia's holds the plate a little tighter.

"And you better not waste one drop of it in my car. Let's go!"

Margaret is very particular about keeping a clean house and a clean car. As they say…"the apple doesn't fall far from the tree." She's got it honest. Nana and Mable are the same way.

Chapter Four

In the car on the way to practice, Amelia's brewing with anger about Bruce, but keeps quiet, not saying one word while she's eating breakfast. Margaret's singing one of her favorite worship songs, "How Great is Our God," the whole way. Rarely will you find Margaret listening to secular music. Generally, she plays worship music when she drives to meditate on the Lord and to keep her spirit lifted, but this morning she needs it to calm her nerves.

Pulling into the parking space in front of the school gym, Margaret turns the ignition off, looking directly at Amelia. Amelia's taking her last bite of food. Despite the rush, they arrived a few minutes early.

Margaret's in a better mood now. The worship music calmed her down. But, looking at Amelia, Margaret can tell she's not calmed down from the incident with Bruce earlier. Before they go into the gym, Margaret addresses the issue.

"Amelia, anger doesn't yield righteousness. I'm your mother and I *know* when you're upset. You don't have to *tell* me that you are, for me to know. I know without you saying *one* word. Sweetie, what you must realize is that by our *own* implication, when we don't forgive…it's the same as not admitting that we're guilty of it in our hearts. The responsibility of a child of God is to *love* others and to *forgive* them, if they hurt us. God's children are called *peacemakers*."

As a believer in the Lord, Margaret doesn't want Bruce or Amelia to be blindsided by the ways of the world or to conform themselves to those kind of ways. So, even though she's still a tad bit upset from earlier, Margaret purposefully rises above her feelings out of concern for Amelia's own spiritual growth to teach her a valuable lesson about holding unforgiveness in her heart. Instead of allowing emotions to harbor, Margaret makes herself an example of what it means to forgive by showing Amelia through her own actions.

Looking out the window at other team members walking in to the gym, Amelia remains quiet.

"Look at me."

"What, Ma?" Amelia turns around, still having a little attitude.

Margaret's trying real hard to control herself, looking upward for a moment.

"*Lord Jesus*, help me please, 'cause my flesh wants to *knock* this child out. OK, OK...let me breathe." Taking a couple of deep breaths, Margaret calms down again.

Looking over at her mom, Amelia's realizing she's pushing it a bit too far.

"OK. I apologize, Ma. I didn't mean to say that."

Looking back at Amelia, Margaret's taking another deep breath, recomposing herself again to get into the *right* spirit, so she can handle this situation as best she can with grace and love.

"Listen, we *grieve* the Holy Spirit when we're disobedient to God. Acting in anger does just that. The Bible says, *'be angry, but sin not.'*"

"Ma, I'm *not* upset."

"*Stop it*, Amelia. You call that look on your face *not* being upset? You know, the one thing you *do* share with your Nana is wearing your feelings on your face."

"Ma…I said, I'm not upset." Amelia's trying to convince Margaret by being calmer, but it's not working.

"Amelia, stubbornness gets us *nowhere*. I tell you and Bruce all the time, the name of 'this *game*' on earth is called 'Get to Heaven,' and there's only *one* way…Jesus. And, it's not by only *knowing* Jesus, but *allowing* Jesus to *live* in our hearts and being *doers* of His Word."

"Bruce just gets on my *nerves* sometimes, Ma."

Finally, Amelia's expressing her frustration. Admitting the truth is hard for her to do most times, because she likes to win all the time, not lose. But, with certain people, she knows she can't play, even though she tries sometimes; her Mom is one of them.

Without Amelia saying any more, Margaret immediately recognizes something much deeper going on with Amelia—unwillingness to forgive.

"Amelia, do you remember when you were ten years old, ruining my brand new outfit for one of the *biggest* job interviews I've ever had?"

"A little. But, what does that have to do with anything?"

"It was a *beautiful* ivory suit I bought on sale from Saks Fifth Avenue specifically for a job interview. The night before my interview, I laid my clothes, shoes, and jewelry on my bed. I was *so* excited, because that interview was for the position of vice president of the northeastern sales division. They were offering me *much more* money than I was making at the time. I'll never forget it. That night, you went into my bathroom and used my red nail polish, without asking. I was so busy running around the house preparing everything for the next day. Then, you *laid* on my bed to watch the *Fresh Prince of Bel-Air*. Without paying any attention at all to my suit on the bed, you rolled over *right* on top it."

Amelia's eyes get slightly big. But, she's still trying to be cool. "Wow. I forgot about that."

"Yes, 'wow.' Needless to say, I couldn't wear that beautiful suit I just bought for the interview the next morning. Can you imagine how disappointed I was with you? I was really looking forward to wearing that suit. But, I thank God, because He blessed me; I got the job anyway."

With her eyes squinted, Amelia's looking at Margaret.

"So, I don't understand why you're bringing this up now."

"Amelia, a person who's faithful in small things, will be faithful in big things. A person who's dishonest when they have the chance of being honest regarding small situations, will likely be the same way in bigger ones. Either you're faithful to God or you're not. You think not forgiving Bruce or anyone else for that matter does something to them, when it's the opposite. Unforgivingness, sweetie, makes you the captive, not the other person. And, God doesn't like it. In fact, He won't forgive you, if you can't forgive another."

"I forgive Bruce, Ma."

"Then, baby, if that were the *truth*, you wouldn't be mad at him right now. Let it go! You haven't *really* forgiven Bruce and a few other people I'm reminded of.

"Maaaa." Tilting her head back and sighing, Amelia's looking up at the ceiling.

"Shhhh! *Listen to me!* You must understand, Amelia, the severity of unforgiveness and how it can cause people to go straight to hell. Being unforgiving is a sin; it's like having debt that people have to pay. This is serious. You need to get this. God will *not* forgive you, Amelia, for things you do, if you can't forgive others for things they do. The Kingdom of Heaven is like that of a king who has slaves that owe him money. And, the king wants to settle his slaves' debts. So, there's one slave, in particular, who owes him a lot of money, let's say...ten thousand dollars. He calls for this slave to be brought to him. Mind you, this slave has *no means* to repay the king what he owes him. So, the king commands him to be sold, along with his wife, children, and *everything* he has. This is the king's way of collecting payment. When the slave hears this, he falls to the ground, prostrate before the king and says to him, *'have patience with me and I will repay you everything.'* The king hears the slave's plea and feels compassion in his heart for him. So, he *forgives* the slave and releases him. The king lets the slave go free and the slave doesn't owe him anything anymore. The slave is debt free with the king. Afterwards, the slave goes out, finds one of his fellow slaves who owes him money. He takes the fellow slave by force, chokes the man and says, *'pay back what you owe.'* So, in great distress the fellow slave does the same thing. He falls to the ground and pleads saying, *'have patience with me, and I will repay you.'"*

"I hear you, Ma, but I still don't get what this has to do with me."

Giving Amelia "that look," Margaret's taking another deep breath.

"Did I not tell you to listen?"

Amelia looks at her and just breathes, because by that look she knows her Mom is really serious now.

"So, as I was saying. The slave the king forgave was *unwilling* to forgive his fellow slave and had him thrown in prison, until he could pay back what he owed. Well, some of the other fellow slaves saw what this slave the king forgave did and were deeply grieved, rightfully so. So, they reported it to the king. Then, the king summons the slave and says to him, 'you wicked slave, I forgave you all that debt, because you pleaded with me. Should you not also have had mercy on your fellow slave, in the same way that I had mercy on you?' And, the king became very angry with the lack of compassion in this slave's heart after what he did for him and handed him over to torturers, until he can repay all of what he owed him."

Looking at Margaret really odd now, Amelia's puzzled, still not understanding the point.

"So, you mean to tell me the slave went to jail after all?"

"Yes, Amelia. He did. That story is an example Jesus told of what God will do to those who don't forgive others from the hearts. God may show mercy the *first* time, when someone repents for their wrong doings and asks for forgiveness, just like the king did with the slave; but, if God sees that you're unwilling to extend the same mercy He extends to you like the king saw in that slave...Jesus said, God will do the same thing to you the king did to the slave, sweetie. Hell is real. You must understand...unforgiveness can lead to offense that *must be* removed from the heart. Wickedness is being unforgiving and holding offenses in the heart, Amelia. Wickedness is also causing others to sin. Forgive Bruce and anybody else that hurt you. Walk with the Lord, Amelia. The Lord loves you."

Looking straight ahead, Amelia's taking a deep sigh.

"So, what if someone keeps on doing the same thing to you over and over again? I'm just so tired of Bruce hogging the bathroom when he *knows* I need to get in there, walking in my room without knocking when I'm on a phone call, and teasing me, sometimes."

"Then, my dear, you have to keep forgiving him *over* and *over* again like Jesus teaches us. The disciples asked Him the same question. God is love, sweetie. If we're His children, then we are too. I'll do my part and talk to Bruce. You do yours…and, *forgive*."

Taking the keys out of the ignition, Margaret's grabbing her purse and opening the door. "Now, let's play some ball!"

Chapter Five

The gym is packed. There are two different teams practicing today. Walking inside, Margaret and Amelia see Coach Marcus, a few of the other parents, and some team members.

"Hey, champ!" Placing his arm over Amelia's shoulder, Coach Marcus hugs her tightly. He's six feet, four and a half inches tall, light brown-skinned, and physically fit. Smiling at Margaret, she smiles back. He's so charismatic that he makes you smile, even when you don't feel like it.

"Margaret! So, how are you doing on this fine day?"

"Awesome, Coach. I thank God for everything! Couldn't be better!"

Looking down at Amelia, he smiles.

He's always happy to see, Amelia. She's one of his star players, like Lynn. With her help they almost made it to the state championship last year, but their team missed it by one game. The score was tied. There were fifty-nine seconds left. The crowd was roaring. The Lake High Falcons had the ball. Amelia dribbles down the court and passes it to Jackie, when out of nowhere a player on the opposing team intercepts, takes the ball, runs up the court, and makes a slam dunk, winning the game. Lake High stood stunned in the bleachers.

"Champ! Go put your bag up in the locker room. Hurry up! I have some big news!"

"Alright, Coach." Amelia hurries off to the locker room, excited to hear about the news while he talks with her Mom about the team.

Coach Marcus is always full of energy; that's what everybody loves about him. Besides that, he's positive and never has anything bad to say about anybody. In fact, he's really great for the team's morale, though he can be a bit hard on them, *sometimes*. That's just my opinion. But, they don't take it personally and neither do the parents, because *everybody* knows he genuinely cares about the girls. Coach never disrespects them or talks bad to them like some other coaches. He's actually been like a second dad to many of them. Hmmmm, come to think of it, Coach might be a good man of God for my Margaret, because he loves the Lord too. If she would only open her heart again, there could possibly be something. I've come to a practice or two. I see the way he smiles and looks at her. A momma has to look out for her baby, you know.

Entering the locker room, Amelia sees Lynn and Mrs. Ellis, one of the team Moms, nearby. She knows she has to act right.

"Hey, Amelia!" Lynn looks up and smiles as she's putting her things away.

"What's up?" Amelia's trying to be polite, but it's not easy, feeling the way she does about Lynn.

"Think we're gonna make it to the state tournament? You know our season record is neck and neck with the Ravens."

Hanging her jacket on the hook in the locker and placing her gym bag inside, Amelia slams the door, turning around.

"That's what we've been playing hard for, *isn't* it?"

With one eyebrow raised and her head slightly slanted now, Lynn looks at Amelia puzzled.

"Yes, we are, but…I was only asking. We're all excited…that's all."

Standing next to Lynn, Connie, Lynn's best friend since kindergarten, turns around, and looks at Amelia with a look on her face as if to say, "who do you think you're talking to like that?"

"What's the attitude all about?" Connie turns back, looking at Lynn.

Lynn grabs her hair twist off the bench to pull her hair back.

"Weird…I don't know. Can't seem to figure her out."

"Why even try with an attitude like that? Don't worry about that girl. Let's go play ball, Lynn."

Connie closes her locker and locks it.

"*Ameeen*." Lynn finishes pulling her hair back.

Feeling slightly light-headed for a second, she sits down on the bench real quick.

"Lynn, you OK?"

With her hands placed beside her on the bench and her head down, Lynn shakes her head yes, then gets back up.

"Yeah, yeah."

Connie's looking at her. "You sure?"

"Yeah, I'm OK. Sometimes, I can get a little anemic, but I'll be fine. My doctor gave me a prescription for iron pills. I just started taking them. Drinking lots of water helps too."

"Oh, girl. You scared me for a minute. You know, my Mom suffered with anemia for a while. She had to take iron pills too. But, it gets better. Just keep taking it. It helps give you the energy you need. You'll be fine."

Lynn stands up, smiling.

"Thanks. I'm better now. Let's go. Everybody's waiting."

Lynn and Connie were the last to come out of the locker room. Seeing them approach the court, Coach Marcus claps his hands as he gathers the girls all together.

"Falcons! Falcons! Falcons!"

Everybody's so excited to hear about the news. Parents sit on the bleachers. Some watch with intensity while others pull out laptops, phones, and iPads. Margaret just watches. She has always felt there was no point of staying at practices with Ameila, if she wasn't going to show any interest. Besides, it makes children feel important and indirectly builds their self-confidence. Nonverbal language can be just as important, if not more important, than verbal language with kids.

"Alright! Alright! Gather around! Before we start practice, I have good news to tell you."

Lifting his baseball cap slightly up. Coach Marcus has a bald head. Pulling it back down, Coach stands in the middle of the team with his arms folded over his chest, smiling from ear to ear.

"Yesterday, I received a call."

With a big smile, he takes a quick glance over at Margaret in the bleachers. Secretly, he likes her, but never says anything out of respect. He maintains a professional relationship with all parents.

"We're going to Monroe to play the Dodgers!"

Everyone's jumping up and down and cheering.

"When we beat 'em, we're moving on to the state tournament!"

"Yes!" Amelia smiles at Coach, high-fiving her best friend, Monica.

"I knew we could do it!" Lynn is so excited, hugging Connie.

Parents sitting on the first and second rows, stand up clapping and cheering. A couple of the dads chant: "Falcons! Falcons! Falcons! Falcons! Falcons!"

All of a sudden, the atmosphere in the gym is full of excitement as the word quickly passes. This is the big moment everyone was waiting for...the possibility of playing in the state tournament. There's so much exhilaration in the gym that it causes the other team to look to the other side to see what's happening. Coach high-fives all of the girls.

After hugging Amelia, Monica looks at her.

"Alright, girl, here's your chance to show 'em what you got! You know they been scouting you!"

Although Monica's one of Amelia's closest friends, she doesn't know that not only have colleges been scouting her, but that they had already offered full basketball scholarships a few months ago to Amelia. Amelia just hasn't told her yet. She's been too preoccupied with Blake and Lynn on her mind.

Amelia pauses looking back at her.

"Yeah, that's right, and *nobody's* going to ruin it."

"What? What do you mean?"

Monica looks at her, not expecting to hear that response, trying to figure out what she means.

"Never mind."

"Never mind?" Monica squints her eyes, giving Amelia a crazy look for a moment.

Amelia's still furious inside, because Lynn tried to speak to her.

In the bleachers, Margaret's clapping her hands with a big smile on her face. She knows how important this moment is for the team having been so close to winning the conference championship last year, but especially for Amelia, since she's graduating. Margaret did whatever she could to compensate for the absence of Joel in Amelia's life. She knows being at Amelia's practices matters, because basketball is a big part of Amelia's life.

Calming the team down now, Coach starts the girls off with the usual twenty-minute warm-up drills. Lynn's Mom, Cheryl, surprises Margaret by quickly sitting down next to her.

"Did you hear about Mrs. Stephens' purse?"

Mrs. Stephens is Amelia and Lynn's biology teacher. She's taught twelfth grade biology class for the past seven years at Lake High. She's strict and stands for no nonsense. Most parents love her.

"No, what happened?"

"Her purse was reported stolen during second period on Wednesday."

"*Girl*, stop, no way! One of the kids stole it?" Margaret is shocked. In all the time Amelia's been going to Lake High, never has she heard about anything like this.

"Apparently." Cheryl looks back at her.

"*Wow.* This is the first time something like this has happened at Lake High since we've been there."

"Yes, and Mr. Smith, the principal, is *very* upset."

Trying to catch her incoming call, Cheryl reaches down in her purse to grab her phone.

"Can you give me a minute? I have to catch this."

"Sure, sure, go right ahead."

"Honeeey!" Cheryl steps away.

"Pass the ball! Pass the ball! Let's go! Let's go!" Coach yells.

Reaching for her iPad, Margaret checks to see if there are any text messages from the office. She was tied up in meetings all week reviewing a new sales campaign. Rushing back toward the bleachers, Cheryl sits back down next to Margaret.

"So, as I was saying, Mr. Smith is calling an assembly together for the whole school at ten o'clock Monday morning in the auditorium."

"How did you find out about this?" Margaret looks at her.

"Lynn told me about it Thursday. Amelia didn't tell you?"

"Huh, no, she didn't."

"Well, to my understanding, Mr. Smith is not *only* angry about Mrs. Stephens' purse being stolen, but also about the school's good standing with the state being jeopardized. He can't *stand* dishonesty, you know."

Since Mr. Smith's been Lake High's principal, the school's notoriety has gone up. He's a devout man of God who believes in the right values. Before he became principal, he used to volunteer much of his time at homeless shelters in Monroe, Georgia, about an hour away from Atlanta. Most people know him in Monroe, because he lobbied for equal rights for the homeless. Even though he's principal of Lake High, at heart he's a real activist. That's why he's so big on values. And, being a man of God, he really holds himself and the school up to higher standards. In fact, some non-Christian teachers have tried to oppose him, because they know where he stands as far as his beliefs are concerned. But, that doesn't scare him; he'll tell anybody, dishonesty is his biggest pet peeve. And, despite the opposition, Mr. Smith pressed to make Lake High second in the state best core principles and high test scores. He always says, "Jesus is the Way, the Truth, and the Life."

"Amen to that truth! So, are you going?" Margaret asks, looking really concerned, putting her iPad back in her purse.

"Absolutely!"

"OK, well, I guess I'll see you there."

"I just want to know who tried to implicate my Lynn."

"What? Are you serious? Implicate *Lynn*? I can't believe that. Lynn would *never* steal anything from anyone. She'd give someone the shirt off her back first. I'm so *sad* to hear this."

"Well, thanks for that. I appreciate your support. Anyway, I'll see you there. I hope the girls win this time."

"Me too."

"OK, Margaret." Cheryl waves goodbye as she gets up to go to talk with some other parents sitting a few rows up.

Margaret just smiles back, thinking to herself aloud, "I wonder why Amelia didn't tell me about this. Ten o'clock, Monday morning. I'll be *right* there."

Hearing the news about Mrs. Stephens' purse and Lynn being accused doesn't settle well with Margaret. Something just doesn't feel right to her.

Although, practice went well, the car ride back home is very quiet. Even though Amelia is happy about the team news, she's still pissed off about Lynn. In her head, she keeps thinking, "the nerve of her…"

At a stoplight, Margaret looks over at Amelia.

"So, Amelia, any new events at school going on I should know about to put on my calendar?"

"No, Ma. Nothing I can think of."

"Aaah ha, OK. Well, hearing the news from Coach Marcus today is great, huh? We get another chance to go the state tournament *and* in your last year at Lake High. What a great way to leave, if you guys win."

After zipping up her jacket, Amelia grabs a water bottle out of her gym bag. As a practice, she keeps extra water in her bag, because she knows how important it is to keep the body hydrated, especially after playing ball.

"Yeah, it's the moment we've all been waiting for. Everybody can't wait."

Taking a quick glance at Amelia again, Margaret knows something is up. She's just wondering why Amelia is withholding information about the assembly.

"Awesome. Can't wait to get there and see you guys play. We'll tell the family, so they can come too."

Turning her worship music back on, Margaret slightly nods her head.

Chapter Six

"Heeeey! How was practice?"

Hearing the garage door open, Uncle Joe looks from around the refrigerator. He's getting a ginger brew, his favorite. Margaret always stocks up on them when she knows he's coming to visit.

Margaret and Amelia walk into the kitchen.

"It was good, Uncle Joe. Did you and Bruce go to Cracker Barrel?"

"Why, as a matter of fact, we did, missy. And by the way…thanks for telling him to meet me in the kitchen after he got out of the shower."

Uncle Joe looks at Amelia holding his ginger brew. She pauses as her eyes get big, knowing she did it on purpose.

Margaret sits down at the island and puts her purse on the chair next to her.

"Joe, can you hand me one of those too, please? I *sure* could use one right now."

Neither Joe nor Margaret drink alcohol. They both try to maintain a healthy lifestyle and prefer all natural beverages that are far more refreshing to them. Ginger brew, by far, is their preference.

Hearing a text message come through, Amelia takes her cell out of the gym bag to quickly check the message. Then, she looks at Uncle Joe again.

"I apologize, Uncle Joe. Bruce made me mad and I just forgot."

"What's with the look on your face?" Uncle Joe is looking curiously at Amelia.

"Yes, that's what I want to know." Margaret says. Uncle Joe and Margaret are both looking at her. They noticed a change in her facial expression.

Amelia's irritated that the text is not from Blake. It's Monica.

"Nothing. Nothing."

"Well, aren't you going to tell your Uncle Joe?" Margaret takes a sip of the ginger brew and puts it down on the countertop.

"Tell him what?" Amelia's standing with gym bag still on her shoulder, holding the cell phone in her hand.

"What do you *mean* 'tell him what'? Only that you guys are one game away from possibly going to the state tournament again."

Uncle Joe's eyes get big this time. He is so happy. "Whaaaat? Really? I'm there! When is it? We've got to tell the family!"

Amelia can't help, but smile.

"In three weeks."

"Good! For that, I'll cancel everything on my schedule!"

"For real, Uncle Joe?" Amelia loves when Uncle Joe comes to her games. He really gets involved.

"Alright! Go 'head with your bad self, babygirl! I knew you guys could do it! Give your Uncle Joe a high five and a hug!"

Margaret takes another sip of her ginger brew and smiles.

"Well, this calls for a celebration this afternoon! Dave & Busters! Four o'clock?" Uncle Joe loves to bowl there.

Margaret watches Uncle Joe hugging Amelia, patting her on the back.

"Fine by me, Uncle Joe. You know I'm gonna to kick your butt at bowling anyway!"

"Bet twenty dollars!" Uncle Joe's smiling, looking at Amelia, so proud of her and the team's hard work.

"Fifty!"

Uncle Joe's eyes get even bigger than before. "Whaaat! High roller, huh? OK, shorty. Fifty it is!"

"Well, alrighty then! Dave & Busters it is!" Margaret lifts up her ginger brew like she's making a toast of it, laughing.

"Go tell your brother, Amelia." Then, Margaret gives her that look as if to say, "Remember what we talked about."

"Me? Awwww, man."

Just then the door bell rings. Amelia looks at her Mom. Margaret and Uncle Joe exchange puzzled expressions.

"I wonder who that is. We're not expecting anyone."

"Don't worry, Sis. I'll get it. Just keep enjoying your ginger brew."

Amelia's putting her bag down, walking over to the refrigerator to get some orange-peach-mango juice. She isn't so crazy about ginger brew.

Opening the door, Uncle Joe looks surprised.

"Hello. May I help you?"

Standing before him are two police officers—one Caucasian and the other black.

"Is this the residence of Amelia Elise Parker?"

"Yes, is there something wrong? I'm her Uncle, Joe." Uncle Joe is stunned, wondering why the police would be looking for his babygirl.

Showing police badges, they verify their identity.

The African-American officer identifies himself first, holding up his badge. "I'm Officer Gaines."

Then, the caucasian officer identifies himself, holding up his badge. "I'm Officer Harris."

"We have reason to believe she's been in contact with a Blake Harrison, a major drug dealer on the streets of Atlanta and we'd like to ask her a few questions."

Now Joe is upset, because he understands, but he doesn't reveal his emotions. Nana told him this guy was bad news.

"Joe! Who's at the door?" Margaret walks up behind him surprised to see police officers standing on her doorstep.

"Why sure. Please, come on in. She's not in any trouble, is she?"

"What's going on, Joe?" Margaret's completely shocked. "Drug dealer? Blake Harrison?"

"Everything's going to be all right, Margaret. They want to question Amelia about a drug dealer named Blake Harrison."

"Officers, you can have a seat right in here. Follow me, please."

Uncle Joe leads them into the living room. Margaret calls Amelia.

"Amelia Elise! Come in here, *right* now!"

Amelia heard the last bit of what the officers said about Blake, just after her Mom walked out of the kitchen. She was about to follow her to the foyer when she saw the police officers standing in front of Uncle Joe.

"Amelia Elise! Now!"

"Coming, Ma."

Amelia's walking slowly around the corner toward her Mom, because she's afraid to answer any questions from the police.

Margaret and Amelia walk into the living room and take a seat on the sofa next to Uncle Joe. Amelia's in the middle.

"Amelia, what's this about you knowing a drug dealer named, Blake Harrison?" Margaret is very upset by this time, to say the least.

Officer Gaines interrupts. "Ma'am, please, may we question your daughter now?"

"OK, OK. I apologize. Go ahead."

The police officers are sitting in the chairs opposite the sofa, looking directly at Amelia. Officer Harris begins.

"Amelia Elise Parker is your name, correct?"

"Yes, sir."

"Do you know a Blake Harrison?" Officer Gaines looks straight into her eyes.

Officer Harris adds, "Amelia, remember anything you say could be used against you, so please answer the questions truthfully." Swallowing her saliva, looking scared, Amelia speaks.

"Yes."

"Yes?" Margaret interrupts loudly.

"Ma'am, please, we know you're upset, but we have to question your daughter. We found her cell number in his phone records." Officer Gaines looks at her, holding his note pad.

Beginning to cry, Margaret quickly wipes her eyes.

"Lord, help us!"

Uncle Joe puts his hand on Margaret's back, patting her. "Margaret, Margaret, calm down. Let the officers do their job."

"When was the last time you spoke to or saw, Blake Harrison?" This time Officer Harris makes direct contact with Amelia's eyes.

"Huh, this morning." Amelia's voice is beginning to crack.

"Can you tell us the exact nature of your relationship with Blake Harrison?" Officer Gaines is looking at her and writing on his pad.

Amelia crosses her feet.

"Friends. We're just friends."

Officer Harris leans forward. "How did you meet him?"

"Hum, we met at Starbucks, over by Walmart."

Margaret looks at Joe, squinting her eyebrows together. Joe gives her a look back as if to say, "don't you dare say a word yet."

"Did you ever participate in any drug activity with him?" Officer Gaines asks this time.

"No. No, sir. I don't even know where he lives. Besides, he told me he was gonna get out of that business."

Amelia's slightly shaking now.

"Did he ever try to sell drugs to you?"

Margaret looks at Uncle Joe again. He just pats her back.

"No! I've never done drugs in my life and don't want to!" Amelia's looking at them like they are crazy. "I'm a ballplayer for Lake High."

"Did he tell you anything about his business?" Officer Harris asks.

"No. In fact, he used to say, 'some things you don't wanna know.' So, I never asked."

"Thank God he didn't." Margaret couldn't contain herself with that question. She sits, wringing her hands, trying to calm down.

"Margaret." Uncle Joe looks at her again.

The police officers just look at Margaret.

Amelia speaks out again, beginning to cry. "I just believed he was going to stop, like he said."

"Do you know any of his friends?" Officer Harris asks, steadily looking at her.

"No." Amelia's shaking her head.

Now, looking at Margaret and Joe, the officers close their note pads. "OK, well, that concludes our questioning. Thank you, sir. Thank you, ma'am, for your time."

Really upset now, Margaret inquires, "Well, is he locked up? And, what does this mean now for Amelia?"

Officer Gaines and Officer Harris look at each other, then Officer Gaines answers, "Yes, ma'am. Blake Harrison was taken into custody today. And, as far as your daughter's concerned, we wanted to question her like we are others whose names were found in his phone records and contacts."

Officer Harris follows. "Ma'am, we're trying to get all the leads we can for this case."

Everybody, but Amelia stands up.

"Well, let me walk you guys to the door. Please, officers, if we may be of any further assistance, let us know."

"Thank you, sir, but we've got all the information we need." Officer Harris and Officer Gaines walk behind Uncle Joe to the foyer. Uncle Joe nods his head, opening the door.

"OK, have a blessed day now."

Margaret walks behind them into the foyer and stands next to Uncle Joe. "Have a blessed day."

Just as he was about to close the door, Office Gaines turns around smiling. "Hey, man, I bought your CD for my mother. She loves it."

Uncle Joe looks surprised, smiling back. "Wow. Thank you. Praise God, my brother! Praise God!"

From the bottom of the stairs, Officer Harris turns and smiles. "Yeah, my wife loves you too, man. Keep up the good work. We need to hear more of your kind of music in the marketplace."

"Amen! Amen!" Joe chuckles.

Officer Gaines reaches out to shake his hand. "God bless, man!"

"God bless you too, brother." Uncle Joe shakes his hand and closes the door. Turning to look at Amelia still sitting in the living room on the sofa crying, Uncle Joe takes a deep sigh. "Young lady, you've got some explaining to do."

"That's for *damn* sure!" Margaret rarely curses, but she's steaming mad.

Uncle Joe walks back over to the sofa. Though he was livid, he remained calm. "Now, what kind of friends, exactly, are you with this dude?"

Walking in behind Uncle Joe, Margaret puts her hand on her hip. "Yeah, that's what I want to know!"

"Hold up, hold up, Margaret. I know you're upset. You have every right to be. But, we need to talk about this calmly. Your pressure is probably already up by now."

"It sure is!" Margaret places her fingers on her temples. When she gets really upset, she usually feels the pressure near her forehead.

Amelia's head is down, still crying, barely able to talk. "We were just friends."

"Amelia, do you know you could have been in serious trouble with the law?" Margaret screams loudly.

"Wait, Margaret." Uncle Joe stops her. "What kind of friends do you mean Amelia? 'Friends' friends? Friends 'I-like-you' kind of friends? Or friends 'I-love-you' kind of friends?"

Amelia stumbles through her words. "Friends, Uncle Joe. Just friends." She can't bring herself to tell them the truth.

"So, if you were 'just friends,' why cry so hard?" Margaret looks at her so mad. Uncle Joe looks at her with a raised eyebrow.

By this time, Margaret's head is pounding. She's so upset at the fact that Amelia was involved with a man like this, that she put them all in danger, and on top of it, that they were probably more than just friends.

"Amelia, haven't your mother and I talked to you about the kind of company you keep and having boyfriends?"

"He wasn't my boyfriend."

"Just almost?" Uncle Joe looks at her. "You know, we weren't born yesterday, Amelia."

With her nose running, Amelia covers her face. "I know. He...he was very nice to me."

"Girl, get a tissue from the box of Kleenex on the coffee table." Margaret's still holding her head.

Uncle Joe lifts up her chin and looks her in the eye. "Amelia, you know better. I'm deeply disappointed with you. Do you know you could have been killed messing with that cat?"

Sobbing harder, Amelia can't even respond.

Then, in walks Bruce holding his laptop, looking at Uncle Joe first, his Mom second, and Amelia last. "What's going on in here? Why were the Po-Po at the door?"

Uncle Joe looks quickly at him, putting his finger up to say, "Wait a minute." Turning back to Amelia, Uncle Joe looks her in the eye again. "I hope you've learned your lesson, young lady, in all of this."

Unable to say a word, Amelia shakes her head, looking down, blowing her nose.

"Joe, I can't take any more of this. My head is hurting and my neck is tight now. I have to go lie down and put the heating pad around my neck. Can you handle dinner?"

"Yes, Sis. I got it covered. Just go get some rest. I'll be up to check on you in a little while. In fact, I think we all need a time out for right now." Amelia looks at Uncle Joe and Uncle Joe looks back, sighing. Walking slowly out of the living room, Amelia's so embarrassed she can't even look at Bruce standing in the archway. She's ashamed, because her relationship with Blake is exposed. She knew she shouldn't have given Blake her number the day they met in Starbucks, but she did it anyway.

Bruce looks at Amelia quietly walk pass him, waits a minute for her to go to the stairs, then looks at Uncle Joe, concerned.

"Uncle Joe! Man, what happened?"

Uncle Joe looks disgusted.

"Your sister is what happened. She was involved with a major drug dealer that just got locked up today."

"What?" Bruce looks wide-eyed. "She's lost it! Trying to talk to a man selling drugs?" Bruce laughs. Of all the things Amelia does, he can't believe this one.

Uncle Joe gets up and walks toward the foyer. Bruce follows him. "Lost it is right! And, it's not funny."

Uncle Joe looks at Bruce.

"I know, Unc, but she does some crazy things, man! She's just out of control!"

"Yes, it seems like it, but I'm going to get to the bottom of what's going on in that head of hers."

They both start walking toward the kitchen.

"So, why were the police questioning her?"

"They found her number in his phone records and wanted to ask her questions to gather information for their case."

"So, Amelia's OK?"

"Yeah, man, she's OK with them, but not with me. I'm upset with her about this." Stopping in the kitchen, Uncle Joe turns around looking at Bruce. "Hey, I need to get my mind off of all of this. I have to leave tomorrow afternoon to get back to LA."

"Why so soon?"

"I have to finish up a new gospel CD we've been working on. I need to go back fresh, and I'm starting to get a little headache. Wanna play a few rounds of pool? I need to clear my head."

Bruce smiles. "Cool! Let's go! I'm gonna whip you anyway!"

Uncle Joe's laughing, turning around to open the basement door. "Man, go 'head! We'll see about *that*." Turning to look at Bruce before he goes downstairs, Uncle Joe holds out his hand. "Betcha fifty dollars you lose!"

With a smirk on his face, Bruce is smiling. "Maaan! You on!" They shake on it.

Heading down the stairway, Uncle Joe's thinking out loud. "See, this is why I haven't had kids of my *own* yet!"

"*Unc*, it ain't me! It's your crazy niece! Besides, you need a wife first to have kids!"

Uncle Joe laughs. "Oh, don't worry about that! She's in the makings!" Stopping in the middle of the stairway, Uncle Joe looks up at Bruce. "But, Jesus comes first!"

"I know that's right! 'Cause these women are crazy!" Bruce laughs.

Holding the railings, Uncle Joe's shaking his head, looking at Bruce.

"Unc! They send me nude pictures on my cell and *call me* at all times of the night. Sometimes, I have to turn my phone off just to get some sleep. And, a few times I found one young lady waiting at my car in the parking lot after class. They crazy man! I'm telling you!"

Looking down and still shaking his head, Uncle Joe looks him straight in the eyes.

"Have you ever seen a few branches lying down around at the base of a tree?"

Bruce looks at him like he's weird, trying to figure out what he's talking about. "Yea, why?"

"People who don't put Christ first...*fall*. Without Jesus, they're spiritually dead. Man, *forget about* those young women. They need Jesus. That stuff they do shows you a lot about who's in them. With *Christ* in you, you'll know who the right one is when the time comes."

"Man, that's deep! I never thought about it *that* way! A branch at the bottom of a tree. Hmmm. I like that Unc. Great comparison."

"Boy!" Uncle Joe laughs looking at him like he wants to slap him upside the head. Turning around, Uncle Joe heads downstairs. "I still got some work to do on you! See, this is what I'm talkin' about! Between you and Amelia...this is why I haven't had kids yet! And, I don't know if I'm going to either!"

Bruce is laughing. "I love you too, Unc!"

Chapter Seven

It's chilly outside Monday morning. With the wind chill factor, it is fifty-nine degrees. It's not like it was over the weekend when Uncle Joe was here, in the low seventies. Typical springtime weather, warm for a day or two, then cool again. Getting out of the car, Margaret grabs her purse and closes the door. The wind is blowing a little.

"Wheew, I need my trench! This weather pattern is crazy!" Opening the back door, Margaret picks up the tan trench coat she ordered online from Burberry in New York this past Christmas as a gift to herself.

Walking toward Lake High's entrance, she thinks to herself, "I sure wish Joe could've stayed until Tuesday. I could really use his support today too."

Already sitting in the auditorium, not knowing her Mom is on the way in, Amelia turns and looks at Monica.

"Mr. Smith must be *real* pissed to call the whole school here today."

"I know, right?" Monica's face looks surprised, wondering what the school meeting is about.

Margaret walks through the doors, smiling at one of the teachers standing in the entrance way.

"Good morning. I'm here for the school meeting."

"Oh, hello, Ms. Parker! Good morning to you. Yes, the auditorium is straight ahead on the left. But, we need you to sign in first, in the office." The teacher smiles back.

"Oh, sure! Thanks!"

Lake High's auditorium is huge and well equipped with advanced technology for plays and sound production. It's practically brand new. The board of education pushed to rebuild it nearly two years ago. It's just like walking into a huge theatre.

Inside, parents are taking their seats in the back.

"Hey, girl, you made it." Cheryl smiles, sitting in one of the seats next to the aisle.

"Yes, wasn't going to miss this."

"Here. Saved you a seat."

"Oh, great! Thanks!" Margaret quickly sits down as she sees Mr. Smith at the podium, waiting to begin.

"Isn't that your mother over there?" Monica whispers.

Quickly turning around, Amelia looks toward the back of the auditorium, feeling like her stomach is going to drop through the seat. She remembers what her Mom asked on the way back home from practice.

"Oh my gosh. What is she doing here?" Amelia thinks out loud to herself, trying to be cool in front of Monica. She doesn't want her to know she's upset.

Knowing her friend, Monica takes one look at Amelia's face and knows right away that she didn't tell her Mom.

"You mean you didn't tell her?"

"No."

"*Girl*, you in trouble now! You know your Momma *does not* play that. I even told *my Momma*."

Turning back around in her seat, Amelia crosses her arms over her chest. Really she's trying to hug her stomach.

"Whatever, OK."

"OK, OK. Enough said." Monica motions one hand in the air with an attitude and looks straight ahead at Mr. Smith standing on the stage. She knows Amelia can be secretive sometimes. She dislikes that about her, but it doesn't stop her from being friends.

"Wow, there're so many parents here this morning." Margaret looks amazed at the turnout.

Nodding in agreement, Cheryl is looking around while putting her bag in the seat next to her.

"Sure is. This is good though. It shows parents care."

"Absolutely."

"Good morning, everyone." Mr. Smith's standing at the podium with one hand holding the mic and the other in his pocket. "Welcome parents, if you can quickly take your seats please, so we can get started, I'd appreciate it. Thank you."

Pausing, Mr. Smith gives the rest of the parents that just came through the door a chance to sit down. For about ten minutes now, all of the students have been seated and Mr. Smith has been ready to begin. Most of the faculty are sitting on the stage behind him.

"I'd like to thank everyone for coming today." Mr. Smith pulls the mic closer to his mouth. "We all know Lake High is known for its core values and responsive educational programs. In fact, many of you know that the state recently ranked Lake High number two in Fulton County. I'd like to think that *you* as parents, *we* as educators, and *you* as students are proud of that fact." Mr. Smith clears his throat.

Everyone claps and cheers.

"The reason why I called everyone here today is, because something bad happened that's *never once* occurred during my tenure here at Lake High. Mrs. Stephens' purse was stolen during second period science last Wednesday."

Mr. Smith pauses, looking around the auditorium with a serious look on his face. The auditorium is really quiet. You could hear a pin drop.

"Needless to say, we're *very* disturbed by this. Now, some people have come forth with suggestions of who the person might be that stole it. And, I shall not give any names. But, I want you *all* to know *we will* get to the bottom of this. Lake High has upheld its ethical standards. For that reason alone many of you students attend this school."

Then, Mr. Smith goes on to review Lake High's history and its many notable graduates.

With a surprised look on her face, Monica puts her hand on Amelia's arm to get her attention. "Wooow. Whoever stole Mrs. S's purse is in some *serious* trouble. Everybody knows Mr. Smith is *strict* about respect."

Slightly smiling with a smirk and a look in her eye, Amelia looks back. "Precisely."

In concluding his remarks, Mr. Smith motions to security standing at the doors to open them now. Looking back at the students and parents, he pauses again, putting both hands on the edges of the podium as he leans forward.

"Now, in the past I've been *very proud* to celebrate the core values *many* of you students have exhibited with regard to respect, honesty, fairness, trustworthiness, and courtesy, all of which embody our school's mission to promote peace and unity. And, you all know, *every* year Lake High gives its Core Value Award to one student in each grade."

Mr. Smith looks at the students intensely. "We would like to continue this program. So, I'm counting on your integrity *to do the right thing.* If any one of you has *any* information *whatsoever* regarding Mrs. Stephens' purse, or saw *anything*, please contact Mr. Manning, the school counselor. Are there any questions?"

"Yes, I have one, Mr. Smith." A parent stands in the back. "What action will be taken against the student who stole Mrs. Stephens' purse?"

"Good question. Thank you for asking.

We recently implemented a new program for students we feel need more assistance in understanding what Lake High's core values and mission are about. He or she will be required to do ten hours of counseling with Mr. Manning after school for one week. Additionally, they must complete five hours of volunteer work with other students to demonstrate their level of understanding. Then, approval to return to Lake High will be determined based upon evaluation by myself and Mr. Manning. *Please*...know that we take stealing seriously here at Lake High. Are there any other questions?"

Mr. Smith pauses. "No? OK, the staff and I would like to thank you, the parents, for coming out this morning. We appreciate it and we appreciate your concern. The meeting is officially adjourned now."

Students start to get up and file out of the auditorium. There's lots of chatter among the students about who stole Mrs. Stephens' purse. Parents stand, waiting for all of the students and teachers to leave first, talking amongst each other.

Cheryl looks at Margaret as she stands up.

"That's why I've always liked Mr. Smith. He's about *values*."

Margaret's looking back at her. "*Yes*, and good ones, thank God."

"Well, girl, I'm going to get out of here. I have to get to the office." Margaret buttons up her trench coat.

"OK, glad you came."

"Glad you told me." Margaret looks at her as if to say, "If you didn't I wouldn't have known about it."

Cheryl smiles, but looks a bit bewildered that Amelia obviously didn't tell her.

By this time everyone is talking louder. Mr. Smith is walking up the same aisle where Margaret and Cheryl sat, talking with some faculty members. Just before Margaret heads to the door, she sees him coming toward her. She waits a few seconds. As soon as Mr. Smith walks right by her, she gently reaches out, grabbing his arm.

"Mr. Smith." He stops and turns halfway to look at her, smiling. "Thank you, for being a *great* principal for Lake High. We really do appreciate the high standard of values you hold the kids to."

The other faculty members stand beside him, smiling too, nodding their heads in agreement. Reaching out to shake her hand, Mr. Smith turns the rest of the way around.

"Thank you. As a matter of fact, do you have a moment?"

Looking at him a little funny, Margaret wonders why he is asking. "Yes, of course."

"Great, let's go to my office where we can talk in quiet."

Slightly slanting her head with a little delay in her voice, Margaret agrees. "OK."

Turning to the faculty members, Mr. Smith puts his hand on a teacher's shoulder, looking at him. There are five of them with him. "See you all this afternoon at the committee meeting."

"Sure, sure, Mr. Smith. See you then." They smile and walk away."

Turning back to Margaret, Mr. Smith smiles.

"Let me lead the way to my office now."

The hallway is jammed with students at lockers, teachers trying to get to their classrooms, and parents trying to leave the building.

Holding her books, standing in front of her locker next to Amelia's, Monica looks shocked. "Amelia, you will *never* believe this."

Amelia's reaching in the top shelf of her locker getting her math and chemistry books. "Believe what?"

"Your *mother* is walking with *Mr. Smith* up the hall." Monica's looking in amazement at them walking together.

"Where? I don't see them." Amelia asks, turning around. Grabbing her shoulder, Monica pulls Amelia over toward her a bit. "There. Up there!" Monica points. Amelia looks up ahead, holding her books up to her chest, and sees them right before they turn the corner. "Oh, OK. So what?" Amelia turns back to her locker.

"'So what?' So, you're not worried?" Monica looks at her like she's crazy.

Shrugging her shoulders, Amelia sets her books on the ground to put on her jacket. "No, why should I be?"

"Well, I don't see anybody else's parent walking with Mr. Smith, except *your mom*."

"And?" Hiding her facial expression zipping up her jacket, Amelia's acting like it doesn't bother her one way or the other.

Monica's looking at her. "*Girl,* I've got to give it to you. You sure do know how to play it cool when you're upset. Don't forget it's me, Monica…your friend. You can act like you're not bothered all you want, but I know you are. If it were me…I'd be a *basket case* right now!" Closing her locker, Monica locks it and straightens her books in her arms.

Picking up her books, Amelia looks back at Monica shaking her head.

"Monica, it's nothing. They could be just walking together—Mr. Smith, to his office, and my Mom, to the front door."

"OK, cucumber! Let's get to class before we're late."

"I'll meet you in there, I have to get something real quick."

Looking at her oddly, Monica turns around and walks off.

Grabbing her cell phone, Amelia taps the Twitter app to open it and types a direct message to Lynn:

> Roses are red, violets are blue, guess who's watching you. The fun is just getting ready to start.

In the front office, Mr. Smith walks through the short hallway to his office and opens the door. "Please, have a seat, Ms. Parker." Mr. Smith motions his arm toward the chair in front of his desk.

"So, what would you like to talk to me about?" Margaret takes a seat and unbuttons her trench coat. It is a bit warm in his office. Taking off his suit jacket, Mr. Smith hangs it on the back of his chair and grabs the water bottle sitting on his desk. Then, he looks directly at Margaret and says, "Amelia came to me the other day with information regarding Mrs. Stephens' purse."

"What? She did? Amelia knows something about Mrs. Stephens' purse?" Margaret sits forward.

"Well, the question is more like, 'why did she give me the information she did?'"

"I don't understand. What do you mean? What was the information?" Margaret looks curious.

Seeing the perplexed look on her face, Mr. Smith clearly sees she knows nothing about this. "Amelia said, she thinks Lynn stole Mrs. Stephens' purse."

"What? I know Lynn, and her mother, Cheryl. Lynn would *never* do that." Slightly nodding her head twice, Margaret remembers what Cheryl said at basketball practice about someone implicating Lynn, but doesn't say anything to Mr. Smith.

"*Exactly.* I've known Lynn for some three or four years now. She's been nothing, but a *blessing* to this school and the students."

Crossing her fingers on her lap, Margaret looks intensely. "Well, why would Amelia say that about Lynn?"

"This is what I want to know and why I wanted to speak with you directly. I was planning to call to you this week concerning this matter."

"Well, I'm certainly glad I came this morning. I'm *really* surprised Amelia would do something like this. Amelia has her issues, as we all do, but this…I'm shocked."

"Yes, Ms. Parker. I am too. Which brings me to my next point. The day Amelia claimed Lynn stole Mrs. Stephens' purse, Lynn was tutoring another student during study hall." Pausing a moment, Mr. Smith leans back with his elbows on the arms of the chair, folding his hands together in front of him. "You know, Ms. Parker, Lynn has been tutoring eleventh grade math to certain students every other Wednesday during second period."

Interrupting him, she sighs, looking baffled. "But, I thought Amelia and Lynn have science during second period together?"

Nodding his head. "Yes, in fact, they do. But, last Wednesday was Lynn's day to tutor during the second period. Like I said, she tutors every other Wednesday."

"Well, how do you know that for sure?" Margaret's getting defensive. She knows Amelia's done some "off the wall" things, but this is a serious allegation. She wants to be sure Mr. Smith has all the facts straight before coming to a conclusion about Amelia.

"I know for sure, because Mrs. Kingsbury, our librarian, accounted for Lynn's presence the entire time during second period on that day. She's known for being a stickler for time. Mrs. Kingsbury said, she clearly remembers Lynn being there, because she saw Lynn walk into the library talking with another student just as second period began. She said, she almost had to kick them out, so they wouldn't be late for third period."

Shaking her head gently, looking down, Margaret sighs. "Why would Amelia lie? Something doesn't sound right."Leaning forward over his desk, looking directly at her, Mr. Smith crosses his fingers. "Ms. Parker, there seems to be something going on between Amelia and Lynn. Has Amelia talked about anything with you at home?"

"Nooo. No, she hasn't." Looking troubled, Margaret doesn't know what to do. "This is the first I'm hearing of this. Cheryl, Lynn's mother, mentioned to me at basketball on Saturday that someone implicated Lynn, but I didn't know it was Amelia."

"Well, it's been brought to my attention by a few teachers from what they've observed, without saying anything, that there seems to be somewhat of an issue between the two of them."

Margaret looks back at him. "You know, every time I've seen, Lynn, she's always so pleasant and nice. I can't imagine what could be going on."

"Yes. Lynn is a *very* nice young lady and works hard to stay in our national honors program, as does Amelia. I'm not sure that there might not be some competition going on with Amelia concerning Lynn. Nevertheless, lying isn't tolerated here at Lake High."

Holding back tears, she's so tired of Amelia's behavior lately. "Of course, of course, Mr. Smith. In no way is it tolerated at home either." Margaret's shock dissipates. "So, what now?"

"Tomorrow morning, I'm going to call Amelia into my office to talk with her. Then, I'll be requesting that she spends an hour after school with Mr. Manning, the school counselor, each day for one week to complete a new program we recently implemented. It's for students we feel need more assistance in understanding Lake High's core values and mission. I mentioned it earlier. Additionally, she'll be required to do five volunteer hours working with other students to demonstrate her level of understanding."

"Well, I don't know what to say, but I support your decision. Right is right, wrong is wrong." Margaret looks really sad for her daughter, but she keeps a straight face as best she can.

Mr. Smith can feel her disappointment.

"Ms. Parker, if I may, off the record, I know you're a woman of God who values righteousness. Personally…I do too. If we don't hold our kids accountable for lying at this stage, God forbid what they'll think they can do when they graduate and go out into the world as young adults. It's best to nip this kind of behavior in the bud while we can. I don't know for sure what's going with Amelia.

But, from what I see, it appears she may have some insecurity issues that need to be worked out. Amelia is a *great* student academically. She's been on honors for two years straight now."

Looking at him, she tries to slightly smile, nodding and agreeing. What can she say? Everything he's saying is true.

"Yes, yes. She has been on the honor roll. We've all been *so* proud of her for that, which is why I don't understand what's going on either."

Taking another drink of water, Mr. Smith crosses his fingers again.

"I heard a few college recruits came here, specifically to watch Amelia and Lynn play ball."

"Yes, they have. I don't know about Lynn, but Amelia's already received full basketball scholarships from UCLA, Brown, and Spelman."

"See...this is exactly what I mean, Ms. Parker." He leans back again, disturbed. "Amelia's a *very* talented young lady, extra ordinarily so indeed."

Margaret takes a deep breath. "Indeed she is. Indeed she is. Well, Mr. Smith, I don't want to take up any more of your time. Thank you *very* much for informing me about all of this. I do understand what you're saying. I'll be talking with Amelia this evening. And, I want you to know again, I'm in full support of your new program and requiring Amelia to complete it. I know it will be hard on her. But, as I tell her all the time, there are consequences to pay for negative actions."

Standing up, Mr. Smith walks around his desk. "There certainly is."

Without him saying, Margaret knows Mr. Smith was trying to say Amelia lied on Lynn for no reason and just got caught. Margaret knows Amelia is very competitive in everything, not only with school and sports. However, this is taking things to a whole nother level.

Standing up, Margaret leans over to pick up her purse. She can't wait to leave his office. She is so embarrassed. That's why she wished Joe could have stayed just a little longer. Between experiencing the police in her home on Saturday and this meeting with the principal today, things are all beginning to become just too much. And, on top of it all, she has no choice, but to go to work this morning. She has a big sales campaign to finalize with her staff.

Reaching for her hand, Mr. Smith gently smiles once again. Pulling her purse over her shoulder quickly, Margaret holds out her hand to shake his.

"You know, no one here knows this, but I used to be a pastor." He looks her in the eye.

"Really?" Margaret smiles, slanting her head to the left. "Who would have ever thought that? But, I must say…I'm not surprised."

"Amen!" Placing his other hand over hers, cupping it, he takes one step closer. "I've seen people who are seekers of themselves reject truth and follow evil." One of Mr. Smith's eyebrows goes up. She looks up at him with her eyes squinted. Mr. Smith is six feet, two inches tall.

"Unfortunately, me too." Margaret shakes her head in agreement.

"But, the wrath of God will be upon those that continue in that way." He looks at her as if to say, "you know what I mean."

Looking at him straight in the eyes, Margaret slowly nods her head again. "I understand. Amen." He nods and slightly smiles.

"Thank you, Mr. Smith. I appreciate that." She smiles back.

"Anytime. Anytime." Releasing her hand, he opens the door. Margaret walks out saying under her breath, "Lord Jesus, help Amelia, because 'no lie is true.'"

"Give me the remote! You've been hogging it the whole time!" Amelia's angry at Bruce. Whenever Bruce is in the living room, he loves to hold the remote, even when he's not watching TV.

"Here! You complain too much! Take it!" Bruce leans back on the sofa with one elbow and a leg propped up, turning on his laptop. Snatching the remote out of his hand, Amelia quickly flips to the local news channel, WSB News. Secretly, she wants to see if there's any breaking news about Blake since his arrest on Saturday.

"Why you want to watch the news all of a sudden? Trying to find out about your boyfriend?"

"Shut up! You always got something to say!" They don't hear their Mom come through the front door. Today, she has decided to leave the car parked in the driveway.

"Well, the question is valid, Amelia." Margaret's standing behind them, putting her keys on the sofa table, taking off her trench coat. Both of them quickly turn around, surprised to see her standing there.

"Hey, Ma. No, I was just looking." Amelia turns the channel.

"Wow, Mom, we didn't hear you come in." Bruce looks up.

"I know. I planned it that way today." Taking off her heels, Margaret reaches into the box on the table to grab one of the melt chocolate cashew caramel patties she loves so much. Ginger brew and good old-fashioned, melt chocolate cashew caramel patties are the two things she always buys for Joe when he comes.

"Wheew, it's been a *long* day. Did anybody cook?"

"Cook? You know the only thing Amelia can cook is a piece of toast!" Margaret enjoyed Bruce still living at home while going to Morehouse. There were times he made her laugh when she needed it the most. And, today she is so tired she can't help but laugh, even though she is still upset with Amelia. "True that."

"See, Bruce, you not right." Amelia gives Bruce the evil eye look.

Bruce yells, "Nana! Ma's home!"

"Nana? Nana's here? How did she get here?" Margaret looks at Bruce with a funny look, because usually when Nana comes over, it's on the weekends.

"She called me earlier today to come pick her up. She said she wants to talk to you in person, so I drove her over after classes."

Nana walks in from the kitchen, holding the last ginger brew. "Huh oh, it's 'bout to be *on* up in here! Nana and Ma in the same room for a talk!"

"Shut up, Bruce!" Amelia looks annoyed.

"He's right, because I had a meeting with your principal today."

Nana takes a seat in one of the oversized chairs across from the sofa. "Well, hell. Oh, forgive me, Lord. I didn't mean to say that! Lord, forgive me, please. I repent, Lord. This is toooo much! What happened now, Margaret? Lord have mercy!" Nana is beside herself about Amelia.

"Nana, you got the last ginger brew!" Bruce looks disappointed, because he's been craving it all day. He wanted to save it for dinner.

Nana looks at him, smiling, taking another sip, propping her feet up on the ottoman. Margaret's living room is very cozy and warm. Designed for family comfort, it showcases beautiful soft, off-white colors with hints of peach and baby blue. An oversized L-shaped sofa; a beautiful glass top, coffee table with a contemporary style, gold base; two large chairs with small tables; pillows; wall art; a tall Bird of Paradise plant; and a sixty-inch flat screen TV perfect the charming, custom-made fire place, wide crown moldings and plush carpeting.

"Nana! I can't believe you did that to me."

"You should have told me, Bruce. I would have saved you half." Nana laughs.

Putting the remote down on the coffee table, Amelia sits back on the other end of the sofa, grabs a pillow, and looks down. She's disappointed she didn't see anything on the news about Blake, and she knows she's in trouble again.

Margaret looks up at Nana and then, Amelia. "Amelia Elise, you know we love you, right?"

"Yes." Amelia speaks lowly.

"So, what's going on with you, baby?"

At this point, Margaret's worn out from everything she's been dealing with around Amelia, especially over the past few days, and work.

Nana interrupts. "Wait a second. What happened in the principal's office?"

"Momma, give me a second, please. There's a lot you don't know."

"That's what *you* think." Nana gives Margaret a look letting her know she knows something.

"OK, Momma. It's been a long day, a long week, and a long life. I'm tired." When Margaret suffers from the lack of rest, she really starts to "lose it," so to speak. Ever since this big ordeal with the police on Saturday, she's not been able to sleep well for the past two nights.

Amelia speaks up. "I'm fine, Ma. I'm fine."

"So why, then, would you tell a lie on Lynn? I had a long talk with the principal this morning in his office."

"What? What are you talking about?" Amelia's starting to get an attitude.

"Watch your tone, child!" Nana gives her a hard look. She's already irritated with Amelia, knowing all she doing. "Don't make me get up out of this chair. It's been a long time since I've whipped some behind. I'll do it again, if I have to. Watch your *mouth*! Do you hear me? Now, answer your mother the *right* way!"

Bruce plays a lot, but he knows now is *not* the right time. He keeps working on his laptop, refusing to look up, waiting for a good moment to exit the living room.

Looking at Nana, Amelia knows not to play with her. She's personally experienced Nana's spankings when she was little and has taken her seriously ever since. Nana's an older woman, but she's a *strong* woman.

"I didn't tell a lie on Lynn. Mrs. Stephens' purse was stolen during second period science class. Sometimes, Lynn hangs around after class."

"But, you know Lynn, Amelia." Margaret looks at her very disappointed.

"Know Lynn? No, I don't know Lynn like that."

"Amelia, you know Lynn well enough to know she wouldn't steal Mrs. Stephens' purse."

"Ma. No, I don't."

"Lynn, couldn't have stolen it." Margaret is angry.

"How do you know, Ma?"

"Because, Lynn was in the library tutoring another kid during second period science class on that particular Wednesday. Mrs. Kingsbury, the librarian, accounted for Lynn's presence from the time second period began to the time it ended. She practically had to kick Lynn and the other student out to go to class."

Bruce looks up at Nana and figures this would be a good time to leave. Nana gives him a slight nod, agreeing. She knows what he is thinking.

Sighing, Margaret takes her hand through her hair. "Amelia, you know Lynn tutors and has been now for some time."

"Yeah, and?"

"Amelia, I am *very* surprised at you *and* disappointed."

"Me too, why would you do such a thing?" Nana looks, putting the ginger brew down on the coffee table next to her.

"I didn't lie, OK? She spends a lot of time in there."

"Did you actually see her in the room that day?" Margaret's looking exhausted.

"No. But, everybody's knows Lynn helps Mrs. Stephens out a lot, so I figured it could be her." Amelia knows she was wrong and has been caught again.

"OK, I see what's going on now." Margaret looks at Amelia, then at Nana, who looks back at her with a cocked eyebrow. "You figured since everybody knows Lynn hangs around science class a lot, they would easily think it was her who stole Mrs. Stephens' purse. But, you didn't consider the fact that Lynn has an impeccable reputation with Mr. Smith and all of the teachers."

Nana interrupts again. "The question is…why would you lie on Lynn? Has Lynn done anything to you we need to know about?" Nana's trying to give her the benefit of doubt at this point, but inside she knows Amelia's lying.

"No, I didn't lie!" Amelia's getting upset.

"But, you didn't tell the truth either." Nana looks at her. Nana already surmised the whole situation without having to hear any more. "You knew that day Lynn wasn't in science class during second period. You can't *tell* me you haven't noticed that Lynn is absent from your second period science class, sometimes. But, because you have a vendetta with Lynn, you thought you could get her in trouble. But, you didn't think it through and you got caught, Amelia." Nana called her out.

Amelia's crying now, not knowing what to say. Nobody can fool Nana. Nana looks over at Margaret, placing her hand up to her head. "Amelia, I need to talk with your mother alone now. You may be excused."

Amelia gets up and rushes upstairs. Bruce passes her in the hallway as he's going to the bathroom and stops. "Amelia, what's wrong? Seriously. I know I joke with you a lot, but what's up? I'm your big brother; you can talk to me."

"I'm fine! Leave me alone!" Amelia walks quickly to her bedroom and closes her door hard.

Back in the living room, Margaret sits across from Nana in the other oversized chair, with her head leaned back and her arms lying on both sides. Her head is hurting from all of the stress Amelia's causing, so she's trying her best to calm down and relax.

Nana picks up her ginger brew and takes another sip. "Margaret, last night I had a bad dream that woke me straight up out of my sleep. And, you know when I have dreams like that, it's the Good Lord speaking to me."

"I know, Momma." Margaret starts crying softly, overcome by what's going on with Amelia and how to help her. "I just don't know what to do anymore."

"I know, I know, baby."

"I do everything I can to raise her *right*, in the Ways of the Lord and look at the things she's doing, Momma. Saturday, the police knocked on the door to question Amelia about a drug dealer she was involved with. I didn't even *know* about Amelia was talking to a man like that."

"What? The police came here?"

"Yes, they arrested him. His name is Blake Harrison. They found Amelia's cell number in his phone records and wanted to question her about how she knew him, did she know about his business, and what kind of relationship they had together. Apparently, they're questioning a number of people who were involved with him somehow to gather more information for their case."

"So, he's in jail?"

"Yes. Thank God." Margaret looks at Nana.

"Thank God he is out of her life now!"

"What do you mean?" Margaret sits up. "You knew about this?"

"Yes, baby. Faith called me the other day concerned about it. She told me everything."

"Faith?"

"Amelia told her, but not everything."

"So, why didn't you tell me?"

"Margaret, why do you think I'm sitting here on a Monday night? I told Bruce to pick me up today, so I could tell you. I couldn't talk to you over the phone about something like this."

"My goodness!" Margaret rests her head back on the chair again. "Momma, this is just too much. I am *exhausted*. Ever since the police left here Saturday, I haven't been able to sleep well. I've been averaging about five hours of sleep a night and you know for me that doesn't work. You know, I need at least six and a half to seven. Work is intense. We have a major a new sales campaign starting. And, this past Sunday, I started my cycle for the month again. You know how that is when you're going through perimenopause, Momma. One night you might sweat out your night gown and the next night you might be cold. I go from pulling the covers on me to taking them off through out the night. Crying at the drop of a hat, sometimes. You're more emotional than you usually are. Trying to control these hormones is challenging, especially with all this major stuff going on with Amelia. Momma, I tell you...I have *never*, in all my years of being a mother, even when Bruce growing up, felt like I wanted to slap the "you-know-what" out of one of my children.

"Well, perimenopause might make you want to slap anybody, baby. Been there, done that. You'll be all right. We all go through it, some worse than others. It's just part of the transition your body is going through. Too bad you don't have a husband though. He could help you work off some of that frustration. You know, like walk around the neighborhood...exercise...in the house...together?"

As bad as her head is hurting right now, Margaret slowly turns it, looking at Nana as if to say, "You had to go there, Momma."

"Don't look at me like that. I know what I'm talking about. Before your daddy passed, we..."

"Momma! Momma! Please! OK! I don't want to hear about you and Daddy. TMI! To much information!" Margaret sighs, gently shaking her head, placing one hand up over her forehead.

"I'm just saying, baby." Nana looks at her, holding the ginger brew.

"OK, Momma. I get it. Okay, thank you."

"Good."

"I just pray God makes a way for this situation, because I've come to my wits' *end*, Momma."

"Baby, God never gives us more than we can handle."

"Well, Momma, I need help *now*, and I need some sleep *now*. It's tough being a single mom."

"That's why I thank God for Joe, Margaret. But, like I said, you'll be fine. It's Amelia I'm concerned about." Nana's getting serious again. "Something *bad* is about to happen concerning Amelia and Lynn, and I don't think it's because of something as simple as lying on Lynn. I don't know what, Margaret, but I tell you, it's not good. In that dream, I saw a *big* accident. Somebody got hurt badly. I couldn't see the face. But, I could see them on a stretcher with blood everywhere. Wheeew! I'm getting chills all over me again!"

Everybody in the family, particularly Margaret, knows to take Nana's dreams seriously.

The phone rings.

"One sec, Ma." Margaret leans forward reaching for the cordless phone on the coffee table.

"Hello?"

"*Girl*, you sound tired!"

"Aunt Mable?" Margaret lifts her eyebrows.

"It's me, honey. I been calling your Momma all day, but I can't get her."

"Oh, she's right here, Aunt Mable. You wanna to speak to her?"

"Yes, baby. Let me speak with her for a minute."

"Ma. Aunt Mable." Margaret hands the phone to Nana.

"Mable? What do you want?" Nana loves to kid with Mable.

"Sissy, the next time you go off somewhere, let me know so I won't be so worried about you!"

"Awwww shucks, Mable! You worried about me? Look at my boo! Mable Ann, look…when it's my time. It's my time, OK?" Nana laughs.

"Sissy, you know I don't like you playing like that! I'm calling, because it's our last day of fasting and prayers for Amelia. Have you told Margaret the news yet?"

"We're sitting here talking about it now."

"Good, because I'm feeling something, Sissy, and it's not good. Something bad is going to happen."

"I'm preparing Margaret for it now. I'll call you when I get home."

"OK, I'll be waiting."

"Bye, boo! I love you, boo." Nana laughs.

"Sissy, you always got jokes." Laid back in her La-Z-Boy chair with the therapeutic massager on and the remote in one hand flipping through cable channels, Mable just shakes her head.

"Mable Ann, with all of this craziness going on in this world *and* our family too, we need to laugh. Talk to you later, girl."

"Bye, girl!"

Hanging up, Nana looks at Margaret leaning back in the chair again with her hand placed over her forehead. She can tell Margaret is really tired.

"I have a slight headache, Momma. I'm gonna get out of these clothes. Are you staying for dinner?"

"Nooooo, baby. I got to get back to the house, because Mable and I are finishing the last day of fasting and prayers for Amelia."

"For who?" Margaret looks.

"Your daughter...my granddaughter."

"Good. Because, she needs it and so do I, for that matter."

Growing up with a Holy Ghost-filled mother and a grandmother from Nigeria who loved the Lord too, Margaret understands the seriousness of days (sometimes weeks) spent fasting and in prayers. The people on her mother's side of the family are devout Christians. They believe with all their hearts in Jesus Christ. In fact, Margaret has quite a few uncles, aunts and cousins who became pastors. She has a big family. When they hold services, the ministration of the Holy Ghost is so powerful.

"Margaret, I might joke and kid around, but you know I'm serious about praying. The Bible says, *'cast your burden on the Lord, and He shall sustain you; He shall never permit the righteous to be moved.'*"

"Amen!" Margaret leans forward to pray. "Father, in the Name of Jesus, thank You so much for Your Grace that carries me everyday. I love You so much, God. I really need You to intervene in this family, God. No one can do what You can. There is none other greater than You, Father. This situation with Amelia is a heavy burden. I'm going to obey Your Word that's infallible, that will never return void and bring this heavy burden on me to You. I know, You'll continue to sustain me and never permit me to fall, because angels from Heaven are working for me, in Jesus Christ's Name. I have the *sustaining* Power of *God* working in me! Ameeeen!"

"Amen! Amen! And, Amen! It is so, in Jesus' Name! *Everything* is going to be alright, baby! I know it, because God *always* gets the glory! We are victors in Christ!"

"I receive that, Momma. I receive that. Thank you. By the way, did you know Mr. Smith was a pastor?"

"He finally told it, huh?"

"What? You knew he was a pastor and didn't tell me? Momma, you withholding information!"

"Mr. Smith's daddy was your daddy's cousin's best friend."

"Get out of here! Oh, my head, my head!" Margaret places her hand back over her forehead. "Are you serious?"

"Yes I am. He took after his granddaddy who was a well-known preacher in Monroe, back in the day."

"Wooow. It's a small world."

"It sure is and a *nastier* one now!"

"Momma!" They both get up to walk to the kitchen.

"Well, it's the truth! Kids killing kids in the classroom! Look at that young boy who was cyberbullied! Came to school with two large knives and stabbed every kid he could get his hands on! More black men are in prison than ever before! Everytime you turn around you here about a young black man shooting another black man! You ride down the street, cameras take pictures of your car, if you go thirteen miles over the speed limit! They collecting money all kinds of ways! And, everybody sings these days and about nonsense! No more good songs like there used to be! Anybody can make a CD now! And, these crazy reality shows are just to much! Women swapping houses with husbands for two weeks! What mess! You got people traveling to the Amazon Rainforest in a boat for money! They get off the boat naked to live in the forest for three weeks to get eaten up by all kinds of unknown bugs and mosquitos. Who are they supposed to be, Crocodile Dundee? What kind of craziness is that? Oh, and you got young people walking around with green strips of hair! And, some just color their head blue! They just don't care anymore! And some people put tattoos over their whole body! We didn't do all of that stuff growing up! We honored our bodies for Jesus! And, the government isn't the same anymore! Did I miss anything?"

Margaret's holding her head, leaning over the island now. "OK, OK, OK, Momma, I get your point and I agree. Please, you're making my headache worse."

"Well, it should!" Nana's picking up her shawl. "'Cause it gives me one just saying it!"

"Bruce! Come on, baby! It's time to take Nana home! Bruce!" Nana yells.

"I'll be right down, Nana!" Bruce yells back.

"Margaret, you never did say how you're going to deal with Amelia and this meeting you had with Mr. Smith."

"I don't have to, Momma. What Mr. Smith is requiring now is enough. He's going to call her into his office in the morning. She's not suspended, but she has to complete a one week program for an hour every day after school with the counselor, Mr. Manning. After she completes that, she has to do mandatory volunteer work with other students to demonstrate that she understands the values of Lake High School's mission. Then, she will be evaluated by Mr. Smith and Mr. Manning. Hopefully, this will teach her a lesson."

"Teach her a lesson? I don't know, Margaret. Embarrass her...yes!"

"Well Momma, embarrassment can teach us lessons too."

"With some people, yes Margaret...with others, no. It just fans the fire. Those kinds of people need a little more heat under their tails!"

"You know what? At this point, I agree with whatever you say, Momma. I have to change clothes and get dinner ready. Then, I'm done for the day. Better yet, I just might order in tonight and call it a day."

Bruce walks in to the kitchen. "I'm here, Nana."

"Good, baby, 'cause I'm ready to go. I'm tired now. I got to go to bed. Margaret, tell Amelia I said goodbye."

"OK, Momma. I love you. Bruce, call me when you're on the way back. I might need you to stop at the store." Margaret's still leaning over the island.

"Awwww, Ma! I wanna get back home in time for *Naked and Afraid*."

"'Awwww, Ma' nothing. What's *Naked and Afraid* anyway?" Margaret's looking at him half cockeyed.

"A new reality show."

"Is that the one where people go on a boat to the Amazon Rainforest?" Nana asks.

"Yeah! See, Ma. Even Nana knows about it!"

Nana points her finger at Margaret. "See what I'm talkin' about! All ya'll crazy! Take me home, boy! Let's go!" Nana's picking up her purse and walking toward the garage door.

Margaret tries not to chuckle, because of her headache, but can't help it. "My head! See Momma? You made me laugh."

"Alright, Ma, be right back."

"Call me, Margaret!" Bruce opens the door for Nana.

"Bruce, I can't believe you watch that dumb show!"

"Why, Nana? It's cool!"

"What's cool about watching people with no clothes on, who can't sleep all night, gettting bit up by a million flies and ants. And, more than that…watch them smack themselves over and over again?"

"I don't know, Nana. It's just cool seeing how they're trying to survive through it all."

Nana's getting in the car. Bruce waits before going to the driver's side to make sure she's in properly.

"Boy, I feel sorry for your generation." Nana's shaking her head. Bruce chuckles and closes the door.

Chapter Eight

"I keep getting these weird direct messages on Twitter." Lynn's looking back at Connie while opening the lock on her locker. Basketball practice just ended. They were both tired. It was the last game before the playoffs, so everybody pushed their hardest. Connie, Lynn's best friend, is sitting on the bench for a quick moment before she gets up to get her things.

"Who are they from?" Connie raises one arm over her head toward the right side of her body to stretch.

"I don't know. It's weird."

"Then, just unfollow them or block them. That's all."

The lock pops open on the door, but before she pulls it off, Lynn turns back around again to look at her. "It feels like this person knows me somehow though. It's crazy."

"Why? What did they say?" Connie's stretching her other arm. One of the team Moms, Mrs. Tatum, peaks her head around the corner. "Have a good weekend, everyone!"

"It's like…they say things that are personal to scare me. It's sick."

"Girl, *block* that person and keep it movin'!"

"Yeah." Lynn pauses in deep thought, wondering who it could be. "I'll do that...tonight."

Just then, Lynn sees Amelia walk in the locker room toward the bathroom stalls. "Hey, Amelia. I think it's awesome how you're helping out the girls in the ninth grade."

Stopping right before she turns the corner, Amelia looks back at her. With the front of her body leaning on the corner and one hand on the wall, she chuckles with a smirk on her face. "Really. I wonder why?"

Lynn loves volunteering to help others. The idea of serving people in one capacity or another has become such a big part of her life over the past two years. So, she really does think that it's great what Amelia's doing. She just doesn't know Amelia's doing it, because Mr. Smith caught her trying to lie on her. Pulling her hair band off to let her ponytail out, Lynn tries her hardest to be nice to Amelia.

"I'm just saying, because helping others is a good thing."

Really angry, seeing the smirk on Amelia's face, and hearing the interaction between them, Connie stops stretching and gives Amelia a look. She would say something, but she doesn't want to make Lynn seem weak, like she can't handle herself.

"So, you want a cookie?" Amelia laughs and walks off.

"Why do you even take the time to speak to her?" Connie's so annoyed.

Looking at her seriously, Lynn props one foot up on the bench and leans forward as she places one arm over her knee. "Connie, to know God is to know love. Jesus teaches us to love God with all our hearts, souls, and minds, and to love others."

"Even the ones who hate us, like Amelia?" Connie's joking with her. Lynn just looks at her. "Look, Lynn, I'm with you. I *do* understand. It's just that she's *so* mean to you *all* the time. She never lets up. It makes me mad seeing people like her be that way for no reason. I personally don't think you should speak to her anymore."

Lynn stands up, putting her hands on her hips. "OK, then. How about this? If we don't represent Christ, then what's the purpose of believing in Him? The Bible says, we should be kindhearted to one another and forgiving. If we don't forgive others, God *won't* forgive us."

Connie is shaking her head. "Wow. You don't get it, Lynn. The girl *does not* like you."

"I know she doesn't." Lynn's picking up her gym bag. "But, I take the Word seriously in my life. I just pray God softens her heart, because I believe deep down inside, she has a good one. She's just tough on the exterior."

Just then, Lynn's cell phone rings. Connie gets up to open her locker really quick to grab her gym bag. Lynn's fumbling through the bag to find her cell phone.

"Okay, if you say so."

After finding her cell and seeing who the incoming call is from, she answers quickly before it ends. "Hello?"

"Is this Lynn Braxton?"

"Yes, this is she."

"This is your doctor's office calling back with your test results."

Lynn's face drops as she drops her bag down beside her. Seeing the look on Lynn's face, Connie stops and whispers, "What's the matter?"

Lynn holds her index finger up, motioning "one second" and takes a few steps away. "OK, go ahead."

"Your pregnancy test came back positive. It shows you're seven weeks pregnant."

Lynn almost faints. Connie steps over to her quickly, catching her from behind. It's a good thing everyone just left a few minutes ago and that no one sees her. The girls usually don't hang in the locker room after practice on Saturdays, because everybody wants to get on with the rest of their weekend.

"Hello? Hello? Lynn? Are you there?"

Stammering, Lynn sits on the bench with Connie's help. "I'm here. Yes, I'm here." She's barely able to speak.

"OK. Are you alright?"

"Huh, yes, yes. I'm OK. Thank you."

"Good. So, you'll need to call us back to make an appointment for your first checkup."

"Huh. OK." The notion of being pregnant is far too great to handle, for so many reasons.

"OK, Lynn. Goodbye."

"Huh. OK. OK. Thank you." Disconnecting the call, Lynn drops her hand on her lap as the cell phone slips out, falling to the floor.

Quickly sitting down next to her, Connie puts her arm around her shoulder, shocked by the look on Lynn's face and her demeanor. She knows it's something serious, because she's never seen Lynn like this before. Lynn looks devastated.

"Lynn, what's wrong? What happened?"

Putting both hands up to her face, she cries really hard, trying to talk.

"I'm...I'm..."

"What, Lynn, What?" Connie's really scared.

"Preg...pregnant." Lynn weeps uncontrollably.

Connie's eyes opened wide. "Whaaaat? How? You're a virgin!" She's shocked and frantic. "Oooooh nooooo! Oooh Lynn!" Tears are rolling down her face now too. Her best friend is pregnant and she doesn't know how or by who, because Lynn doesn't even have a boyfriend. She and Lynn took a vow in church, at the age of fifteen with a group of other teenagers, to remain celibate until they got married. Their youth pastor even presented them with chastity rings.

Lynn's sobbing and Connie's thinking out loud. "This can't be!"

Amelia's walking toward the corner of the entrance to the locker room, when suddenly she hears Lynn crying and Connine talking loudly. Anyone listening would clearly know Connie is very upset about something. Amelia had left a few minutes ago with the other girls. In a rush, she left her jacket hanging in the locker. On the other side of the corner wall are the lockers. Inquisite about what's going on, Amelia's standing quietly listening.

Weeping profusely, Lynn murmurs trying to explain what happened.

"My…my…my uncle."

"What? What about your uncle? Lynn talk to me?" Connie's desperately hoping Lynn's not saying what she thinks.

"Unc…Uncle Richard," Lynn murmurs, leaning over her lap with her hands covering her face.

"Your Uncle Richard? Lynn? Answer me. Your Uncle Richard, what?" Connie's being sure she's hearing correctly what she thinks Lynn's trying to say. "Lynn, calm down. It's going to be OK. What are you trying to say about your Uncle Richard?

"He…he…" Lynn says. She can barely talk or even see. Tears flood her face.

"He what, Lynn?" Anxiety is building up fast in Connie, hoping Lynn is not getting ready to say what she thinks she is. Dropping her gym bag from her shoulder on the bench next to her, Connie speaks in a soft tone, hoping to calm Lynn down a bit. Usually she's pretty good with calming people down when they're upset, but this is an unusual situation. Lynn's crying harder by the moment to the point of almost hyperventilating.

"Lynn, Lynn. Just take a moment and breathe. It's going to be OK. You're going to be all right. Just try to calm down, so you can breathe better. Please, Lynn. I don't want you to hyperventilate."

Really worried about Lynn now, Connie closes her eyes and prays. "Lord Jesus, please help Lynn. Comfort her. Calm her down, and give her strength, Lord, to get through whatever this is, in the name of Jesus."

Hearing Connie pray, Lynn's wiping her eyes as her breathing slows down a little from going so fast. Reaching in her gym bag, Connie grabs a tissue really quick and hands it to Lynn. Then, she grabs another to help Lynn wipe her face. Connie's mother taught her to always keep a small pack of Kleenex in her bag.

"Here, let me help you. It's going to be OK. Now, what are you trying to say about your Uncle Richard?"

Lynn feels so ashamed. Still sobbing, but not as heavy…Lynn looks at Connie. Her eyes are red and puffy. She speaks softly, holding the tissue up to her right eye, looking down at the floor again, reluctant to say what she's been trying to say, because she's scared.

"He raped me."

Connie gasps, sitting up straight on the bench with her eyes wide open. Connie screams in disbelief. She was praying it wasn't what Lynn was trying to say. "Noooo! Lynn! Noooo! Noooo! Noooo! *When* did this happen? *How* did this happen? I can't believe this!" Connie loses complete control for a moment. Anger consumes her. "That bastard! How could he!"

Lynn bursts into tears again, crying from the deepest part of her soul.

Gasping, Amelia's stunned. Quickly, she's covering her mouth with her hand and she doesn't move an inch. She can't believe what she's hearing. With the other hand, Amelia quietly pulls her cell phone out of her gym bag to turn the ringer off. Then, she peeks her head around the corner. Neither Lynn nor Connie see her. Holding her cell phone up, Amelia quickly snaps a photo of them. She has the latest Samsung Galaxy; the camera takes awesome high resolution pictures.

Standing up in a rage, not knowing what to do at this point, Connie paces back and forth for a few seconds, gathering herself and her thoughts. Looking at Lynn still crying, Connie sits back down next to her. Lynn looks up, helpless. Connie puts her arms around Lynn's, hugging her tightly. Lynn hugs her back with her arms around Connie's back, sobbing deeply on her shoulder. Connie realizes she has to hold it together right now, for Lynn's sake.

Stroking Lynn's hair, Connie weeps again with her softly, "Listen, we're going to get through this, OK? We'll face this together. You are not alone."

Lynn nods her head, sobbing, with tears rolling down her cheeks.

"Does your Mom know?"

"No!" Lynn immediately becomes frantic, pulling away Connie's shoulder. "And, I can't tell her yet either." Lynn looks frightened.

"Well, Lynn, we have to file a report with the police!"

"Noooo! He'll come after me or my Mom! No! He said, if I told anyone, he'd come back for me! The police can't know about this! Connie, *promise* me you won't say a word to my Mom?"

"Are you serious?"

"Yes, Connie, pleeeease! I just need some time to figure this all out. If I tell my Mom, she'll go after him. I *know* she will. I know her. I don't want him to hurt her either. I need to tell someone who I can trust first, so they can talk to her with me, to help keep her calm and level-headed."

"OK, OK. I promise, you have my word. But, we have to figure this out, Lynn."

"OK, thank you." Lynn takes a deep.

Switching thoughts in her head. "Connie, *how* am I going to raise a baby? I don't know the first thing about being a mother."

Grabbing Lynn's hand, Connie's looking straight at her. "Lynn, you're going to be fine. You're an amazing person. God is with you and He'll see you through this. Remember, what you always say to me? 'All things are possible through Christ.'"

Taking another deep breathe, Lynn looks, nodding her head. "Yes, I believe that. I just have to trust God like I always do." Taking another tissue, Lynn's wiping her eyes again, trying to calm down, but it's hard and scary thinking of human being growing inside of her.

Connie wipes her eyes. "It's so hard to believe he would do that to you. I'm shocked. How did it happen?"

Lynn sits up a little, taking another deep breath with a somber look on her face. "One day, I was home alone. My Mom was still at work. I heard a knock at the door. I never answer the door when my Mom isn't home. But, I heard him calling my Mom's name."

"Who?"

"Uncle Richard. So, I peeked outside the window and saw him at the front door. He kept knocking and knocking. I thought something was wrong. So, I went to the door and asked who it was even though I knew it was him. He yelled, 'Richard!' so I opened it. He came in the foyer and asked if my Mom was home. I said, 'no, not yet, but she'll be here soon.' It seemed like he was a little drunk, but I wasn't quite sure. Everybody in the family knows he has a drinking problem. It's been that way with him for years. Then, looking at the way he was standing, I was sure he had been drinking again. So, I started feeling a little uncomfortable, because he started looking at me with that strange look he's always looked at me with growing up."

Connie gently shakes her head in disbelief with tears in her eyes looking at Lynn.

"So, I said to him, 'Well, I have a lot of homework to do. I'll tell Mom you stopped by.' But he said, 'I have to use the bathroom and then I'll go.' I looked at him and said, 'OK, I'll wait in the living room till you're done,' and closed the front door. Then, he walked to the bathroom by the kitchen and I went into the living room to wait for him to finish. I sat on the sofa to start reading my book for English class and the next thing I know he's standing in front of me. So, I stood up to go open the door and he pushed me down. I looked up at him surprised after I fell down on the sofa. I was shocked, just totally shocked. Then, he grabbed my shoulders and turned me around real quick, and pushed me really hard back on the sofa. I tried to get up, but he pushed me back down again. He put my hands behind my back and held them there with one hand, bending over me. I yelled at him, 'what are you doing? Stop! Stop! Stop!'" She stops for a moment. The recall is making her sick to her stomach. Connie takes a deep breath, fighting back more tears, trying to be strong for Lynn.

"But he told me, if I didn't shut up and stop yelling, he would hurt me. Then, he pulled a pocket knife out of his pocket and threw it on the coffee table and said, 'don't make me use it.' I looked at him in fear, crying hard pleading with him to stop. He's big, about six feet three inches tall, and bulky."

Connie can't help it and screams, "I'm so sorry this happened to you! Why? Why? OK, OK, OK, OK. Let me calm down. Go ahead."

By this time, Lynn's sobbing again.

Amelia's shocked. She's still easedropping hiding behind the wall.

"Connie, there was nothing I could do! Nothing! He had my hands tight behind my back." Lynn cries deeply. "I begged him, 'please, Uncle Richard, don't do this! *Please* stop! *Please* stop! *Please* stop!' Then, he took my hands and raised them over my head, opened his pants, and…and…and….he…" Lynn's breaking down remembering.

Connie's holding herself, wanting to scream again. With tears flowing out of her eyes, she feels totally helpless and full of anger. She sits speechless, looking at Lynn, wanting to take all of her pain away.

Looking back at Connie, Lynn wipes her eyes again.

"Connie, I couldn't move! I couldn't move! So, I closed my eyes and all I could hear was him grunting in my ear! And, it hurt so bad! It hurt so bad, Connie! It hurt so baaaaad!" Lynn couldn't stop repeating it, putting her head down on her lap again.

Getting up, Connie screams, crying, holding her hands up in the air, making fists, punching them downward, three times. "Noooooo! Noooooo! Nooooo! I'm so angry with him! I hope he goes to jail for this!"

Quickly sitting back down on the bench, Connie rocks back and forth with her arms folded, crying. Lynn's crying more softly now, still leaning her head down over her hand on her lap. She's exhausted from crying so hard. They both sit in silence for a few minutes. Putting her hand on top of Lynn's head, Connie strokes her hair, trying to calm her down.

"I can't believe this. *How* could he do this to you? You're his niece."

Tilting her head up first, Lynn sits all the way up on the bench. Speaking slowly and softly with barely any energy to talk, "yeah. I ask myself that same question every day, over and over again. I guess I have no choice, but to deal with this now." She shrugs her shoulders gently. "How do I? I don't know, but I have to. And, what am I going to tell my Mom about who did this to me and who the person was? I just don't know."

Connie's furious about what Lynn's Uncle did. "What do you mean? You *already* said it. Find someone you can trust to talk to her with you and tell her the truth, Lynn! Your Mom needs to know the truth! And, he needs to be locked up for what he did to you!"

"No! Connie, you promised me you wouldn'tt say one word about this to my Mom! She can't know about this yet, or that it was my Uncle Richard who did it! I'm *telling* you! I *know* her! She'll go after him!" Lynn's looking desperate again, because she's afraid of what he told her.

"OK, OK. Calm down. You know I'm not going to do that. We'll think of something together. But, first let's get you out of here." Taking more tissues out of her gym bag for Lynn and herself, Connie hands some to her. "Here, wipe your face. We'll figure the rest out later." Standing to help Lynn up, Connie swings her gym bag over her shoulder.

Behind the wall, Amelia drops her cell phone.

Turning round real fast to look toward the wall, Connie squints her eyes, wiping them again. "What was that?"

Lynn looks, shrugging her shoulders, wondering. "I don't know. I thought everybody left."

"Me too."

"You stay right here, let me check." Connie's disturbed, hoping no one heard the conversation. She's really protective of Lynn. They've been friends since they both were five years old.

Amelia quickly picks up her cell phone and runs toward the door fast. As soon as Connie turns the corner, the door shuts. But, when she looks at the door, it was closed. Standing on the other side of the door, Amelia sighs a sigh of relief that she made through without any noise.

"Hmmmm. Nobody's here. I don't see anyone." Connie looks around. Walking back toward Lynn, she sees her trying to stand up.

"Wait. Let me help you." Making sure their lockers are closed, Connie grabs Lynn's gym bag.

"OK, we've got to get you out of here, girl. I got your bag. Come on. Hold my arm. I'm driving."

"OK." Lynn's grabbing her arm, feeling so weak now from crying.

"Now we know why you were feeling light-headed at the last practice."

"Yeah. Isn't that something? I thought it was anemia, which I really do have."

"Well, it could have been both. But, either way…it's going to be alright. You're not alone in this."

"Thanks. I really appreciate having you as my best friend."

"We've always been and always will be best friends forever."

"Amen."

Holding each other's arm, they walk out of the locker room together, connected deeper as friends than they ever been.

Chapter Nine

Two and a half weeks flew by. Amelia completed her program and passed Mr. Smith's evaluation with flying colors. Things have calmed down a bit. Margaret's high blood pressure issue is doing much better. Even Amelia is a little more pleasant around the house. And, you know Bruce? He gets a kick out of it. He can't believe it. He keeps saying, "something's up with Amelia, Nana." Even Faith notices a little change in Amelia's behavior. Amelia's still prideful, but a little less angry these days. I don't know who she thinks she's fooling, because I know a cat in the bag when I see one. Anyway, me and Mable have long finished our fasting and prayers for Amelia. But, both of us keep feeling like something is still terribly wrong. The night before Amelia's spring dance, God showed me the same dream I had before. It was *really* bad. I woke up from the dream *panting* this time. It made me *so* nervous that I got out of bed and got on my knees to pray in the Holy Spirit. It was about one o'clock in the morning when I woke up and about three AM before I fell back to sleep again.

"So what are you wearing tonight?" Monica's in her room talking to Amelia on the phone, dancing to Jason Derulo's "In My Head" on Majic 107.5, looking at different dresses spread all over her bed.

Balancing the cell phone between her shoulder and ear, Amelia looks in the closet, pulling out two of her favorite dresses. "I don't know, yet. I can't decide. It's between either my black sleeveless dress with a black and silver bolero, and black heels, or my red dress with a bolero, and red heels. How 'bout you?"

"Well, I think I'm wearing the black dress with silver embroidery that my Mom gave me for Christmas. Oh! And, my black heels I just got for my birthday. Girl, they are niiiice! I got them from Lord & Taylor, where my Mom shops."

"You go, girl!"

Monica stops dancing in the middle of the floor for a quick second, noticing a shift in Amelia's tone; it's a good one. "You seem happy this evening. What's up with you?"

"I am, as a matter of fact." Amelia's smiling, holding her black sleeveless dress up to her shoulders, looking at it.

"That's good, because we're going to *"paaaaartey"*!"

"Party we are, indeed!" Amelia looks over at the note on her desk she wrote earlier.

"OK, so what time are you and Bruce picking me up?"

"Hmmm, let's see." Amelia's looking at the watch. "We should be there in about two hours and ten minutes."

Monica's dancing again, hanging up the other clothes spread out across her bed. Her Mother hates an untidy room. "*Alrighty then!* Call me when you're on the way!"

"OKAAAY!" Click. They hang up.

Amelia's standing by her closet, smiling for a moment.

Bruce knocks on the door. "Amelia! Be ready in two hours!"

Walking to the door fast, Amelia opens it with a big smile.

"I *sure* will, bro!"

Bruce looks confused. She's happy. "Are you alright?"

"Why? Should I not be?" Leaning on the door in a pair of Bruce's old boxers he gave her and an oversized T-shirt, Amelia's holding her black dress in one hand and her cell phone in the other. She can't *wait* to get to the dance.

Bruce hasn't seen Amelia this happy in a long time. "No, sis. Just asking, that's all. I'm glad that you're happy for a change. I'll be in the living room watching TV, waiting for you when you're ready. And, make sure you tell Monica to be on time, because she's slow, sometimes."

"*Already* done! See you in a little while!" Amelia smiles, closing the door. Bruce squints his eyebrows, looking at her weird, before heading downstairs.

Amelia turns on Majic 107.5. Then, her cell phone rings. "Hellooo!"

"Wow, you sound chipper!" Faith is surprised.

"Thanks! I am!"

"I just called to say I hope you have a good time tonight *and that* everything goes well for *everyone, Amelia.*" Faith repeats, "*Everyone.*" What she really wants to say is, "don't start any trouble, and there won't be any trouble," but she holds her peace as Nana says.

Knowing what Faith's talking about, Amelia speaks up quickly. "And, it *will!*"

"OK, girl. I still love you even though I haven't heard from you."

"Love you too, cuz!"

"OK, I'll be preparing a presentation for class while you're out partying, so dance some for me too!"

"I most definitely will!" Amelia laughs.

Faith smiles. "Bye, girl. Have fun."

"Byeeeee!" Amelia disconnects the call and turns up the radio.

Downstairs in the living room, Bruce is watching *Transformers 3.* He and Amelia love the first one. They keep up with the sequels. Margaret's relaxing in her bedroom, something she doesn't do very often. Usually she's lying down to go to sleep for the night around this time or to help bring her blood pressure down. But, tonight her pressure is normal, so she's enjoying some real R and R. Wearing her favorite pair of soft cotton pj's, Margaret props pillows behind her back and along her side to finally do some long awaited reading. With easy listening music playing in the background on cable TV, Margaret dives into the new book she just bought from Barnes & Noble.

"I can't think of the last time when I got a chance to relax in my bed and read a good book," Margaret thinks aloud, as she stops reading and reaches over to grab her cup of hot peppermint tea.

Meanwhile, Bruce is watching *Transformers 3* with great intensity. There's so much action, but that's why he loves it. Then, his cell phone rings.

"Bruce, baby!"

"Nana. Is everything OK?"

"Yes, yes, baby. Isn't tonight the night of Amelia's spring dance?"

"Yes, it is, Nana. I'm driving Amelia and her friend Monica to the dance. We're leaving soon."

"OK, baby. Listen to me. Be very careful driving tonight, OK?"

"OK, Nana. What's up? You know I'm a good driver."

"Sweetheart, I know you are. I just want you to be *extra* careful driving tonight. You hear me?"

"OK, OK, Nana. I will. But, is there something I should know about?"

"I just want you to be *very careful* on the road tonight, that's all." Nana's very concerned, because she knows something is going to happen, but she doesn't know what, when, or to whom.

"Nana, don't worry, I will. How about this? I'll call you when I drop them off at the school and when we get back home, OK?"

"That would be wonderful, baby."

"OK, Nana. Talk to you in a little bit."

Pressing the END button, Bruce looks at his cell phone, saying to himself, "OK. Something *really* weird is going on. Amelia's acting *too* nice, and Nana's worried about something."

"Bruce!" Margaret calls from the stairs on the way to the kitchen to get some Biscoff cookies to eat with her tea. She loves those. After traveling so much over the years, she finally found a place near the house where she can buy them in bulk…Sam's Club.

"Yes, Ma! I'm in the living room!"

Standing behind the sofa now before she goes into the kitchen, Margaret looks at him with one hand on her hip. "Does Amelia seem extra happy to you tonight?"

Bruce turns around. "Yeah. She does. When I went to her room a little while ago to remind her about the time we're leaving, she had a big smile on her face. It was weird. I haven't seen Amelia like that in a *long* time."

"Hmmmm. Yeah. Me neither. I just walked past her bedroom on the way downstairs and I heard her singing a song out loud on the radio."

"I don't know, Ma. Something weird is going on; even with Nana. She just called me about being extra careful while driving when I take Amelia and Monica to the dance. Something's going on." Bruce shrugs his shoulders and turns back around.

Margaret's still standing there. "Hm. Well…OK. Call me when…"

Bruce interrupts, turning back around. "I know, I know…when I drop them off and when we're on the way back. Nana told me the same thing. I don't know what's going on. But, I'm going to apply the Blood of Jesus over me before I leave out of here. I know that!"

Margaret just looks at him with a playful eye, then laughs. "You better! I'm going to cover you and Amelia too, and thank Jesus for it."

Meanwhile, Amelia is blasting her radio, singing while she's doing her hair. On the way back upstairs, Margaret knocks on the door. "Amelia, turn that music down some, sweetie. And, I hope you've picked out something appropriate to wear tonight!"

"OK Momma! And, I did! Don't worry!"

Amelia's cell phone rings again. "Heeey, it's Uncle Joe."

"Uncle!"

"Heard you're going to the spring dance tonight?"

"Yep! I can't wait. Bruce is driving me and Monica. We're leaving in an hour or so."

"Good, good, babygirl. I want you to have a good time, behave yourself, and remember our talk about dancing with the fellas."

Amelia laughs. "Don't worry, Uncle Joe. I know how to dance appropriately."

"Alright, now. Call me tomorrow and let me know how it went. I'm expecting a good report!"

"I will! Love you!"

"I love you too, babygirl." Hanging up the phone, Uncle Joe looks, wondering what's going on with Amelia, because she seems so happy.

After reading a few chapters in her new book, Margaret gets up to make more tea and reminds Bruce that it's almost time for them to go pick up Monica for the dance. Margaret stops at the bottom of the stairs, holding her empty tea cup.

"Bruce, honey, it's almost time to go."

"Yeah, Ma. You're right!" Bruce looks at his watch and jumps up. Margaret walks to the kitchen to brew more tea.

"Amelia! You ready?" Bruce yells from the bottom of the stairs, "Amelia!"

"Yes! I'm coming!"

Bruce walks over to pick up his keys from the sofa table. Margaret walks back into the living room.

"Wow! Don't you look beautiful?" Margaret's standing with her arms folded over her chest, smiling.

"I do look marvelous, don't I?" Amelia laughs, talking with an English accent.

"Bruce, take some pictures on your phone and text them to me."

"Bruce, the camera man! Why does everybody always ask me to take pictures?"

"'Cause you're an expert photographer, dear." Margaret smiles.

Bruce looks at Amelia. "Sis, you do look nice. By the way, you're quite happy tonight. What's up with that? You sure you don't have something up your sleeve?"

Amelia's posing and smiling. "Just been waiting for the spring dance for a long time, that's all."

"Well, baby, it's finally here! And, you look great! I want you and Monica to have a *good* time tonight. OK?"

Bruce is taking pictures with his cell phone and Amelia's steadily posing.

"Alright, alright...enough now." Bruce puts his cell phone back in his pocket.

"Awwwww, Bruce? Just one more!"

"We gotta go pick up Monica or else you'll be late."

Margaret chuckles. "Bruce, when you get back, please text the photos to my iPhone. And,..."

"I know, I know, Ma...don't forget to call you *and* Nana."

"You got it!" Margaret's smiling, hugging Amelia as they're walking behind Bruce to the garage door.

"Amelia, you better hope you're not late!" Bruce opens the door.

"OK, dear. Have fun. Dance for me. And, tell Monica I said hello, Amelia."

"OK, Ma. Love you." Amelia walks into the garage, making sure her purse is closed. Bruce starts the car and pushes the button on the garage opener attached to the windshield visor.

"Love you too, baby!" Margaret's standing in the doorway waving goodbye. She sighs a sigh of relief and smiles, because finally there's been a little peace in the house. It feels good hearing everyone say "I love you" to each other again. Little does she know what's about to happen next…Nana's dream.

Chapter Ten

Pulling into the school parking lot, they hear loud music outside the doors from the dance. People are parking their cars and walking through the parking lot. There's so many people that Bruce can barely find a space.

"Looks like a whole lot of people showed up! I just might join you guys!"

Amelia looks at Bruce like, "no, you didn't just say that." She's in a good mood, but that's taking things a bit far.

Monica's in the back seat looking out the window. "Alright! We're finally here! Oh my gosh! Amelia, look! There's Craig over there!"

Amelia nods and chuckles. She knows that ever since tenth grade, Monica's had a crush on him.

"He is so *cute!*"

"Cute? You better watch out for these guys!" Bruce comments.

Monica chuckles.

"Yeah, well maybe you and Craig can get your dance on tonight." Amelia laughs.

Amelia looks over at Craig as he's getting out of his car. It's a black Range Rover. His family is well known in Atlanta and very wealthy.

"Oh my goodness! I hope I didn't leave it!" Amelia's talking to herself, swirling things around in her purse.

"Leave what? I'm telling you, right now. We aren't going back home." Bruce looks at her.

"Oh! Whew! I have it."

"Whatever it is, it must be important." Monica looks at her from behind.

Bruce is still driving, looking for a space.

"Oh, Bruce, there's a space! You can drop us off right over there." Amelia's pointing.

"Finally." Bruce pulls over and turns the engine off. His cell phone rings. It's a young lady he met at a football game a few months ago. She's been trying to get close to him ever since. But, after talking to her for a while, he realized she's not quite what he thought. She's beautiful, but very different from him. She says she believes in Christ, but her family doesn't believe in the Lord. And, he's not willing to be with just any woman just because she's pretty, especially after what Uncle Joe told him that day on the stairs. So, he talks to her as a friend, because she really is a nice person, in hopes that he can encourage her walk with Christ.

"Hey! What's up, Sherry? I have to call you back in a few minutes. I'm dropping my sister off somewhere…Alright, later."

Bruce disconnects the call and puts the cell phone back in his pocket. Then, he turns to look at Amelia and Monica. Both of them are fixing their hair in the mirror before they get out of the car.

Playing with them, he puts a serious look on his face, talking in his "daddy" tone.

"I'll be back here at eleven o'clock sharp! And, remember— no slow dancing, standing close to guys, or giving them your phone numbers. You understand me?" They laugh.

Amelia's smiling, ignoring him. "Was that your boo on the phone?"

"No! Don't worry about that. Worry about doing what I told you or else!" He smiles and laughs.

"Yeah, right. Whatever you say, brother!"

Amelia and Monica open the car door to get out. Bruce gets out too. They look at him surprised.

"What are you doing? You don't have to get out of the car." Amelia's looking at him, squeezing her eyebrows together.

Bruce looks back at her, locks the car doors, and pulls his cell out to respond to a text message while he walks over to them. "I know, but if I don't, Ma will have a fit. Don't worry, I'm not going in. I'm just walking you guys to the door."

"OK, but stay back some."

"What! You don't want to be seen with your big brother?" He's talking a little loud, playing with her.

"Shhhh! Don't so talk loud."

Monica looks at Bruce and smiles. She's always liked him secretly.

Close to the door, Amelia turns to Bruce.

"OK, here is good."

"All right, then. See you guys in there!"

"Stop playing around!"

Holding his hands up in the air, Bruce smiles. "I can do my Michael Jackson impersonation!"

He laughs, Monica chuckles, and Amelia gives him an eye.

"Dance like Usher? Sing like Robin Thicke? Pharrell Williams? Oh! What about Ne-Yo?" Bruce laughs, remembering how much Amelia used to love Ne-Yo a couple of years ago.

Amelia rolls her eyes at him and walks through the door. Monica looks back, chuckling, waving bye.

Inside the gym, "Alingo" by P-Square is playing. Everybody's dancing, talking, and having a good time. Amelia and Monica are amazed at the turnout and how great the gym looks. In only three days a few students and faculty members transformed it into a club scene with round tables and chairs covered with red tablecloths and candles; a custom dance floor; a refreshment table with drinks; a buffet with different finger foods; and balloons everywhere hanging from the ceiling. It looks amazing. The DJ even has his own spot decorated with trees adorned with lights next to his table.

"Monica, let's go check out the buffet table!"

Before they can take two steps, Timothy, the star linebacker on the football team, walks up in front of them. He's so full of himself. He's about six foot two, big and bulky, wears dreadlocks snatched back in a rubber band, and has a tattoo on his arm. A promising athlete with lots of colleges after him, but the problem with him is that he's real arrogant.

"You look *good*, ma. Mmmmmm! You look like you 'bout ready to turn it up in here. Wanna dance? What's up?" He's rubbing his hands together, licking his lips.

"Ah, no thanks. We're just getting here. You go ahead and turn it up." Monica slightly smiles.

"Oh! So, it's like *that*, ma! You gonna turn a brother down?"

Monica speaks louder over the music, so he can hear her clearly. "No, it's not. I'm just not feeling up to it. But, thanks. I appreciate the offer."

"Alright, *then*. Later."

"He's such a jerk!" Amelia's looking at him with disgust as he walks over to Lesley, one of the cheerleaders.

Monica shrugs it off, excited to be there. "He thinks he's all that. So, let him. I don't plan on dancing with him anyway. I can't stand his attitude. Come on, let's go."

Just then, "Happy" by Pharrell Williams comes on. One of Amelia's all-time favorites. She can't stop herself from dancing. So, Monica joins in.

It might seem crazy what I'm about to say

Sunshine she's here, you can take a break

I'm a hot air balloon that could go to space

With the air, like I don't care baby by the way…

Clap along if you feel like a room without a roof

Because I'm happy

Clap along if you feel like happiness is the truth

Because I'm happy

Clap along if you know what happiness is to you

Because I'm happy…

As the song ends, they laugh with each other as they're about to head over to the buffet when John from Amelia's math class places his hand on her shoulder from behind. They didn't see him walk up.

"I like the way you dance."

John is really cute. He's about five feet eleven, slender build, smooth olive skin, straight black hair, half-Brazilian, half-Cuban. He's a straight-A student in the honors society and the vice president of the twelfth grade. Amelia has always liked him, because he's so nice to her.

She turns around real quick, wondering whose hand is on her shoulder.

"I saw you from across the room. Wanna dance again?"

She's pleasantly surprised and smiles. Monica nudges Amelia on her back with her elbow and looks the other way. She's trying to let her know it's OK, she'll wait.

"Oh! Hi, John. Thanks." Amelia's smiling from ear to ear, remembering how she had such a crush on him last year. "I would love to, but we just got here and were on our way over to the buffet table when Pharrell's song came on. It's one of my favorites."

"I can tell. You look happy, *and* you look good too."

Monica whispers on the other side. "If you don't, I will."

Amelia nudges her back, smiling at John.

"Well, how about a little later? We just want to get some food first."

"Alright, sure. That's cool. I'll see you later then."

"OK. Sure thing." She can't stop blushing.

He smiles back at her and walks away.

"*Girl*, why didn't you dance with him? I could have waited! He is so *cute* and *such* a gentleman!"

"Yes. He is." Amelia's looking dreamy eyed. "He really is. I'll dance with him later though. I just want us to check things out first. Come on. Let's see what kind of food they have."

"Alright. Let's go then!"

The real reason why Amelia wants to check the place out first is to find out where Rihanna, the editor of the school newspaper, and Lynn are.

Walking toward the buffet table, Amelia spots Rihanna standing by the gift stand with her crew. Then, she sees Lynn sitting with Connie at one of the tables near the buffet.

"Hey, Monica!" Amelia grabs her arm. "Wait a minute! Let's see what they're selling at the gift stand real quick before we get something to eat."

Rihanna's at the gift stand holding out her hand in front of everyone, showing off her commitment ring Joshua, her boyfriend, gave her last night. Everybody knows about Rihanna and Joshua. They've been together for nearly two years now.

"Wow! You go, girl! It is gorgeous!" Kim, Rihanna's best friend, is holding Rihanna's hand, staring at the ring in amazement with a look of approval on her face. Kim is very domineering and thinks she knows everything. She's conceited too, although she really is pretty. She's mixed with Japanese and African American. Swinging her long, silky black hair over her shoulder, Kim laughs and says. "I wonder what you had to do to get this."

Rihanna laughs. "Love him!"

"I bet!"

Kim doesn't realize her hair hit Amelia in the face when she swung it over her shoulder. So, when Kim turns around for a moment, Amelia gives her a not-so-happy look, but doesn't say anything. Amelia's trying to get past Kim to Rihanna, so she keeps her cool. She doesn't want to blow her plan to slip the note she wrote earlier into Rihanna's purse. Pretending like she's interested in one of the gift items on the table, she takes a few more steps a little closer to Rihanna.

Rihanna's so excited as she's telling Kim and her other friends about all of the details of how Joshua gave her the ring yesterday and how they're both planning on going to the same college together in the fall.

Monica's a few steps away from Amelia, looking at all of the gifts on the table. The purpose of the gift table is help raise additional funds for the twelfth grade graduation party. She thought Amelia was behind her, but instead Amelia walked closer to Rhianna toward the other end of the table. Just as Monica turns around to show Amelia a beautiful glass paperweight in the shape of a turtle, Sterling, from their English class, walks up and compliments Monica on her dress. So, they talk for a few minutes.

With her back to Rihanna, Amelia quickly pulls the note out of her purse and looks over at Monica to see if she's looking at her. Kim and the other girls are engrossed in Rihanna's story about the commitment ring, so they don't even notice Amelia standing right in back of Rhianna. Quickly scanning the area to see if anyone else is watching, Amelia slowly turns to her left, looking downward toward Rhianna's purse. Rhianna's friends are holding her arm out toward them, so the purse is dangling on her side. Rihanna's purse has a small flap on top, but the flap is tucked inside, leaving a small opening. Looking as if she's looking past Rhianna, Amelia quickly slips the note in her purse and turns around quickly toward the gift table. No one sees her.

Seconds later, Monica grabs her arm.

"Amelia! Look at this!" Monica's holding the cute small glass turtle paperweight she found at the other end of the table.

"Oh yeah. I like that." Amelia's smiling, trying to be cool, thinking, "that was a close call."

"Dang! I left my money at home!" Monica's rummaging through her purse.

Amelia grabs the twenty dollar bill she tucked in a small pocket on the inside of her purse. "Girl, you know I got your back. Here's twenty."

"Awwwww, Amelia. Thanks. I'll pay you back on Monday."

"No. Here, just take it. Don't worry about it."

Handing the attendant the twenty dollar bill, Monica looks over at the buffet they've been trying to get to.

"Girl, I'm so hungry! We still haven't made it to the buffet table."

"Me too. So let's hurry up, so we can go get some food before it all disappears."

"Hey, beautiful. You look gorgeous." A deep voice speaks from behind Amelia. It was so close that the vibration of the sound tickled her ear a little. Really curious, she turns around. It's Robert, the quarterback of the football team who is also a member of the National Honors Society . Robert's about six feet three inches tall, medium brown in complexion, has a body like a body builder, and short black hair. He's very "clean cut," has a charismatic smile, and a great disposition; he's very warm, gentle, and friendly. And, he loves Jesus. He always wears a cross around his neck. All the girls at Lake High and in the community love him. His family is well known around town, because his dad is known as a very wealthy businessman and philanthropist. He owns a major technology company.

Looking at Robert, Amelia smiles.

"Would you like to dance?" He's smiling back at her.

By this time, Rihanna and her friends have walked away. Monica turns around with the gift bag in her hand, putting it in her purse, shocked to see Robert. Her mouth almost drops wide open, but she catches it in time, looking with her eyes slightly wide open. Amelia's stunned; she was totally unprepared for Robert to walk up to her. But, she's trying her hardest to play it cool.

Monica steps a little closer to Amelia, poking her in the back with her elbow a couple times, trying to signal her to dance with him.

Amelia blushes. "Thank you."

"You're welcome. So, would you like to dance?"

Then, all of a sudden, everything and everyone around her disappears and the only person she can see in the room is Robert.

Monica pokes Amelia again, realizing she's almost in a daze.

Clearing her throat some, Amelia quickly comes back to reality. "Huh? Sure."

But, she can't help from melting inside. He looks so debonair dressed in his medium-gray, single-breasted Italian jacket with tailored, medium-gray trousers, a light-gray shirt opened at the neck, and black Bruno Magli dress shoes. With that charming smile, he takes one hand out of his pants pocket and extends it toward her.

In that moment, the DJ plays another one of her all-time favorites, "I'm In Love" by Ne-Yo. People rush to the dance floor.

Monica clears her throat, smiling at Robert, waiting for Amelia to take his hand.

Then, Amelia slowly raises her hand and places it in his.

Holding her hand softly, but firmly, he leads Amelia onto the dance floor. She can hardly feel her hand in his. Its as if both of their hands are one. This will surely be a moment she remembers forever.

Turning around to take a quick look at Monica, she blushes harder. Monica's waving her hand close in front of her chest, smiling back at her with excitement.

On the dance floor, Robert pulls her close to him, being careful to be respectful of the amount of space between them, and looks into her eyes.

"You are *so* beautiful and you smell *so* good too. What perfume are you wearing?"

Amelia's in a daze. She can't believe it. She's dancing with Robert, who she's had a crush on all year long. And, to top it all off…she's dancing with him to one of her favorite songs.

Looking at him, she tries to stay focused. "Thank you. It's my favorite. First by Van Cleef & Arpels."

She looks back into his beautiful light brown eyes thinking of how elated she's feeling in his arms right now. Then, she remembers how sometimes after school she used to sneak out to the bleachers just to see him play football during practice.

"Well, I love it on you. Good choice. So, who did you come here with?"

"Oh, my girl Monica."

"I'm glad. I was hoping you would make it."

"Me?" Amelia looks surprised.

"Yes…you." He smiles.

Robert loves this song too. One of his favorite parts is coming up so he starts singing.

Does anybody understand

That I'm in love? (love love)

And, I think I found the real thing (real love)

Kind of love to make your heart say (love love)

You got me singin' lalalalala.

"You're the quarterback of the football team, in the honor's society, *and* you can sing too?"

Robert blushes. "Singing has always been one of my passions. I been singing with the choir at church since I was five years old."

"Wow! You have a *really* good voice." Amelia is amazed. She didn't know he could sing.

"Well, if you let me call you sometimes, maybe I can sing to you over the phone."

She smiles, with her hands placed around the back of his arms. "That would be nice. Like before I go to sleep?"

"Anytime you want." He smiles, looking into her eyes, holding her with his arms around her lower back.

Amelia's feeling so good that she can't keep from blushing. So, she drops her head a little, being shy. Then, he gently presses it on his chest, so she can lay her head on him. Raising his hands up toward her shoulders, he lightly squeezes and hugs her while they're dancing. She feels so comfortable that she actually forgets to answer his question.

"Well, may I?"

Lost in another world, she snaps back and answers in a soft voice, "yes."

Then, he pulls her a little closer to him, squeezing her a little tighter. She's speechless. As they're dancing, it feels like they're one. It's weird; she's never felt anything like this before, not even with, Blake, who she thought she was falling in love with.

Then, Robert lifts her chin up, looking deep into her eyes with his captivating smile that makes her melt. For a quick moment, she thought he was going to kiss her. But, he just stares at her.

"You're so beautiful, Amelia."

As the song ends, they slowly stop dancing. Still holding one another, they look into each other's eyes. For both of them it's as if the world stopped and no one else is around them.

Then, grabbing her hands, he says, "thank you for dancing with me. You made my night."

She smiles back. "Thank you, as well. I enjoyed it."

Taking her hand, he leads her back toward the gift stand area. Monica sees them heading off the dance floor and rushes over toward them.

He puts his hand in his jacket pocket and pulls out his cell phone.

"So, shall we exchange numbers now?"

"Oh, yes, of course."

"OK, what's your number? I'll call it now. That way you'll have mine."

"OK, mine is two-nine-three, seven-seven-four-one." Robert calls her phone, so she pulls it out of her purse to catch the ring.

"You got it?" He looks.

"Yes, I do…it's seven-four-four, one-one-five-two?"

"That's it. Don't forget to log me in."

"I won't." She blushes and he smiles back.

"Alright. I'll call you soon so, I can sing to you while you go to sleep?" He takes her hand again.

"OK. I'm going to hold you to it, Ne-Yo," she smiles.

He sees Monica waiting for Amelia. Then, smiling, he lets her hand go and walks away, turning back again to look at her.

Quickly walking up to her, Monica is so excited.

"OK, details, details! Give me details!"

Amelia's laughing.

"Girl, he is fine! How was it?"

"I know! I know! It was awesome! It felt like I was in another world. He is so strong, yet so gentle. I could have laid on his chest all night."

"You laid your head down on his chest?!" Monica's eyes get big.

"Yes, and it was amazing!" Amelia turns around and sees him looking back at her smiling while he's talking to his buddies.

"Woooow! I love it! I love it! I love it!" Monica's talking fast, smiling, because she is so happy for her. "Did he ask you for your number?"

"Yes, he did." Amelia smiles back at him and turns around.

"So, did you give it to him?"

"I sure did. I'm not a fool." Amelia's regrouping now, seeing Rihanna and Kim walk toward them.

"You go, girl! Watch out world! Rihanna and Joshua are here! There's a new couple in town!" Kim always talks loud.

Walking right pass Amelia and Monica, Rihanna and Kim join Joshua at close by. "I can't believe Lynn is pregnant," Rihanna says loudly.

"I know! I'm shocked! Let me see that note again."

Rihanna pulls the note out of her purse, handing it to Kim.

"I wonder who put this in your purse." Kim looks puzzled.

"I don't know, but whoever did has it out for Lynn!"

Pausing after hearing what Rihanna and Kim are saying, Monica looks at Amelia. "Did you hear them?"

"Hear what?" Amelia's looking at Monica as if to say, "what are you talking about?"

"Rihanna and Kim just said that Lynn is pregnant!"

"What? Are you sure that's what they said?"

"Yes! That's what I heard them just say. I'm shocked…Lynn? Of all people, she's the last I'd expect to be pregnant."

"Are you sure, Monica, you heard them say that?"

"Yes, Amelia! I am!"

Amelia's good at making others question and doubt things.

Meanwhile, Lynn and Connie are sitting at one of the tables with their friends, enjoying the music, when they both decide to get something to drink. Little do they know, the news about Lynn being pregnant is quickly spreading around the gym. Rihanna and Kim have already told a few people.

"You thirsty?" Connie looks at Lynn, making sure she's OK.

"Actually, I am. Let's go get something to drink."

"OK." Getting up to leave the table, Connie lets their friends know they'll be right back. Walking toward the drink stand, they pass Rihanna and Kim's table. They're talking about how good it is that Lynn's finally able to release a little bit of stress from her situation by being at the dance with her friends. At first, Lynn didn't want to come, but Connie practically forced her to go.

By this time, Amelia coaxes Monica to walk over near the dance floor away from Rihanna and Kim's table. All she cares about is that she did what she came to do; her mission is accomplished.

"Wow, if that's the truth, I really feel sorry for her." Amelia pretends like she's just as surprised as Monica.

Monica zones out for a few moments in her mind, standing by the edge of the dance floor, watching people dance. The music is loud, but it's drowned out by her thoughts.

"It doesn't make sense though. How would Rihanna and Kim know? Everybody knows they aren't friends with Lynn." She has a funny look on her face.

With one hand placed over her forehead like she's wearing a sun visor, Amelia's pretending like she's looking for someone. What she's really doing is trying to change the subject.

"Hey, is that John over there?" She's pointing. "I promised him a dance."

Monica turns back to look over at Rihanna and Kim. "Ah, what did you say?" She turns back around.

"Come on, let's go! I love this song!" Amelia pulls Monica by the arm onto the dance floor. Another song she loves plays. It's "Remember the Time" by Michael Jackson.

Back at the table, Kim sees Lynn and Connie approaching.

"Rihanna, look, there she is." Kim's tapping Rihanna's arm quickly. Rihanna's looking at Joshua who just got up to go to the bathroom, but turns around real fast. She's so in love with him.

"I cant believe it! Lynn—of all people…pregnant! I wonder who the father is." Rihanna's just staring at her.

"Come on! Let's go over there!"

They both get up quickly to approach Lynn and Connie.

"Hey, Lynn!" Kim yells, walking toward Lynn with her arms folded over her chest. Lynn and Connie look.

"Soooo, we hear *congratulations* are in order. Who's the father?" Rihanna's standing in her ever so confident-looking pose, smiling with a sly look on her face.

"Yeah, Lynn. I'm surprised. I heard you *had* a chastity ring."

Instantly, Lynn's eyes swell with tears. She can't believe they know about her being pregnant. She's so overcome and embarrassed that she can't speak.

Connie looks at them, shocked for a moment. In her mind, she remembers that day in the locker room; nobody else was there. But, she does remembers hearing someone before they were going to leave.

"Cat got your tongue?" Rihanna grins.

Connie brakes out of her moment of bewilderment and angrily jumps to Lynn's defense. Lynn still can't talk. She's in shock and doesn't know what to do.

Stepping forward, Connie looks straight into Rihanna's eye with a mean look. "You never stop, do you? Enough evil is never enough for you, is it?!" Then, she looks at Kim. "And you! You're just part two of the evil, drama saga!"

Rihanna looks back at Connie, taking a step forward. "I eat drama for breakfast."

"Yeah, it's good." Kim looks, smiling.

"You both are evil!"

Rihanna laughs. "No! Just truthful! Come on, Kim."

Then, Kim smiles, taking a step closer. "Hey, Lynn. If you need a babysitter, let me know. You can hire my niece." Then, they both walk away laughing.

Connie immediately turns around to look at Lynn. Lynn's doubled over, holding her stomach, sobbing.

"Connie, I feel like I'm going to throw up," Lynn whispers.

"Oh no!" Quickly, Connie puts her hands around Lynn's shoulders to help her stand back up.

"Oh my gosh, the whole school is going to find out now! How do they know?" Lynn's wiping her eyes.

"Lynn, listen let's get you to a chair, so you can sit down! Don't pay them any attention! They're devils! They always have been and always will be devils, unless they let Jesus change them!"

"I can't believe this!" Lynn's going through her purse looking for her car keys.

"What are you doing? Let's get you to a chair. You need to sit down quickly." Connie's concerned, because she looks weak now.

Connie can see by the look on Lynn's face that she is really upset again like she was in the locker room the day she found out she was pregnant.

"Lynn! Please! Don't let them get to you! I *know* you're upset. I am too. It doesn't matter how they found out, right now. What matters is you!"

Lynn's frustrated looking for her car keys. "Where are my keys?!" Lynn's weeping harder and harder, feeling totally embarrassed.

"Lynn, I need for you to calm down, please." Now, Connie's getting really upset seeing Lynn like this, because she doesn't want her to hyperventilate again.

All of a sudden, Lynn finds her car keys in her purse, grabs them, drops her purse on the floor, and runs as fast as she can toward the door without saying a word to Connie. Connie's in shock for a couple of seconds seeing Lynn run. She quickly looks at Lynn's purse on the floor and back up at Lynn to see where she's running so fast. Picking up her purse, Connie yells, running after her, "Lynn! Wait! Stop running! Wait!"

The music is playing loud. With every one talking, dancing, and having a good time, no one sees or pays attention to Lynn running toward the door.

Stopping for a second, Lynn kicks her shoes off, so she can run faster.

Connie's close behind. "Lynn! Lynn!"

At the door, Lynn pushes it open fast.

"Lynn!" Connie sees the door swing open. Connie looks over and sees faculty members standing by the buffet table talking, but they didn't see Lynn running to the door. There're so many people standing around.

The door closes as Connie pushes it open fast to run after Lynn who is headed to the parking lot. Up ahead, she sees Lynn approaching her car. Running faster, holding both her purse and Lynn's, Connie's yelling louder, "Lynn! Stop! Wait for me!"

Lynn runs even faster and before Connie knows it, Lynn is already near her car, unlocking the door with her keys. Connie hears the sound of the car unlocking. Chirp-chirp! Lynn swings the car door open, gets in, and starts the engine. Just as Connie makes it to the car on the driver's side, Lynn locks the door and backs out of the parking space quickly. Connie's banging on the window.

"Lynn! Lynn! Stop! Stop the car! Let me in!"

Lynn doesn't even look at her. She's in a daze, looking straight ahead. Shifting gears, Lynn speeds off fast toward the traffic light at the entrance of the parking lot. It's a three-way intersection.

"Lynn!" Connie yells running after the car. Then, stopping for a moment to catch her breath, still holding both purses, Connie sees a car in the distance coming toward the traffic light at the intersection of school's entrance. It's very dark outside. She can't see the color of the car coming, only the head lights.

Lake High is located in a rural part of Atlanta. At night, the only lights people can depend on are a few street lights around the school and lights in the school parking lot.

Immediately, she starts running again towards Lynn's car that's approaching the entrance fast, screaming at the top of her lungs. Her throat is beginning to feel funny inside from running so fast and screaming so hard, but she pushes past the feeling to try to get to her best friend.

"Lynn!! There's a car coming!! A car's coming!! Lynn!!"

Lynn's speeds faster toward the entrance. Connie's heart is pounding seeing the oncoming car moving faster. Lynn pulls up to the traffic light and makes a quick left without seeing the oncoming car.

"Nooooooo!!" Connie stops and screams loudly. "Noooooooooo!!! Lynnnnn!!!"

BANG!?X!)! The cars collide. It sounds like an explosion. The oncoming car collided directly into the driver's side of Lynn's car, pushing her car back a few yards.

"Nooooooooooo!!" Connie screams as she runs faster to Lynn's car.

"Nooooooooooo!!"

Almost out of breath, Connie reaches Lynn's car. She stops for a moment. Steam billows from both engines. She runs to pull Lynn's door open. In her mind, she's thinking she has to help Lynn get out of the car right away. Swinging the purses onto her back, she pulls and pulls on the door, but it's stuck. "Oh nooooo!! Nooooo!! Nooooo!! Open!!" She frantically pulls on the door handle several more times.

Quickly cupping her hands on the window, she looks in. Lynn's head is cocked to the left, facing her. Blood is running down her face on both sides. She doesn't have her seat belt on.

"Lynn!!" Connie bangs on the window. "Lynn!! Can you hear me?!!" She bangs a few more times.

Quickly, she stands back up and runs to the other side of the car. Pulling on the door handle of the passenger's side, Connie gasps, beginning to break down at the thought of her best friend being locked in the car. The impact of the collision jammed both of Lynn's doors.

"Nooo!! Not both doors!!"

Breathing hard, she reaches for her purse and pulls out her cell phone to call 911.

"Please work!! Please work!! Please work!!" She's dialing the number quickly.

"This is nine-one-one. Can you please state the nature of your emergency?"

"Hello!! Hello!! There's been an…" The call drops. "Hello?! Hello?!" The battery died.

"OK!! OK!! Lynn's phone!! Let me use Lynn's phone!!"

She grabs Lynn's cell phone in her purse, almost dropping her phone on the street.

"Nooooo!! Nooooo!! This can't beeee!!" The screen is black. Lynn's battery is dead too. Lynn forgot to charge her phone in between all of the stress and drama of deciding whether or not to come to the dance.

"Lord!! *Please* help me!! I don't know what to do!!" She throws both phones back in her purse and in that instant, she hears a voice.

"Run to the school."

Looking back at Lynn really quickly, Connie takes off running back to the school for help.

Through the parking lot she's screaming. "Heeeeelp!! Heeeeelp!! Somebody heeeeelp!!"

Robert looks up as he's opening his car door. He just walked out to his car to get something. He's parked off to the side of the lot. Squinting his eyes, looking over the roof of his car, he sees Connie running fast toward the school.

"Heeeeelp!! Somebody heeeeelp!!"

"Connie? Is that you?" Robert yells loudly from his car door. She can't hear him. As she gets closer, he realizes it's her for sure. Bam!! Chirp-Chirp!! Robert slams the door, locks it, runs through the cars toward her.

"Connie! Over here! It's Robert! What's going on?!"

Connie turns her head looking back at Lynn's car as sees Robert running toward her. She stops running and puts her hands on her knees for a minute, panting.

Running up to her, Robert stops. "What's happened?" Clearly he sees Connie's distress and that something bad just happened.

"It's Lynn!!" she pants. "She's been in an accident!! Her car collided into another car!! We need an ambulance!! The doors won't open!!"

"What!!" Though Robert isn't really close to Lynn or Connie, he knows them well from classes and school activities over the years.

"At the light!! It looks like she's unconscious!! My cell phone is dead and hers too! We need to call an ambulance *now!!*"

"Okay! Come on, let's go! I'll call with my phone!" Robert pulls her up by the arm and they run toward Lynn.

Meanwhile, Mr. Franklin and Mr. Bates, teachers at Lake High, are standing outside the gym, talking and smoking cigarettes.

Suddenly, Mr. Franklin sees two people running through the parking lot. He can't see who they are.

"Wonder if something happened." Mr. Franklin looks curiously. Mr. Bates is puzzled. He didn't see anyone; Mr. Franklin did.

"Let's check it out real quick to make sure there's no trouble."

"You're right. Let's go."

Dropping their cigarettes and smashing them on the ground with their shoes, Mr. Franklin and Mr. Bates run toward the parking lot. About halfway, they see the collision at the intersection of the parking lot entrance.

"Looks like a major accident happened!" Mr. Franklin's surprised.

They stop for a moment. "And, is that Robert and Connie over there?" Mr. Bates looks concerned.

"It sure looks like it." Mr. Franklin puts his hands on his hips; it's been a while since he's exercised. He's a little out of breath, even with running a short distance.

Mr. Bates yells, "Robert! Connie!"

Robert and Connie are at the scene of the accident now. They hear someone calling them and turn to look.

"That's Mr. Bates and Mr. Franklin!" Robert walks a little closer to Lynn's car, pulling his cell phone out quickly.

Connie screams, "Lynn's been in an accident!!"

Robert's calling 911.

"Oh no! Hold on! We're going to get Mr. Smith!"

Shocked, the Mr. Franklin and Mr. Bates run back to the school.

Rushing through the gym doors, they see Mr. Smith, the school principal, standing near the buffet table, chatting with Mr. Manning.

Running over to him, they yell. "Mr. Smith! Mr. Smith! There's been an accident at the light! Robert and Connie are out there!"

Mr. Smith turns around quickly with a concerned look on his face. "What?" He's a bit surprised. There's never been an accident at the school entrance before. "What's going on?"

Quickly putting his plate down, Mr. Manning is looking with concern also at Mr. Franklin and Mr. Bates running fast toward them.

Mr. Bates repeats himself, slowing down as he and Mr. Franklin approach Mr. Smith and Mr. Manning at the table.

"Mr. Smith, you have to go right away! There's been an accident at the light! Robert and Connie are out there, right now!"

Mr. Smith responds quickly, looking confused by what's happened. "OK! Is anyone hurt?"

"It's Lynn, sir!" Mr. Franklin's feels almost out of breath from running so fast.

"Whaaat?! Lynn Braxton, are you sure?!" More concerned now, Mr. Smith moves quickly. "You and Mr. Bates and the other faculty cover the dance while Mr. Manning and I run to get help!"

"OK, OK, sir! We'll be right here!" Standing there, both Mr. Franklin and Mr. Bates are breathing hard, trying to catch their breath. There are only a few faculty members monitoring the dance tonight, so they have to trade places with Mr. Smith and Mr. Manning to watch the students. A very large number of students turned out for the dance.

Mr. Smith and Mr. Manning run through the crowd toward the gym door to go meet Robert and Connie at the scene of the accident.

Meanwhile…at the intersection, Robert is talking to the 911 operator on his cell phone.

"This is nine-one-one…"

Robert doesn't wait for the operator to finish her sentence before he yells. "We need an ambulance, quick! There's been an accident! It looks like a head-on collision! Both drivers need help—quick!"

Robert's standing by Lynn's door. He looks in and sees that Lynn is unconscious. Connie's crying profusely, standing by him.

"What's your location, sir?"

"The parking lot entrance at Lake High School on Wilmington Street! It's a three-way intersection!" Robert's trying to pull Lynn's car door open while he's talking to the operator, but it won't open.

"Can you see the drivers in both cars, sir?"

"Yes, I can see them, but neither one of them are moving!" He's frustrated, looking at the door, trying to open it. He tries pulling on the handle again.

"I'm trying to pull open the driver's door, but it's stuck!"

"OK, sir. We're going to need you to remain calm. Hang on. We're dispatching two ambulances to the location now."

"OK. OK. Thank you!" Robert's pulling and pulling, but the door won't open. Connie's still crying, becoming more nervous, because Robert can't even open the door.

"They'll be there in a few minutes, sir. Hold on. OK?"

"Yes! Thank you! Thank you!"

The operator disconnects the call. Robert puts his cell phone back in his jacket pocket and turns to look at Connie.

"The door is jammed!"

"I know! I tried to open it too!"

"Thank God, the ambulance is on the way!"

Crying harder, all Connie can do is shake her head. She can't even talk anymore. The thought of losing Lynn, the closest friend she's known since kindergarten, is frightening. They always used to talk about life in the future, seeing each other with kids, married, and serving the Lord.

Looking at Lynn's car, Robert can see that the whole left side of the front of her car, all the way to half of the driver's door is completely crushed. If only the windows were cracked, he's thinking, maybe he'd be able to get in. With tears flowing down his cheek, Robert feels helpless. By the position of both cars, he can tell the impact of the collision was pretty bad.

Then, frantically, he tries again to open Lynn's door, pulling really hard, but the door doesn't budge.

"The door won't open!" he screams, hitting the top of the car. Again, he steps back looking at the whole car, frustrated, because he can't do anything to help, Lynn. He can see, but not so well, because it's so dark outside. His eyes are filled with tears and the street lights don't seem to give enough light.

Holding her arms over her chest with both purses hanging from her shoulder, Connie looks at Robert and yells, "what else can we do?!"

She's never felt so helpless in her life. Looking at Lynn lie unconscious with blood running down her face is a very traumatic sight.

Quickly, Robert walks around to the other side of Lynn's car to see, if he can open the passenger door.

"No way!" he screams. "This door is jammed too." He's pulling on the handle, but the passenger door won't open either. Putting both hands on the window, he leans forward looking inside the car to check on Lynn. She's still lying back with her head leaning sideways on the seat.

Sirens are blaring loud and lights are flashing in the distance. Two ambulances, three police cars, and a fire truck are near by. Robert looks and yells, "they're here!!"

Just then, Mr. Smith and Mr. Manning arrive at the accident. They ran as fast as they could. The ambulances, police cars, and fire truck pull up.

Robert bangs on the window again, screaming. "Lynn! Lynn! Can you hear me?! Lynn!! Lynn!! Hang in there!! We have help!!"

"What happened?!" Mr. Smith and Mr. Manning see Connie crying and Robert banging on the window of Lynn's car. They run quickly to Robert on the passenger side of Lynn's car.

Robert looks up desperately, glad to see help. "It's Lynn, sir!! She's locked in the car!! I can't get either of the doors open!!"

Connie yells, "Lynn's car collided with the other one!! We tried to open the driver's door and the passenger's door, but they're jammed!!" Robert's frantic, trying to figure out what else he can do.

Mr. Smith loves Lynn's spirit so much and just can't believe this happened to her.

"Here, let me try!" Mr. Manning runs over to the driver's side.

"I can't get the door open! I can't believe this! Lord Jesus, help us!" Mr. Smith's pulling on the passenger's door as hard as he can, but the door doesn't open.

Mr. Manning yells, "Mr. Smith! It's jammed like Robert says."

Getting out of their vehicles, the paramedics, police officers, and firefighters, are quickly running toward the collison. One of the police officers is holding a walkie-talkie, speaking to the dispatch unit. The paramedics are pushing stretchers and the firemen are walking quickly with them.

One of the paramedics call out while pushing the stretcher to the car, "can anyone tell us what happened?!"

Connie's still standing on the driver's side of the car with tears streaming down her face, praying someone can get Lynn out of the car soon.

"Yes!! I'm the principal of Lake High. It appears there's been a collision. The passenger in *this* car is one of my students! We've tried opening both doors, but they're jammed!"

The paramedics quickly look inside the car. One of the police officers, Officer Neil, turns and yells to the other officer, Officer Turner, who is getting a crow bar out of the trunk of the police car, "Turner! We need that crow bar and a wedge too, quick! Everybody, please stand back!" Officer Turner figured they might need both as he quickly surveyed the scene when they arrived, so he ran to the trunk of the police car while the other officers ran to the scene.

Officer Rucker runs to the passenger's side of Lynn's car to try to open the door. Two of the firemen follow him.

Officer Mason and a few other firemen run to the other vehicle to check on the driver. "He's alright over here! He's conscious! The door is jammed though! Officer Turner, we need a crow bar and a wedge over here too!" Officer Mason yells.

One of the paramedics looks at Mr. Smith, realizing there's nothing they can do until Lynn's door is either opened or removed.

"Sir, we're going to stand by while they work on the door. And, don't worry. We're going to do everything we can to help your student and the other driver."

"Yes. Yes. OK. Thank you." Mr. Smith's nodding his head agreeing, very concerned for Lynn now.

"Here's the crow bar and wedge, Neil!" Officer Turner says. He grabbed two sets when he heard Officer Mason yell that he needed a crow bar and wedge for the other car also. Quickly, he runs to Officer Mason to hand him his next.

Mr. Manning and Robert move to stand with Connie. She backed up, so the police officers and firemen could get to the door. Mr. Smith waits with the paramedics watching anxiously. Then, he yells, "Connie! Get Lynn's mother on the phone, right away!"

"OK, sir!" Connie yells back.

Robert reaches into his jacket pocket to hand Connie his phone, remembering the battery on her cell phone is dead. He's a quick thinker.

Ms. Braxton's phone rings, Connie's crying saying, "I tried to stop her! I tried to stop her, but I couldn't!" She cries uncontrollably again waiting for Lynn's Mom to answer.

"Connie, Lynn's going to be alright, Okay. God is with her." Robert's hugging her, trying to console her and calm himself down at the same time. "The paramedics and police are here now. They're going to get her out."

Closing his eyes for a few seconds, Robert prays. He remembers what his Mom and Dad preach all the time to him: pray, not just with words, but from the heart. *"Lord Jesus, I love You. There is none other like You. Thank You, Lord for Your Grace. Touch Lynn, Lord and help her. She needs you."*

Looking at the police and firemen who are trying to pry open Lynn's door, Mr. Manning shaking his head with both hands placed on his hips. "Man! This collision is unbelievable!"

On the other side of Lynn's car, Mr. Smith stands close by the paramedics, waiting with one arm folded across his chest. The other is propped on top with his hand under his chin. As a man of God, he understands some spiritual principles of God and therefore, the power of declarations. So, he's always careful about things he says. He declares, *"in the Name of Jesus Christ, Lynn Braxton shall live and not die. The Power of God is working in her. She shall live, in Jesus' Name."* He knows Lynn very well from her attending Lake High over the past few years and knows she is a true child of God. He's witnessed (as many others have) the Nature of Christ in her and knows she loves the Lord very much; she doesn't just say it.

Meanwhile, the police and firemen are working hard trying to open Lynn's door. The door is almost open.

"I'm going to push the crow bar into the crack of the door! You guys pull on the other end!" Officer Neil yells.

Lynn's Mom finally answers. "Hello?"

"Ms. Cheryl! Ms. Cheryl!" Connie is crying hysterically.

"Connie? What? What, baby? What's wrong?" She's watching a movie. Cheryl picks up the remote and turns the TV off.

Connie can barely talk. "Ms. Cheryl! It's Lynn! She's been in a terrible accident!" Connie's crying harder.

Feeling sympathetic, Mr. Manning puts his hand on Connie's back. "Here, Connie, let me speak to her."

Robert continues hugging Connie as she weeps on his chest. "Lynn is going to be alright." He's really trying to hold it together himself, so he can be strong for Connie. Anyone seeing someone in Lynn's condition would be devastated too. It's not good.

"Ms. Braxton. This is Mr. Manning, the school counselor. Lynn's been in an accident. It looks like there's been a collision."

"Whaaat!! Noooooo!! Not, Lynn!! How did that happen?! Is my baby OK? Where is she?" Instantly, Cheryl feels sick to her stomach. Jumping up out of her chair, she runs to get her car keys while she's still talking to Mr. Manning.

"We're still at the school, at the intersection in front the entrance to the parking lot. The paramedics, police, and firemen are here now. Both of Lynn's car doors are jammed. They're trying to pry the driver's door open now to get Lynn out."

"Oh Nooooooo!! My baby is stuck in the car?!"

"Yes, but they're working on the door now. It looks like they almost have it opened. Mr. Smith wanted us to call you right away. He's with the paramedics."

Mr. Smith sees Mr. Manning on the phone and Connie crying in Robert's arms. "Is that Ms. Braxton?!" he yells.

Mr. Manning looks over. "Yes!"

Mr. Smith looks at the paramedics. "Which hospital will you take her to? There are two very good ones in the area."

They look at each other. "What about Lake View? It's known for it's excellent service in the trauma unit."

"Good. Lake View, then." Mr. Smith says.

Officer Neil yells out, "we almost got it open!"

"Manning, hold on!" Mr. Smith rushes over to take the phone.

"Hello, Ms. Braxton?! This is Mr. Smith! The ambulance is taking Lynn to Lake View Hospital and I'm riding in the ambulance with them! It looks like the officers and firemen almost have the door open! Her door was jammed shut from the accident!"

Feeling like she's about to "break into pieces," Cheryl grabs her purse and runs as fast as she can to the front door to get to the car.

"Thank You, Jesus! OK! OK! I'm getting in my car now!"

"Good! Drive straight to Lake View Hospital! We'll meet you there!"

"OK! OK! I'm on my way right now! *Please*, Mr. Smith, stay with my baby!" Cheryl quickly locks the front door and runs to her car.

"Don't worry, Ms. Braxton, I'm not leaving Lynn's side! See you at the hospital!"

Mr. Smith hands the phone back to Mr. Manning and drops his arms to the side of him with anguish in his eyes. He looks with great anticipation at the officers and firemen, as they push hard to pry the door open.

As Mr. Manning takes the cell phone, he sees the agony on Mr. Smith's face. Lynn is more than just a student to Mr. Smith; she's been a wonderful friend and a great help to the faculty.

Looking at Robert now, Mr. Manning hands the cell phone back to him. "Here you go, Robert. Thanks, man." They look at each other with the same hope in their eyes that Lynn will be OK. Connie's still leaning her head on Robert's chest, holding her hands over her face.

Meanwhile, a few students who saw the accident when they went to the parking lot, ran inside to tell others. A few faculty members saw many of the students leaving the gym to go outside and went to go see what was going on. The students gathered near the scene of the accident on the school parking lot. Mr. Smith hears the students and turns around. Then, he sees Mr. Bates running toward him.

"Mr. Bates, tell everyone the dance is over! Prepare to go home."

"Yes, sir! Right away, sir!" Mr. Bates clearly sees there's been a bad accident, but doesn't know Lynn is involved.

Officer Neil yells again, "It's open! It's open!" It took fifthteen minutes. It was a lot of work, but they finally got Lynn's door open.

Slightly letting his head fall back for a quick second, Mr. Smith sighs, putting his hands in prayer position. "Thank You, Jesus! Thank You, Lord!"

Mr. Manning sighs, placing his hands on top of his head.

Robert closes his eyes for a quick moment and squeezes Connie. "Thank You, Jesus." He says.

Still leaning on Robert's chest, Connie turns her face just enough to see the police and firemen. She's so devastated, she can't say a word.

The paramedics rush toward the driver's side of Lynn's car with the stretcher. The officers and the firemen are still pulling the rest of the door off of the car. They had no choice, but to take the whole door off. It was the only way to get it open.

Looking inside, the police officers and the firemen can see blood everywhere. Lynn's is still unconscious. Her head is still leaning to the side. Her leg is partly crushed under the dashboard. It takes five minutes for the paramedics to pull her out.

Connie turns her face into Robert's chest again as the paramedics lay Lynn's body on the stretcher. Then, all of a sudden, she bursts from Robert's arms and runs toward Lynn.

"Lynn! Lynn! Lynn!"

Robert dashes after her and grabs her just before she reaches the stretcher. "Connie! Come back!"

"Please, let me touch her!! Lynn! Please, God! Don't let her die! Please!" Connie's crying uncontrollably in Robert's arms.

"It's OK! It's OK! They got her out now! She's going to be alright!"

Connie grabs the side of his sleeve tight and sobs loudly. Robert holds her head close to his chest.

"It's not fair! It's not fair! It's not fair!" Connie repeats over and over again. The pain of seeing her best friend laying on a stretcher is just too great to handle.

"I know! I know! But, she's going to be OK! She's going to be OK!" Robert holds her close to him, placing his chin above her head, rubbing her hair. "She's going to be OK, Connie."

Mr. Smith runs up to the paramedics. Mr. Manning follows.

Pushing the stretcher in a hurry to the ambulance, one of the paramedics yells to Mr. Smith, "We're ready to go!"

"OK!" Mr. Smith runs with the paramedics toward the ambulance, yelling back to Mr. Manning, "Manning, you, Robert and Connie follow the ambulance to Lake View and let Lynn's mother know we're on the way now!"

Sirens are blaring loudly and lights are flashing. The other crew managed to get the other driver out of the car, as well and into the other ambulance. Students who drove to the dance are getting in their cars and lining up at the school's parking lot entrance waiting to leave.

Mr. Manning quickly looks at Robert. "Did you drive?"

"Yes! Yes!" Robert looks, hugging Connie.

"OK! Then, you and Connie follow me! Where did you park?"

"Over there!" Robert points in the direction where he parked his car.

"OK! Me too!"

At the ambulance, the paramedics quickly push the stretcher in, hooks Lynn up to monitors and puts an oxygen mask over her face. Mr. Smith looks back real quick before he gets in. "Call Ms. Braxton *and* Connie's mother also!"

"Don't worry! We will!" Mr. Manning yells back.

Then, Mr. Smith jumps in the ambulance and sits across from Lynn. The other paramedic slams the door shut and runs to the front of the ambulance to drive.

"Robert, call Ms. Braxton to tell her the ambulance is leaving now! Connie! Call your parents after he calls Ms. Braxton!" Connie shakes her head unable to talk.

"OK, Mr. Manning! Right away!" Robert turns Connie around. "Quick! Let's go!" Connie nods her head, yes. They run to their to the cars quickly, so they can follow the ambulance to the hospital.

Robert looks at Connie. "I'll call Ms. Braxton to let her know we're on the way, then you can call your Mom, OK?"

"Yes," Connie says softly.

They reach Robert's car. Robert quickly opens the door for Connie, makes sure she's seated, closes the door, and runs to the other side to jump in. Mr. Manning jumps in his car and pulls out of his parking space quickly. Driving by Robert's car, Mr. Manning yells out of the window, "Robert! Follow me!" Robert nods his head, backs out of his parking space, and pulls behind him.

Quickly looking at Connie, Robert takes her hand. "She's going to be alright, Connie. Don't worry."

Connie just looks at him and nods.

Robert reaches for his cell phone to call Ms. Braxton.

"Hello?"

"Ms. Braxton?"

"Yes, this is she! Who is this?"

"This is Robert. I'm a friend of Lynn and Connie. Mr. Smith wants you to know the ambulance is on the way to the hospital now!"

"OK! OK! Thank you, Robert!"

"I'm following Mr. Manning with Connie in my car!"

"OK! I'm almost there!"

"Yes, ma'am."

Cheryl disconnects from Robert and immediately calls her parents.

Robert hands his cell phone to Connie.

"Here Connie, call your Mom."

Connie nods, taking the phone, wiping her eyes. She lays both Lynn's purse and her purse on her lap. Then, dials her mom.

"Momma!" Connie sobs.

Connie is breaking down again. She can't get the vision of Lynn lying on the stretcher with blood all over her out of her mind.

"Mija! What happened? Are you OK?" Connie's Mom and Dad are both from Venezuela. Spanish is their primary language at home. They call Connie "Mija," which is short for "my daughter" in Spanish.

Mercedes, Connie's Mom, is standing in the kitchen, looking bewildered, wondering what's going on. She can tell by Connie's voice something is horribly wrong.

With tears flowing down her face, Connie can barely speak. She feels like something welling up in her throat.

"It's Lynn, Momma! She's…" She can't get the words out at first. Connie's trying to clear her throat.

"Did you say 'Lynn,' Mija?" Mercedes can barely understand her, because Connie's crying so much.

"Yes, Momma!"

"What! Tell me, Mija! What happened?!"

"She's been in an accident, Momma!"

"Oh noooo! Noooooo! Baby, are you OK?! Where are you?! Your Dad and I are leaving now!" Mercedes loves Lynn like her own daughter. Over the years, Lynn spent a lot of time with them as a family and accompanied them on many family vacations. Likewise, Connie hung out at Lynn's house quite a bit with Lynn and her Mom and went many places with them too.

"Yes, Momma! I'm OK! But, Lynn's not! She looks like she's unconscious! I'm riding in the car with Robert on the way to the Lake View Hospital now! We're following Mr. Manning, the school counselor! Mr. Smith, the principal, is riding in the ambulance with Lynn!"

"Who is Robert?" Mercedes pauses for a quick second. She and her husband are very protective of Connie.

"A friend at school." Connie's whimpering now, starting to calm back down some.

"Oh, OK, OK. Which hospital again?"

"Lake View, Momma." Connie talks softly.

"OK, *listen* to me, Mija." Mercedes is a very reserved woman. Experience in Venezuela as a nurse in the ER taught her how to remain calm in heightened situations. "I want you to calm *down*, OK? Lynn is being cared for now. Me and your Dad are on the way right now. We'll meet you at the hospital. Tell your friend, Robert, thank you."

"OK. OK, Momma."

"OK, baby. One second."

"Papi! Papi! Ven aquí, quickly!" Mercedes calls for her husband, Eduardo, to come quickly.

"Yes, Mami. What's going on?" Eduardo rushes into the kitchen from the living room. He hears the urgency in her voice.

"We gotta go *now*, Papi to meet Connie at the hospital! Lynn's been in an accident!"

"*What?*" He pauses for a moment. "OK, OK! Let's go!" Eduardo runs to get the car keys.

"Baby! We're leaving now!"

"OK, Momma. See you there." Connie's crying softly, taking a tissue out of her purse to blow her nose.

Meanwhile, Cheryl is on the phone with her Dad.

"Daddy?"

"Yeah, baby, everything alright? It's late." Her dad leans over in the bed to turn the light on. He and Cheryl's mother just fell asleep.

"Daddy! It's Lynn! She's been in a horrible accident! You and Momma have to come to the hospital! Now, Daddy!"

"Whaaat? Our Lynn? Well, is she OK, Cheryl?" He's sitting up in the bed.

"Daddy, I don't know! I'm in the car *right now* on the way to Lake View Hospital!" Cheryl's driving as fast as she can. *Hooonk!* She blows the horn at a driver who almost crossed in front of her car.

Her momma wakes up and turns over to look at Cheryl's daddy. "Leroy, did you say Lynn's name?"

"Yes, baby." He looks at her with great worry on his face, trying to be calm. "We have to get dressed and head over to the hospital. Cheryl said, Lynn's been in a horrible accident."

"*What?*" She can't believe it, because Lynn is such a careful driver. They helped teach Lynn how to drive a few years ago when she took driving classes.

"Oooh noooo! I've got to get to my baby." Lynn is her only grandchild and she loves her grandbaby.

Cheryl's crying, trying to keep it together. Thinking of what Lynn must be feeling having been in an accident and if she's okay is overwhelming. Lynn is her only child. Being a single mother, she's had to be strong on many occasions for her daughter, but this one tops them all. She loves Lynn so much; they're so close. They have an unusual relationship. More than mother and daughter, they're friends too.

"OK, baby." Cheryl's Dad says. "It's gonna be alright. Don't you worry. You hear? There's *nothing* Jesus can't do. He's our Healer. We're going to throw some clothes on and meet you at the hospital as quick as we can."

"OK, Daddy. 'Cause I can't do this without you and Momma. I need you both with me." Cheryl's always been able to depend on her parents through good times and bad.

"Listen, you be careful driving out there. OK?"

Cheryl's crying. For a moment, Cheryl's mind goes blank and her body feels numb. While both of her hands hold the sides of the steering wheel, she feels like somebody else is driving the car, not her.

"Cheryl! Cheryl!" Her Dad's calling her name loudly.

"Yes, yes, Daddy! I'm here!" She quickly snaps out of the daze.

"Are you alright?"

"Yes, Daddy! I'm OK. I'm OK. Please hurry, Daddy."

"OK, now! Be careful out there. We're on our way."

"OK, Daddy." Cheryl can barely speak. She's feeling weak inside. Weeping harder, she's trying hard not to think the worst.

Chapter Eleven

"We're one minute away with the victim!" The paramedic disconnects the call with a nurse in the emergency room. He gave her details about Lynn's case, so they can prepare for her arrival. Pulling in front of the emergency room doors, the sirens blare loudly as the paramedics stop the ambulance to race to get Lynn inside. They unlock and swing the doors open quickly.

"I'm ready! Got this end!" the paramedic inside of the ambulance yells to the driver and the other paramedic outside.

"Alright, here we go! One, two, three…lift!" the driver yells.

Swiftly, but gently, they pull the stretcher out of the ambulance and proceed into the emergency room unit.

Mr. Smith jumps out of the ambulance, running behind them. In a flash, another set of emergency room doors fly open as the paramedics rush to push the stretcher down the hallway. The Code Blue alert is sounding loudly to let the emergency room doctors and nurses know to prepare. Swinging back the curtain of a cubicle, one of the on-call doctors leaves a patient and rushes toward them. A nearby nurse follows him.

Really anxious now, Mr. Smith stands behind the medics. The emergency room is full; three other stretchers with people line a wall. Nurses are walking swiftly back and forth from the main desk to cubicles. Wearing green plastic gloves, they're carrying charts, needles and vials to draw blood, and give medicine. The telephone at the main desk is ringing. People with various kinds of sicknesses are lying in beds, looking very sick.

"What's the condition?" The doctor quickly puts his stethoscope around the back of his neck. The nurse stands next to him taking notes.

The paramedic that was on inside of the ambulance quickly walks up from the other end of the stretcher.

"Broken left leg, lacerations, damage to the cranial, appears to be unconscious, blood pressure is up, vitals are low, little oxygen."

"Full name?" The doctor looks intensely, as he's used to handling these types of emergencies.

Mr. Smith speaks up quickly. "Lynn Braxton, Doctor. She's my student at Lake High."

The doctor looks at Mr. Smith. "OK, we're taking her into surgery immediately."

Turning back to the nurse, he says. "Let's go! Prepare the team for surgery!" The nurse runs, holding her clipboard of notes to prepare the others. The doctor disappears behind two big swinging doors. Everything's happening so fast.

Mr. Smith wanted to let the doctor know Lynn's mother is on the way, but he didn't get a chance. The severity of Lynn's situation calls for immediate attention.

"What do I do now?" Mr. Smith turns to one of the medics.

"Well, sir, you have to wait. She's unconscious. Her vitals are low. They're going to work on her immediately."

"OK, I understand."

"The best thing to do now is to go to the emergency waiting room. Let them know who you are and that you rode in the ambulance with the patient. Does she have family?"

"Yes, her mother is on the way here." Mr. Smith answers.

"Good. Give them the patient's name and let them know that her mother's on the way. A nurse will inform you from there about what's going on."

"Alright. Thanks! I appreciate all you guys did to help."

The paramedics slightly smile, nodding their heads. "That's what we're here for," one says.

Mr. Smith nods as he sees the EMERGENCY WAITING ROOM sign and rushes off towards the door below it.

Meanwhile, everyone else is pulling up outside into the emergency room parking lot about the same time. Cheryl makes it into the emergency room a minute before Mr. Manning, Robert, and Connie. Connie's parents are still on the way. They live a little farther out than Cheryl does. And, Cheryl's parents are getting into their car to leave.

Running fast through the sliding glass doors into the emergency waiting room, Cheryl's screaming at the top of her lungs, "where's my baby? Where's my baby?"

Immediately, Mr. Smith turns around, seeing Cheryl running, he rushes over to her from one of the windows. He was talking to administrative personnel that handles intake.

Seeing Mr. Smith, Cheryl rushes towards him. "Where is my baby?" she cries loudly.

"They just took her back for surgery."

"What?! What happened?! What's wrong with my baby?!" Cheryl's looking at Mr. Smith with tears running down her face.

"Lynn's unconscious and she has a broken leg." He places his hands on her arms.

"Noooooooo! Noooooooo!" She falls into Mr. Smith's chest, feeling like she's going to faint. Lynn has never been unconscious before. Mr. Smith puts his arms around her and hugs her tightly. He's feeling so sad for Lynn and Cheryl.

Just then, a nurse walks up. "Are you Lynn Braxton's mother?"

Turning around quickly, Cheryl looks with anticipation of hearing news about Lynn. "Yes! Yes! I am! What's happened to her?"

"Ma'am, currently your daughter is in surgery. We need you to fill out some paperwork in the meantime."

"OK! OK! But, first I need somebody to tell me exactly what's going on with my baby!" Cheryl's frantic.

"Ma'am, I really wish I could, but that's the doctor's responsibility. We have to wait until he comes out."

"What do you mean?!" Cheryl becomes more upset with the fact that there's no more information the nurse can give.

"Ms. Braxton, I understand you're upset, but please try to calm down. We can't proceed until we have this paperwork filled out." The nurse tries to sympathize, understanding she's in great pain.

Mr. Smith interjects, "The doctors are working on Lynn right now. She's going to be OK." Cheryl looks up toward the ceiling, crying.

"Yes, ma'am, they are, and we won't know anything until the doctor comes out. But, in the meantime, we really do need you to give us some information and sign some forms for your daughter."

"OK! OK!" Cheryl looks at her, realizing she's just trying to do her job and that she won't know anything more until the doctor comes.

"She's going to be alright, Ms. Braxton. Let's just give them the information they need, so we can help move the process along." Mr. Smith gently places both of his hands on her shoulders. Cheryl's wiping her eyes now, nodding her head, trying to calm down.

"It'll only take a few minutes of your time, ma'am. I promise." The nurse is standing in front of her, holding a clipboard with the forms on it.

Cheryl's annoyed with the system, but understands. Sobbing lightly now, taking a deep breath, she looks back at the nurse. "OK, what do you need?"

"First, I need to know your daughter's full name."

"Lynn Michelle Braxton."

"Is your daughter allergic to any medicines?"

"No. Not that we know of."

"Has she ever had any operations before?"

"No."

"That's good. Is she pregnant?"

"Pregnant?!" Cheryl looks at her like she's crazy. "No! She's not pregnant. Why would she be pregnant? She's only eighteen!"

"Ms. Braxton, you'd be surprised. We get young women who come in here all of the time pregnant at her age and younger girls too. These questions are just standard protocol."

Cheryl looks at her, taking another deep breath. Mr. Smith gently squeezes her shoulders again, letting her know it's alright.

By this time, Mr. Manning, Robert, and Connie are walking swiftly toward them. As they approach Cheryl and Mr. Smith, they hear the nurse asking questions and stand back to wait until she's finished.

"We're almost done now, ma'am. Who is your daughter's primary care doctor?"

"Freeman. Dr. Freeman." Cheryl crosses both arms over her chest and shakes her head thinking out loud, "Why my baby?"

"OK, great. We're all done now, ma'am, with this part. I just need you to sign right here, please." The nurse hands Cheryl the clipboard.

"OK." Cheryl takes the board and signs the form.

The nurse flips the paper over to another. "And, right here." She's pointing to the signature line on the second page.

Cheryl signs and hands the clipboard back to the nurse.

"Ma'am, as soon as the doctor is finished, he'll be out to speak with you, OK?" The nurse tries to reassure her before she leaves.

"Yes, yes. Thank you." Cheryl looks at her with tears flowing down her face.

The nurse slightly leans her head to the left side, holding the clipboard up to her chest, looking at Cheryl for a moment with compassion. Although, she encounters these type of unfortunate situations in the ER all of the time, there's something different about Lynn's that draws her to Cheryl. She can't describe it; she just feels it.

Mr. Smith nods his head at the nurse as she reaches out to touch Cheryl's right arm in compassion for the pain she's going through before walking away.

Gently squeezing her shoulders again, Mr. Smith consoles Cheryl the best he can. "It's OK. Lynn is going to be alright, Ms. Braxton." Looking at the seating area, Mr. Smith directs Cheryl. "Here, let's wait right over here for the doctor to come out." Then, he motions with his head to Mr. Manning, Robert, and Connie, who are still standing nearby, to have a seat.

Taking her seat, Cheryl puts her purse on the left side of her in the next chair and looks at Mr. Smith with tears in her eyes. "Thank you, Mr. Smith, for riding with Lynn to the hospital. I *really* appreciate it."

Grabbing her right hand and holding it in his, Mr. Smith slightly smiles and looks back. "Ms. Braxton, you don't have to thank me. We *all* love Lynn, and we all want to see her well again. Don't worry. I'm gonna to stay here with you until we find out what's going on."

Nodding her head okay, Cheryl looks down, sobbing again, putting her left hand on top of Mr. Smith's. A few seats from Cheryl, Connie sits leaning on Robert's shoulder, looking at Cheryl and Mr. Smith. Cheryl looks over at them for a quick second, crying, and slightly smiles as a gesture to thank them for being there. Connie gets up and goes to hug Cheryl. Without saying a word, Cheryl and Connie weep in one another's arms. Mr. Manning and Robert look at

Cheryl and Connie, sadden by all that has happened. Mr. Smith takes a deep sigh and rests his hands in his lap.

"Ms. Braxton?" The doctor quickly walks up from around the corner.

Cheryl jumps up with anticipation. Connie, Mr. Smith, Mr. Manning, and Robert all stand up, eager to hear the news.

"Yes! Yes! I'm Ms. Braxton! How's my daughter, doctor?" Cheryl's looking anxiously at the doctor with her eyes wide and mouth open.

"Well first, I'm Dr. Hagan, the on-call doctor. I examined your daughter when the paramedics brought her in. The accident your daughter was in was pretty bad. I'm sorry to tell you this, but she's in a coma."

"What?! Noooooo!" Immediately, Cheryl drops to the floor.

The doctor looks. "Ms. Braxton!"

"Oh noooooo!" Connie gasps. Mr. Manning puts his hands up to his head. Robert puts his arm around Connie, looking really upset by the news. With shock on his face from the update, Mr. Smith quickly leans down, helping Cheryl back up to her seat.

The doctor continues, "Ms. Braxton, I know you're upset, but *please* try to be strong for your daughter. She's going to need you. Her left leg is broken. She's suffered some major trauma to the head and has lacerations on both her face and leg. But, her vital signs are stabilized now. However, she lost the baby."

"Baby?!" Cheryl's face almost changes colors. She looks at him, stunned. "*What* baby?! Lynn isn't pregnant." She sits up a bit in her chair.

"Ms. Braxton, I'm sorry to tell you this, ma'am, but your daughter was about seven weeks pregnant."

Cheryl screams and weeps, at the same time looking at him. "Noooooooo! Nooooooooooo! That couldn't be! Not, Lynn! Not my baby!"

It's clear to Dr. Hagan that this is the first time Cheryl is finding out about the pregnancy.

Shocked even more, Mr. Smith stands a moment thinking, "Lynn?"

Connie turns her head into Robert's chest, unable to hear any more.

Cheryl leans forward in the chair, propping her elbows on her lap and her face in her hands, sobbing. Mr. Smith sits back down slowly in disbelief, but remembers he too must be strong...for Cheryl. Gently, he moves Cheryl's long hair over to the other side of her back. With a sad look in his eyes, he rubs her shoulder lightly.

"We're here for you, Ms. Braxton. We're working every second with your daughter," the doctor says.

Looking at the doctor, who's waiting a moment for Cheryl to settle from the news, Mr. Smith clears his throat. "So what happens now, doc?"

Cheryl's weeping with her face in her hands.

The doctor looks at Mr. Smith. "Well, right now, we're preparing to operate on her left leg and as soon as we're done, she'll be moved to the intensive care unit. The nurse will come over and give you all the details. But, I'll be back out to let you know how the surgery went."

Cheryl's crying even harder.

Mr. Smith nods his head. "OK, doc. Thank you. We'll be right here waiting."

"OK, good." The doctor puts his hands in the pockets of his medical jacket, turns around and leaves.

Mr. Manning plops back down in the chair, leaning forward with his legs spread to both sides of the chair, putting his elbows on his thighs and hands together. He deeply wishes he could do something to help. Robert's still standing, rubbing Connie lightly on her back. "It's going to be OK, Connie." Robert repeats. "Lynn's going to be alright." Connie's sobbing on his chest.

Cheryl sits up in the chair now weeping, feeling completely overwhelmed. She doesn't know whether to lean forward or sit back. She can't get comfortable. Everything in her feels like screaming. Putting his arm around her back, Mr. Smith pulls Cheryl into his chest and just holds her. Everyone's quiet, stunned by the news about Lynn. Then, all of sudden, Mr. Smith begins singing a slowly, "What a Mighty God We Serve," worshipping God in his heart. He knows with God, not man, but with God…anything is possible.

What a mighty God we serve.

Angels bow before Him

Heaven and earth adore Him

What a mighty God we serve.

He holds the winds in His hand

And He is the great I am

He is the bright and morning star

And without Him I would fall

Angels bow before Him

Heaven and earth adore Him

What a mighty God we serve

Angels bow before Him

Heaven and earth adore Him

What a mighty God we serve

Jehovah Jireh, my provider

Jehovah Shalom, my peace

Jehovah Tsidkenu, my righteousness

What a mighty God we serve

Connie looks at Mr. Smith, still crying with tears rolling down her face, feeling some relief. Mr. Manning nods his head in agreement and smiles, still leaning in the same position. Robert looks at Mr. Smith with a gentle smile, then he closes his eyes and prays, *"I love You, Jesus. Please, let Lynn live."*

Cheryl lifts her head up and looks at Mr. Smith. "I needed that." Her voice cracks. "Oh, God! Let my baby live, and make her whole again."

Slightly smiling at her, fighting back tears, Mr. Smith's moved in the Spirit. This song always moves his heart with faith in what only God can do.

Looking directly into Cheryl's eyes, Mr. Smith looks full of peace in his face. "Ms. Braxton…there's a protective place of peace…and, that's the secret place of God Almighty…Christ in us, our hope of glory. When Christ lives in us, we're under the covering of His Blood…the Blood of Jesus. We can't let doubt slip in, even in times like this. We may be weary, but we know we have a Master whose a Healer. The responsibility is ours to renew our minds in Him…Christ, and to declare the workings of God with our mouths. In Christ, we're free. So, when anxiety comes, we have to go to Him…the Master…the Good Lord, Jesus. I'm reminded of what God says He will do for those who believe in Him when I sing that song. God is a covenant-keeping God. One thing God will never do is forsake us. So, I know…Lynn is gonna to be just fine."

Finally, feeling a little strength flowing in her body, Cheryl smiles as best she can. Inside now, she's renewing her own mind in Christ with the help of the Holy Spirit by thinking about the Power of the Blood of Jesus and the Power in His Name.

Nodding her head. "Yes, our God can do *anything*. Through Christ *all things* are possible. By His stripes we're *healed*."

Smiling more at Cheryl now, Mr. Smith hugs her closer. "Ameeen!"

Wiping her eyes a bit, Cheryl looks back at him. "The Holy Spirit is helping my baby."

"Yes, He is, Ms. Braxton. Yes, He is. And, I praise God for it. He loves us."

"Yes, thank You, Lord." Cheryl's calming down a lot now, sniffling. Her mind is being renewed and refreshed in the Lord.

Just then, Mercedes and Eduardo, Connie's parents, rush through the emergency room doors looking for her. Eduardo looks to his right. Mercedes is standing next to him, throwing her beautiful, thin purple shawl over her back. She's looking very worried. They're both anxious to find Connie.

"Honey, there she is…over there!"

"Mija!" Mercedes is running over to Connie. Connie sees her parents and bursts out of Robert's arms to run to them. Eduardo comes behind Mercedes and puts his arms around his wife and daughter.

"Thank God, baby, you're OK!" Eduardo looks at Connie.

"We're here now, baby. Calm down." Mercedes kisses Connie's forehead. Connie's so glad they're finally here.

Then, Mercedes walks over to Cheryl and leans down to hug her.

"Cheryl, honey, we're here for you."

Cheryl's trying to be strong, but she struggles to say, "Lynn's in a coma and has a broken leg." She sobs some more, remembering the talk she just had with Mr. Smith.

"Oh no! Not, Lynn! I'm *so* sorry to hear this, Cheryl." Mercedes is really upset hearing the news. "Listen, Lynn's going to pull through this. Don't you worry. God can do anything. Don't talk anymore, just calm down, honey. We're here, OK? We're going to stay with you, OK?"

"OK." Cheryl nods her head. "Thanks. I appreciate it."

Mr. Smith smiles slightly at Mercedes and nods his head once, acknowledging Eduardo.

Mercedes joins Eduardo and Connie as they sit down. Robert and Mr. Manning sit, waiting patiently with the rest of them.

Chapter Twelve

"Amelia! Monica! Over here!" Bruce yells, motioning to them as they come out of the gym. Students are standing around waiting to be picked up and others are walking to their cars. This time, Bruce parks directly in front of the gym, instead of looking for a space. He came right away when Amelia called.

"So, what's up? How was the party?" Bruce leans his elbows over the top of the car, looking at them open the doors. "And, isn't it a little early to be picking you all up? Wasn't it supposed to be in another forty-five minutes?" He looks at his watch and hops back in the driver's seat.

"Yes, it is." Amelia looks disappointed, leaning to get in the car as she fixes her dress underneath her.

"It's a bummer!" Monica adds, settling in the back seat, placing her purse beside her.

"The DJ was *good* though, wasn't he, Monica?" Amelia turns, looking at Monica and then Bruce. "Everybody was having a good time. Then, all of a sudden the dance ended, because a bad accident happened."

Turning the music down some, Bruce puts his arm on the armrest, looking at both of them surprised. "Wait a minute. What happened again?"

Monica looks at Bruce. "I mean, I feel for whoever was in the accident, but it was the *best* school dance we've ever had." Not to concerned about the accident, Monica leans back in the seat, looking out of the window, disappointed.

Squeezing his eyebrows together a little not understanding, Bruce looks at Amelia.

"Evidently, there was a big accident a little while ago." Sometimes, Amelia can be difficult. Instead of giving all of the details, you have to pull them out of her.

"Where and what happened?" Bruce looks really concerned.

Amelia looks at the radio to see what station Bruce is playing.

"One of the faculty members said it happened in front of the parking lot at the light." Amelia's looking out of the window now at other students leaving.

"One minute we were dancing and the next minute everybody stopped dancing when the DJ stopped playing music. We were all wondering what was going on."

Monica sighs. "Yeah, then they told us the dance was ending early, because of a big accident occurred."

Bruce looks forward, nodding his head, starting the engine. "So, that's why you called me early?"

"Yes." Amelia's reaching over to change the radio station.

"Well, it must have been a big accident." Bruce is driving off.

"Bye!" Monica puts the window down quickly when she sees Craig walking to his car.

"Call me!" he yells back, smiling.

"When did you talk to him?" Amelia quickly looks back at Monica.

Monica's blushing. "Oh! I forgot to tell you. While you were dancing with Robert, Craig walked up to me and we talked for a little."

"Whaaat!" Amelia's face lights up.

"We only talked for a few minutes though, but we exchanged numbers." Monica can't stop blushing. She's liked Craig for a long time.

"You go girl! Wow! They finally exchange numbers!" Amelia laughs.

"So, who was in the accident?" Bruce glances at Amelia with his hands on the steering wheel.

"Don't know." Amelia shakes her head. "They didn't say. All we know is that they ended the dance." Amelia lays her hands over her purse on her lap.

"Wow." Bruces looks. There's a long line to get out. Lots of cars are leaving at once. When its his turn at the light, Bruce makes a right out of the parking lot to drive to Monica's house to drop her off.

Ten minutes later, they arrive at Monica's. She lives around the corner from their house.

"Bye, guys." Monica's in a somber mood getting out of the car; she's really disappointed about the evening.

"Bye, girl. Talk later." Amelia looks at her closing the door.

The light at the front door of her house comes on before Monica makes it to the steps. It's her dad. He's very strict. Every time Monica goes out, he waits in the living room until she comes home.

Bruce waits a minute to see her Dad open the door.

"Good night, Mr. Williams!" Bruce waves.

Mr. Williams waves back and closes the door.

"Well, at least you got to dance a little." Bruce looks at Amelia.

"Yeah, I guess." Amelia leans her head back. At this point, she doesn't care about messing up her hair. The night is over as far as she's concerned.

Back at the hospital, everyone's still waiting in the emergency room for Dr. Hagan to return after Lynn's surgery.

"Would anybody like anything to drink?" Eduardo looks around getting up. "I'm going to the vending machines."

Cheryl shakes her head no.

"I'll take some water, please." Mr. Smith reaches in his pocket to give Eduardo some money.

Eduardo sticks his hand out. "No, don't worry."

"I'll go with you." Mr. Manning's getting up.

Connie and Mercedes don't say anything, because they know he's going to bring them something back. He's always been a thoughtful person, always thinking of others.

Putting his arm around Cheryl again, Mr. Smith leans back in the chair and sings another song softly. Except this time, it's one he wrote a few years ago.

When I gave my life to Jesus

When I gave my life to Jesus

He received me and He loved me

When I gave my life to Jesus

When I gave my life to Jesus

When I gave my life to Jesus

He covered me and protected me

When I gave my life to Jesus

When I gave my life to Jesus

When I gave my life to Jesus

He promised me He'd bless me

When I gave my life to Jesus

"That was simple, but *so* beautiful. Thank you." Cheryl smiles a little, feeling greater comfort.

Mr. Smith squeezes Cheryl on the shoulder and slightly smiles back.

"Mr. Smith, have you considered making your own CD." Mercedes smiles. "We didn't know you could sing like that. Your voice is so Anointed. You're really gifted."

Mr. Smith smiles back, still singing, worshipping God in his heart.

Robert gently smiles, looking over at Mr. Smith. "Yeah, Mr. Smith. When you sing earlier, I didn't know you had pipes like that."

"And there's a whole lot more you'll learn as you grow, son." Mr. Smith smiles back at Robert. "And, thank you, Mrs. Meldes." Mr. Smith looks at Connie's mother. "To answer your question…no, I never considered it…never even thought of it actually."

Robert nods his head. This is the first moment since the accident occurred earlier that he's beginning to feel a little peace inside. Mr. Smith helped them all by reminding them of what it means to have faith. It's no doubt that the Holy Spirit is moving in the ER tonight.

Thinking to himself now, Robert is wondering if Amelia knows about Lynn. At the scene of the accident, for a quick moment, he saw students gathering behind them while the paramedics were pushing Lynn on the stretcher to the ambulance. He glanced back when he heard some of the students talking. Now, he remembers hearing Mr. Smith instruct one of the teachers to end the dance. At the time, his focus was on Connie, trying to calm her down. So, he's not sure if Amelia was out there or not. Pulling his cell phone out from the inside of his jacket, Robert notices there's only one bar of battery life left and sends Amelia a quick text before his phone dies. It reads:

Hello, Amelia. Did you see the accident outside the school tonight? It was Lynn. I'm at Lake View Hospital with Mr. Smith, Connie and Lynn's Mom.

In the car on the way to the house, Amelia and Bruce are singing songs on the radio. The windows are down and the cool breeze is blowing on them. Since it's not quite summer yet, the temperature has been dropping at nighttime. Pulling into the driveway, Bruce hits the garage opener when a text notification chimes on Ameila's cell phone.

"Is that mine or yours?" Bruce is reaching for his phone. They both have the same text notification chime. Bruce has been meaning to change his.

Reaching in her purse to check, Amelia sees the light on her phone shining. "It's mine."

Picking it up, she looks at number of the text message, but doesn't recognize it. She didn't have a chance to log his number in. It's a text from Robert. She wasn't expecting one from him so soon. His number doesn't register in her mind until she reads the text and finds out that it's him.

"Oh my gosh!" Ameila gasps. The calm facial expression from the song they were just singing turns to fear. She thinks back to the moment when she put that note in Rihanna's purse.

"What is it?" Bruce is pulling into the garage and putting the car in park.

Quickly, Amelia texts back:

Robert?

In the emergency waiting room, Robert's sitting, holding his cell phone in his hand, hoping she'll respond. He didn't put it back inside of his jacket pocket yet, just in case. Feeling the phone's vibration from a text notification in his hand, Roberts looks quickly to see if it's from Amelia and it is.

He texts back:

Yes, it's me, Robert.

Margaret opens the garage doorway from inside the house in her pajamas, eager to hear all about the evening. She heard the garage open from her bedroom and quickly came downstairs to meet them. The kids always tease her about having ears like a canine. "Hey guys!"

Before Bruce opens the car door, he turns around, looking at Amelia holding the car keys in one hand with his other hand on the door handle. "What's going on?" He can see she's all of a sudden distressed about something.

"One second! One second!"

Amelia's texting Robert back, texting as fast as she can. She's shocked, hearing the news. Never did she think putting that note in Rihanna's purse would come to this.

Her text back to Robert reads:

No, I didn't. Was inside. You mean, Lynn Braxton?

Quickly, she turns her head looking at Bruce, scared. "It's Lynn!"

"Lynn what, Amelia?" Bruce is trying to understand what she's talking about. Margaret's wondering what's taking them so long to get out of the car.

Looking at him intensely with big eyes, Amelia takes a deep breath and swallows. "I think she's the one that was in that accident."

Bruce looks at her, first trying to make sure she's talking about Lynn on Lake High's basketball team. She's the only Lynn he knows around Amelia. Secondly, he's wondering why she's so frightened about the news, knowing Amelia doesn't care so much for Lynn. He has seen the way Amelia acts toward Lynn at basketball practices; something isn't quite adding up.

"You mean, Lynn, on your basketball team?"

In the meantime, Robert texts back:

Yes, Lynn. She's in a coma.

Amelia gasps deeper for air. All of a sudden, it feels like a deep hole is forming in her stomach. She stares at the screen for a moment.

With her eyes still big, Amelia looks back at Bruce, shaking her head. "She's in a coma at Lake View."

Margaret's still standing in the doorway. "What are you guys doing in there? Come on inside!" Margaret yells. She's fixing her soft cotton pink pajama shirt that matches her cotton pink pajamas pants. She loves cotton pj's. "Wheew! It's a little nippy out tonight. Put the garage down, Bruce!" Margaret says. The night breeze coming through the garage is quite nippy.

"Wow!" Bruce's eyes get big, opening the car door. He knows Lynn's Mom, Ms. Braxton, from basketball practices and games, because his Mom and she always talk. "So you mean Lynn! Lynn is in a coma?!" Shaking his head, he gets out of the car, making sure he has his cell phone that was on the charger. "I can't believe that."

Margaret folds her arms. "Bruce, what's going on? You guys are taking too long just to get out of the car."

Bruce looks up at Margaret. "Hey, Ma, let Amelia tell you."

Grabbing her purse, which fell on the floor, Amelia slowly gets out of the car and closes the door. The expression of happiness Amelia had on her face leaving to go to the school dance clearly isnt' what Margaret is seeing. Standing for a moment, Ameila leans over a little, because her stomach feels like it's going to sink. Then, swinging her purse over her shoulder, she walks around the back of the car toward the stairwell. The thought that Lynn could die, because of what she did is unthinkable.

Margaret's looking really puzzled. She didn't expect to see Amelia return home like this. "Amelia, what's wrong?" Margaret's looking at her from the top of the steps in the garage.

"Wow! That's sad!" Bruce locks the car and walks behind Amelia. He just can't believe it. Standing behind Amelia, shaking his head. Amelia stops at the bottom of the stairs, frightened, looking at her Mom.

"Ma, I just found out Lynn's in a coma. She got into an accident earlier tonight during the dance." Her stomach feels like it's in knots now.

"What?! Lynn?? Lynn Braxton?? Are you sure, Amelia??"

Amelia gets another text from Robert. It reads:

Are you there?

Amelia looks at it real quick, assuming it's Robert again, but doesn't answer. The shock of it all is sinking in.

"Yes, I'm sure. Robert just texted me. They're all at the Lake View Hospital. The school ended the dance early, because of it. I didn't know til just now. Robert is a friend of mine who goes to Lake High." Looking up at her Mom, Amelia feels sicker and sicker in her stomach.

"What?! Oh noooo!" Margaret gasps, looking at Amelia, placing both hands around her face quickly. "I've got to get to the hospital right away! Cheryl must be a wreck! Oh my! She'll need support! She's always been there for me!" Running to change her clothes, Margaret yells back, "You guys come on inside!"

Bruce yells back, seeing his Mom run, "Ma, I'm going with you! And, I'll drive!"

Quickly, Bruce walks back to the car. Amelia stands there thinking about what she should do for a moment...stay home or go to the hospital with her mother and brother? Her stomach's cramping from the thought of her note being responsible. Leaning her head on the banister, she sighs. "I can't believe this."

A few minutes later, Margaret's rushing back down the stairs to grab her purse from the kitchen.

Amelia's still leaning forward with her head down. She keeps feeling pulled to go to the hospital with her Mom and Bruce, instead of staying home, despite the pain in her stomach building. While Margaret's turning the kitchen lights off and running to the garage door to lock it, Amelia walks to the car and gets in the back. But, this time in the back seat.

Locking the door to the house in the garage, Margaret turns and sees Bruce in the driver's seat. It didn't take her long to change. She threw on a pair of jeans, a baby-blue silk blouse, slipped on a pair of sandals and grabbed a long, comfortable gray cardigan. "You guys sure you want to go?!" she yells.

"Yeah, Ma! I'm sure." Bruce looks over.

"OK, where's Amelia?"

"The back seat!"

"OK! Let's go!" Margaret rushes down the steps over to the passenger side of the car.

Starting the engine, Bruce backs the car out carefully. Margaret looks back at Amelia, turning the radio off. "Amelia, are you OK, baby?"

Amelia looks, nodding her head, trying not to show much emotion on her face. Her stomach is really cramping. She's only felt this type of pain in her stomach during her menstruation. "Yes, Ma. I'm fine." Really she wants to cry, but she fights back the tears.

In the front seat, Margaret pulls her cell phone out of her purse to quickly call Nana.

"Hello?" Nana's in the bed doing her nightly Bible study and prayers.

"Momma!"

"Yes, Margaret. What is it, baby? You sound like something's wrong." Nana places the Bible and her reading glasses on the bed beside her, looking concerned. She hears a sense of urgency in Margaret's voice.

"You know that dream you had?! The accident you saw, Momma?! And the feeling of something bad happening?!"

"Yes, baby. What about it?" Nana's clearly remembers.

"Well, it happened tonight! It was about Lynn! She evidently got in a serious accident tonight!" Margaret's looking out the passenger window. She trusts Bruce driving.

"Oh my! Are you sure, Margaret? Nana knew her dream would come to pass and shakes her head. She really likes Lynn.

"Well, we're all on the way to Lake View Hospital now. I need to get there for Cheryl. Amelia said, Lynn's in a coma!"

"Whaaaat? It's that bad? Oh no!"

Margaret's shaking her head. "I know Cheryl's a basket case, Momma. I would be if it were Bruce or Amelia."

Nana looks up to the ceiling, speaking from her heart. *"God, in the Name of Jesus, please help Your precious daughters, Lynn and Cheryl."*

"Yes, Lord! Help them, Lord! They both need You." Margaret props her elbow on the edge of the window, placing her hand on her forehead.

"Look, Margaret, call me when you guys find out more about what's going on with Lynn."

"OK, Momma. I will. Love you."

"Remember, God is in control, Margaret. I'll be here praying for you all. And, tell Bruce to drive carefully."

"I will. Call you as soon as I know something, okay. Bye Momma."

"I love you. Talk soon, baby." Nana hangs up.

Amelia hears Margaret end the call with Nana and looks out the window saying in a low voice, "what have I done?"

Placing her cordless telephone on the nightstand, Nana leans back on her pillows and prays.

"Father, Your are the Great I AM. I worship You, my Father, my God. Thank You, God, for Your Love and Grace. When You raised Christ from the dead, you raised us up also to be co-heirs with Him. Your Word says, all who believe in Jesus and His Name are given the right to become Your children, O'God. And, in Christ, we have authority to use His Name, to dominate in the earth for Your Good Pleasure and Will. In the Name of the Lord Jesus Christ, I cut Satan off from Lynn's life. I destroy Satan's power over Lynn's life by the Power of the Holy Ghost and the Blood of Jesus Christ. I declare that Satan's power over Lynn's life is destroyed now, in Jesus Christ's Name. No weapon formed against Lynn shall prosper, according to Isaiah 54, in the Name of the Lord . Lynn, shall live and not die, in Jesus Christ's Name. She belongs to the Lord. Move in her body, Holy Spirit. Revive Lynn. Bring her out of that coma, Holy Spirit, and back to her mother. Restore her back to normal. Let this be a testimony for all who don't believe in You, Lord, to come to You and the Holy Spirit. Lord, comfort Lynn's mother and help Margaret to calm down. And, open the eyes of Amelia's heart, Lord. Oh Lord, deliver Amelia from those evil influences. Help her too, Lord. Protect them as they drive to the hospital and keep all of them safe, in Jesus' Name, I pray." Nana pauses. She feels chills all over her body. It's confirmation the Holy Spirit always gives her. *"I trust You, Lord. Thank You, Precious Holy Spirit."*

At the hospital, everyone's still in the emergency waiting room waiting to hear more from the doctor about Lynn's surgery.

Although Cheryl's calmed down some, she still can't believe what's happened to her baby. The fact that her only child is lying in the hospital in a coma is very hard to accept.

"Holy Spirit, *help* my baby. Holy Spirit, *help* my baby. Holy Spirit, *help* my baby…" Cheryl's shaking her head slightly in disbelief with tears in her eyes, swaying a little side to side.

"The Holy Spirit *is* with her." Mr. Smith's still holding her in his arms.

Running through the hospital's doors with Bruce and Amelia trailing behind her, Margaret stops, quickly scanning the room for Cheryl. Lake View has a large emergency waiting room. There're lots of people sitting down and a few nurses passing by. The security desk is right in front of her.

"Can I help you, miss?" The security officer puts his pen down and looks up.

"I'm looking for my girlfriend. Her daughter was in a serious accident."

Looking at her, Bruce, and Amelia a little funny, the security officer doesn't know whether she's referring to a "girlfriend," as in just a friend, or as in an actual girlfriend.

Over to the right, past a tall plant just before the vending machines, Margaret spots Cheryl and Mr. Smith sitting with everybody else in a small nook. "There they are!" Margaret points to her right.

Margaret quickly turns back to the security officer. "Thanks, sir. I found her." Then, she rushes over to Cheryl who doesn't see her coming.

Approaching Cheryl, Margaret immediately kneels down, looking up at her, grabbing her hands. Mr. Smith removes his arm, giving them their moment. Bruce and Amelia take seats across from them.

"Oh, Cheryl! When I heard what happened, I rushed right over! I'm here for you! We're not going *anywhere*." Margaret glances up at Mr. Smith. He nods and smiles. "We're going to stay *right here* with you and Lynn."

Beginning to really cry again, Cheryl's so thankful to see Margaret. With tears in her eyes, unable to say anything, she can barely say, "thank you, Sis." They hug each other for a long time.

"Thank you. Thank you, Sis. I'm so glad you came." Cheryl says.

Hugging Cheryl, Margaret cries with her, gently rubbing her back. She can only imagine what Cheryl's going through not knowing what's going to happen to Lynn.

"It's gonna be OK. *God's* got this. *God* is in control." Margaret pulls back and looks directly into her eyes. Cheryl isn't moving, just crying. Sniffling, she shakes her head.

"Yes, yes, Margaret. He is. My baby is in His hands."

"That's right, Cheryl. And, she's *covered* by the Blood of Jesus." Looking Cheryl in her eyes, Margaret feels her pain as a mother. She grabs Cheryl's hands and holds them in hers. Gently squeezing Cheryl's hands, Margaret looks, slanting her head a bit, as if to say, "I'm here for you, girl," and stands up. Cheryl slightly smiles, being very appreciative, understanding exactly what Margaret means without her saying one word.

Across the way, Amelia glances at Robert, then looks away from everyone. Her stomach's getting worse now, because they're actually in the hospital where Lynn is lying unconscious. Margaret looks over at Amelia and Bruce and back at Cheryl, then Mr. Smith.

"OK, we're going to be sitting right over there." She points to the seats where Bruce and Amelia are sitting. Before Margaret walks over toward Bruce and Amelia, she looks around, gently smiling, acknowledging everyone. Then, she looks back at Mr. Smith as if to say, "I'm so glad you're here to help her."

Looking at him, Margaret remembers what Nana told her about him being a pastor, and the day they met in his office. She knew then he was a great man of God. Mr. Smith nods and smiles, reaching for her as if to say back, "everything is going to be OK." Taking his hand, Margaret nods. For an instant, they both feel great warmth in the power of their touch, but there's too much intensity from the situation to make anything of it.

Sitting next to her parents, Connie sees Amelia and gives her a hard look. She's so angry with Amelia for the way she's treated Lynn. In her mind, she's thinking, "how dare she even be here?"

As Margaret begins to walk over to Bruce and Amelia, Dr. Hagan walks up.

"Ms. Braxton?"

Quickly, Margaret turns around and walks back to Cheryl and holds her arm. Everybody stands up, including Bruce and Amelia who take a few steps toward them to hear the doctor.

"Yes, Dr. Hagan! How's Lynn doing? Can I see her now?" Cheryl's looking with desperation at Dr. Hagan. She's been waiting for a long time.

"Yes, Ms. Braxton, your daughter is doing better, and yes, you can see her now, ma'am."

Cheryl gasps, putting one hand over her chest, sighing with relief.

Margaret and Mercedes say, "thank You, Jesus!" at the same time. Mr. Smith glances upward for a moment, praising God silently in his heart; then, he places his hand on Cheryl's upper back. Connie looks hopeful for her best friend. Robert lightly slaps his hands together in the air, holding them in a prayer position, closing his eyes for a quick second. Everyone else looks intensely at Dr. Hagan.

Taking a deep breath, Dr. Hagan looks at everyone and then back at Cheryl.

"The operation on Lynn's leg was successful, but I'm sorry to say…" He pauses. "She's still in a coma."

The sigh of relief among everyone quickly turns back deep sorrow as they all let out a slight sound of a groan. Cheryl doesn't respond. She just nods her head okay, beginning to cry a little more. She feels like every ounce of energy has drained away again. She was hoping to hear that Lynn woke up.

"We've managed to stabilize her condition. So, now she's being moved up stairs to the intensive care unit."

"So, can I go to see her now, doctor? I *need* to see my baby." Cheryl's still crying and a bit agitated with all of the waiting.

"Yes, you can, Ms. Braxton. They're moving her as we speak. If you follow me, I'll personally walk you up to her room myself. The intensive care unit is on the fourth floor. There's also a family waiting room there up there."

Cheryl takes another sigh of relief. At least she's finally able to see Lynn.

"OK." Cheryl nods.

"Now, we only allow two to three people at a time in a patient's room when they're in the intensive care unit."

"OK, I understand. Just show us where everyone can wait, please." Cheryl's trying to control herself from crying uncontrollably again. She's beginning to get a headache.

"Thank you, doc." Mr. Smith nods.

Nodding his head back at Mr. Smith, Dr. Hagan turns with his chart in his hand to lead them toward the elevators to go to the intensive care unit. Everyone follows Cheryl and the doctor, except Robert; he lags behind. Bruce and Amelia remain.

Touching Connie on the arm as she walks by, Robert gently says. "Connie, I'll see you up there in a little while."

"OK." She tries to smile a little, but can't. Understanding why, Robert nods. Connie walks ahead next to her parents, forgetting to pick up her purse from the chair.

Margaret lets go of Cheryl's arm, so she can follow the doctor, but pauses for a second. "Bruce…Amelia…you guys want to come up or stay here? I'm going up with Cheryl."

"No, Ma. We'll wait down here." Bruce looks up, pulling his cell phone out of his pocket, realizing they're going to be there for a while.

"Yeah, Ma. Imma wait here with Bruce." Amelia looks at her Mom, trying to hold back tears. Hearing the news reconfirms everything. A part of her wants to disappear. So many emotions are running through her mind now.

"OK, then. I'll be upstairs. If you need me, come to the fourth floor, OK? The doctor said the intensive care unit is on the fourth floor." Margaret's looking at both of them.

"OK, Ma." Bruce shakes his head, yes, and Amelia shakes hers too.

"That must have been some serious accident." Bruce is slowly sitting back down, realizing the impact it had on Lynn.

"Yeah." Amelia gulps, looking at Robert. "I'll be right back." Slowly, she walks toward Robert, who's standing with his hands in his pockets, looking at her.

Still fighting back tears, Amelia tries to smile slightly. Robert notices a glaze in her eyes, but just thinks she's upset like everyone else.

"Hey, thanks for texting me and letting me know about Lynn. My Mom and Lynn's Mom are friends."

"You're welcome." Robert looks, sighing. "Man! That was a *horrible* accident and frightening too. I pray to God I never see anything like that ever again."

"You were there?" Amelia looks surprised, feeling the cramps start to worsen in her stomach; they are coming and going.

"Yeah, just after it happened. I was getting something out of my car when Connie came running toward the school, screaming for help. I ran back with her to the scene of the accident, at the light right in front of the parking lot. It was a *really* bad collision. Lynn's car is totaled. I tried to get the doors open, but they were jammed. It was *so* frustrating, looking at Lynn lying unconscious in her car."

Amelia's stomach feels like its sinking more just listening to Robert. She's fighting so hard to conceal the pain.

"We called nine-one-one and after they got there, it took two police officers and a couple of firemen about ten to fifteen minutes to pry Lynn's door open." Robert's shaking his head in disbelief, thinking about it again.

"Wow." Amelia says softly, looking at him with her eyes wide open and her mouth dropped. "I can't even imagine that. I feel *so* bad for her." In her mind, she's thinking all of this probably happened, because of that note she put in Rihanna's purse.

"Yeah, well…I just pray Lynn comes out of the coma." Robert says.

"Did the doctor say he thinks she'll come out of it?" Amelia's voice is beginning to crack a little as she's folding her arms over her chest, leaning forward a little bit. The pain in her stomach is growing stronger. The stress of thinking about what she did is beginning to cause muscle spasms.

"No." Robert's looking at her, noticing something's wrong.

All of a sudden, Amelia's feeling a little dizzy and sick all over her body. "I think I need to sit down."

Really quick, Robert takes her arm and helps her to a chair. A nurse rushes past, brushing up against him by accident.

"Oh! Excuse me, sir!"

"No problem." Robert looks back.

Feeling like she's going to throw up, Amelia leans over her lap in the chair.

"Are you OK?" Robert's looking at her really concerned now.

"I feel sick."

"Wait a sec. Let me get someone." Robert puts his hand on the chair rail, quickly standing up. He sees two nurses standing with a patient a few feet away.

Quickly, Amelia reaches for his arm to stop him. "No! No! Not that kind of sick."

"I don't understand." He looks at her. "You said you feel sick."

For the first time in her life, Amelia feels sorrow and real regret in her heart for something she did wrong. Covering her face in her hands, she cries out loud. "*I'm* the cause of Lynn's accident!"

Robert's shocked by what he hears Amelia say. Looking at her, he sits back down.

The guilt of what she did is to much; she can't take it anymore. It's so great that she can't hold it in. She feels awful knowing all she did to Lynn. With Lynn's life hanging in the balance, the guilt is consuming her. She crying harder and harder.

"Amelia, what do you mean you're the cause of Lynn's accident? You weren't even there." Robert's looking at her stunned, confused by what she's saying.

Bruce looks up from texting on his cell phone, hearing Amelia cry, wondering what's wrong.

"*I'm* the cause of Lynn's accident!" Amelia cries out again, still holding her face in her hands.

"Amelia, calm down. You're not making any sense." Robert gently places his hand on her back.

Bruce gets up and walks over and stands in front of her.

"Amelia! What's wrong?" Bruce has never seen his sister like this before. Instinctively, he knows something is seriously wrong. Before sitting down on the other side of her, Bruce quickly introduces himself to Robert. But, Bruce has a weird look on his face, looking at Robert, wondering what's wrong with Amelia.

"Hey, man, I'm her brother, Bruce."

"I'm Robert. I'm a friend of Amelia's at Lake High." They shake hands quickly.

Bruce looks at Amelia while sitting next to her.

"Sis! What's wrong?"

"I can't take it! I can't take it anymore! I hate myself!" Amelia's sobbing now.

"Sis! What are you talking about?" Now Bruce is really concerned.

"*Hey. Hey.* Calm down now. Tell us what's wrong, Amelia." Robert's gently rubbing her back.

Bruce is totally perplexed by Amelia's outburst of crying. He knows this is *no* time to play.

"Yeah, sis! Calm down and tell us what's wrong."

"I've hurt *so many* people, in the past, and for *no* reason! And now Lynn! I can't take it! I just can't take it anymore!" Sitting back, Amelia wipes her eyes, still weeping, trying to talk. It seems like life has stopped. The only thing she cares about, in this moment, is telling the truth, because she can't take the weight of carrying guilt inside.

"If it wasn't for that note I put in Rihanna's purse, Lynn wouldn't be in this hospital right now or in a coma!" Then, she bends forward again, propping her elbows on her thighs, covering her face with her hands. She's *so* ashamed.

Bruce looks at Robert with one hand up, wondering if he knows anything about this. Robert gives a look back to Bruce like, "I don't know what she's talking about, man."

"What note, Sis?" Bruce leans forward on his lap closer in to Amelia.

"Yeah, what note?" Robert's confounded by this.

Amelia's crying so hard, realizing all of the pain she's caused. She can barely speak. The thought of Lynn losing her life is weighing heavily on her conscience now.

Putting his cell phone back in his jacket pocket, Bruce gets up quickly, and kneels in front of her. "Sis! Look at me. Breathe. It's going to be OK. Calm down."

Amelia looks at him with her eyes full of tears, crying hard.

"I did it, Bruce! I did it, Bruce! It's my fault!"

"Wait a minute! What note are you talking about that you put in somebody's purse, Sis?"

In the intensive care unit, Cheryl receives a call from her parents. "Cheryl! We're in the lobby! Where are you?" Her Mom sounds frantic; she wants to get to Lynn right away.

"Momma?!" Cheryl can barely hear. The reception on the fourth floor is bad.

"Yes, baby! We're here in the lobby!"

"Oh good!" Cheryl takes a deep breath. Instantly, she feels a little relief having her parents at the hospital. "You guys are in the ER?"

"Yes! Yes! Tell us where to go."

"I'm with Lynn in the intensive care unit on the fourth floor. But, *stay* there! I'll be right down to get you!"

"OK, baby!"

Cheryl looks at Margaret, disconnecting the call, taking another deep breath. Mr. Smith went to the rest room. Margaret and Mr. Smith were the first two people to come in Lynn's room with Cheryl. The others are in the family waiting area.

"Margaret, I'll be right back. I've got to go meet my parents. They just got here. They're waiting in the lobby downstairs."

"OK. Don't worry. I'll be right here." Margaret touches her shoulder to console her. Cheryl smiles as best she can, taking a quick look at Lynn. Rushing, she grabs her purse on the chair and leaves. Margaret turns back around toward Lynn who's lying listless on the bed. She looks so peaceful though. It's like God Himself is holding her. She's such a beautiful young woman, Margaret thinks. Tightly, squeezing her hands together under her chin, Margaret prays. A few minutes later, Mr. Smith walks back in the room.

"Hey, how is she, Margaret?"

Margaret looks up, barely smiling, but believing in the Power of the Holy Spirit. It's so sad seeing Lynn in this condition. "She's the same. We just have to keep praying and declare healing over her. The Lord will heal her."

"Amen. Amen. She's going to be just fine. I *know* it." Mr. Smith rests his hand on her pillow, looking down at her. The nurses cleaned up the laceration on the side of her forehead and bandaged it.

"Yes, she is. Well, Cheryl's parents just arrived a few moments ago. She went downstairs to get them. I think I'm going to go check on my two."

"Oh sure. Go right ahead. I'll be up here. In fact, I'll go check on everyone else in the family waiting room really quick while you guys are gone."

Margaret slightly smiles, repositioning her purse on her shoulder. "OK. I'll be right back. Oh! If Cheryl gets back before me, please let her know where I went."

"Sure thing." Mr. Smith smiles.

Downstairs in the emergency waiting room, Bruce and Robert are still trying to find out about the note Amelia's talking about.

"Amelia, please try to calm down some. I know you're upset. But, we don't know what note you're talking about?" Robert's talking gently to try to calm her down.

Slightly lifting her head, Amelia looks up again with tears streaming down her cheeks. Bruce is still kneeling in front of her.

"A few days ago!" She pauses, sniffling. "After ball practice, I found out Lynn was pregnant! I overheard her conversation with Connie in the locker room!" Amelia starts bawling again, because she knows Lynn got pregnant by her Uncle Richard who raped her, not by a guy, and that she used the information against her.

Bruce takes a deep breath, looking at her in amazement. He's quickly starting to put the "pieces of the puzzle" together. Robert looks very surprised.

Catching her breath some, Amelia wipes her eyes again.

"So, before the dance I wrote a note about Lynn being pregnant to give to Rihanna, because I knew she would gossip about it! The note read: 'Lynn Braxton is pregnant.'" She pauses again to wipe her eyes. "When Rihanna wasn't looking, I slipped the note in her purse!" She sobs even more, feeling horrible.

Robert is stunned. He never saw Amelia as the type of person who would do something like this.

Bruce stands up, looking at her, because he's so disappointed. "Amelia!" He's finally putting it all together, remembering her looking for something in her bag before she got out of the car that night.

Robert leans forward, holding his head between his hands. "Why would you do something like that, Amelia?! I thought you were different!"

Amelia stands up and turns around, looking at them both. "I know! I know! I know! It's *all* my fault! *I'm* responsible for Lynn being here!" Amelia screams, crying even harder now, not only feeling completely guilty and ashamed, but embarrassed too. And, to top it all off…embarrassed in front of the guy she likes so much.

Holding her hands out, she screams, "God, *please* forgive me! *Please* forgive me! Forgive me, God!"

Bruce is standing with his wide mouth open, thinking, "She's done it again."

With a perplexed look on his face, Robert stands up after thinking about everything she just said. "So, wait a minute." He says calmly. "Let me try to understand this."

Amelia's standing in front of both of them with her head down, crying profusely, holding her hands around her head. The guilt is too much. And, the stress of it all is taking its toll on her very quickly.

Down the hall, Cheryl's quickly approaching them on her way to the emergency room lobby doors. She came back the same way, because she didn't want to waste time asking a security guard about a different way. She wants to get to her Mom quickly, because she could hear how upset she was on the phone by the tone of her voice.

Amelia screams as Cheryl's walking toward the area where they're standing.

"It's *my* fault! I know…It's *my* fault! *I'm* responsible for Lynn being here!"

Hearing what Amelia's saying, Cheryl stops dead in her footsteps, turning to look at her. For a moment, she can't believe what she's hearing. Her eyes get as big as saucers.

Amelia's bawling and screaming from the deepest part of her soul. "It's my fault! It's my fault! It's my fault! I'm so sorry! Lord, I'm *soooo* sorry!"

Despite his disappointment in hearing this, Robert sees something deeper going on with Amelia. Although, he's really upset about what she's done, he can tell she's *really* hurting.

Bruce sits down, burying his head in his hands. He doesn't know what to do. He's so upset. The thought of consoling Amelia hasn't even entered his mind. All he keeps thinking is that Lynn's lying in a coma, because of something evil his sister did. As Robert reaches over to touch Amelia, Cheryl walks over.

"*What* did you just say?" Cheryl looks at her and says.

Amelia's startled. She recognizes Cheryl's voice and immediately turns around. With her eyes red and puffy, she puts her hands down, feeling completely empty, and faces Cheryl with great humility,…a virtue she's never expressed. In the past, she always let pride get in the way.

"Did I just *hear* what I think I heard?" Cheryl looks confused and very upset. Cheryl's countenance is changing from sorrow to *deep anger* as she's looking at Amelia intently.

"Ms. Braxton!" Amelia looks with tears running down her face. "*Please*, forgive me! *Please* forgive me, please! I did something terrible to Lynn! *Please* forgive me!"

Coming up the hall toward them, Margaret sees Cheryl next to Amelia and Amelia crying. "What's going on?" Margaret's looking baffled, seeing Amelia's face and Bruce looking upset.

Bruce looks up and shakes his head with disappointment. Immediately, Margaret gets a feeling in her gut that something's not right. Robert just stands there, not knowing whether to say something or not by the look on Cheryl's face.

"How can *you* be responsible for Lynn's accident? The medics told Mr. Smith Lynn was in the car by herself. Connie wasn't even in the car. I'm not understanding something here." Cheryl's voice sounds *very* irritated.

"Wait a minute! What is going on, Amelia?!" Margaret steps beside Cheryl, puzzled by what Cheryl's now saying.

Feeling a big lump form in the back of her throat, Amelia gulps. Looking at her Mom now, Amelia cries out, "Ma! I'm so sorry! I did something horrible! I *can't* keep it in anymore! *I'm the one* responsible for Lynn's accident!"

"Wait! Wait! Just wait a minute! Calm down and explain what happened!" Margaret's looking like, "I can't believe what I'm hearing."

Cheryl's getting more upset by the moment, having to remind herself that if it were not for Jesus, she would slap Amelia across her face. Her only child is lying in a hospital bed fighting for her life and Amelia is admitting to be the cause of it. Bruce is looking in amazement, but now he's beginning to see how Amelia's *really* hurting inside.

Looking at her Mom, Amelia tries to calm down some to talk. "Remember the other day after practice when I came to the car ready to go?"

"Yes, go ahead."

"Well, then I said to you I needed to go back to the locker room for a minute?"

"Yes. I remember. Go ahead." Margaret's looking bemused and speaks sternly.

"Well, when I went back into the locker room, I overheard Lynn talking to Connie, telling her she got pregnant by her Uncle who raped her."

"Her Uncle?" Cheryl screams.

"I stood behind the wall, so they couldn't see me." Amelia's almost shivering now, afraid to keep going, but she does.

Cheryl gasps, almost dropping her purse, thinking how all this time that Lynn didn't tell her. Margaret's eyes are huge. Bruce and Robert just stand there, more stunned than before. Amelia didn't tell them Lynn was raped.

"So, what did you do?" Margaret's shocked, but she's trying to keep her cool, so Amelia can continue telling them what happened next.

Amelia looks over at Cheryl. "I wrote…" She can barely talk, because she's stammering now. Every time she thinks about that note, she's ladened with more guilt.

Just then, Connie walks up behind Cheryl and Margaret. Thirsty and exhausted, she came downstairs to buy some water and to look for her purse. Walking towards them to get her purse, she heard what Amelia said and is *very* angry. But, she's more concerned about Ms. Braxton, in the moment, knowing that she didn't know about the pregnancy. So, she quickly interrupts.

"Ms. Braxton, Lynn didn't want to tell you, because she was afraid! Her Uncle said he would hurt her, if she spoke! She said, you would go after him!"

Cheryl gasps again, turning around. Everyone's looking at Connie now. Amelia looks at her, weeping harder by the minute.

Cheryl screams out loud, "that bastard! That bastard! How could Richard *do* such a thing?!!"

Connie looks at her, terrified by the whole evening. "Lynn said, it happened one day while you were still at work. He came by to see you, so she let him in."

"Wait till I get my hands on him!!" Cheryl's steaming inside now. "For touching my baby!! I can't believe he would do such a thing!!"

Seeing the impact on everyone was to hard now for Amelia. Coming clean wasn't easy, but for the first time in her life, she wanted to do the right thing…and, tell the truth, no matter how much it hurt or the cost.

Margaret turns back to Amelia calmly. She realizes everything has quickly become "unhenged" with all that's been said. She's been through so many of Amelia's escapades. By far, none have topped this one. "So, what did you do, Amelia?!!"

Connie gives her a mean look. Cheryl, Bruce, and Robert look back at her, waiting to hear what she's going to say.

Amelia clears her throat, barely able to speak again, because the pain of what she did is now unbearable.

"I wrote a note before the dance to give to Rihanna, the newspaper editor. It said, 'Lynn Braxton is pregnant.' Rihanna's a big gossiper at Lake High. During the dance…" She pauses, looking at Robert." Right before you came up to me…" Then, she looks back at her Mom. "I slipped the note in Rihanna's purse without her noticing. I knew Rihanna got the note, because Monica overheard her talking to her friend Kim about it. They were sitting at a table nearby us." Amelia's sobbing.

"But *why*, Amelia?! Why would you do this?!" Margaret begins to cry. Amelia's done a lot of bad things, but this takes the cake. Enough is enough.

Looking at her Mom, Amelia's feeling more pain now than she felt when her Dad left years ago. With tears in her eyes, in a sorrowful voice, Amelia answers, "I was looking for anything I could use against Lynn, because I didn't want her to be crowned Queen of Lake High. I know, I was wrong! I was wrong! I was wrong! I admit it! It's *my* fault! It's *my* fault!!" Everyone's looking at her in disbelief. Amelia closes her eyes for a moment. "God, *please* forgive me! *Please* forgive me, Gooood!!"

Opening her eyes, she looks around at everyone in a daze and sees great disappointment on their faces. Her heart's pounding; she can barely see. Connie's very angry, but she can see the desperation in Amelia's face. Margaret's crying, but puts her head down for a second and takes a deep breath. Cheryl has a look of shock on her face. She's beyond anger; she's enraged. But, she too can see despondency in Amelia's eyes and doesn't know what else to say at this point, except...

"You should be ashamed of yourself, young lady! How could you do such a *low* thing to someone?! How could you stoop so *loooow*?! Do you not have any love in your heart at all?! If I didn't love the Lord, I swear I'd say some things I *know* I shouldn't say! Let me get out of here! Lord, help me! I've got to go get my parents who've been waiting in the lobby for me!" Cheryl loves Jesus and understands the ramifications of sinning in anger. Withholding herself, Cheryl turns abruptly and leaves, shaking her head, throwing one hand up in the air saying, "Lord, help me!! Help me, Lord!!"

Bruce looks at Amelia and for the first time, he recognizes something in her he's never seen before...real remorse. Robert looks too, but doesn't know what to say. Despite his disappointment in her, he rises above it to try to hug, Amelia. It's obvious she's struggling with great pain inside from what she's done that's real, not fake. Amelia can't take the guilt, shame, pain and embarassment anymore. The feeling is overwhelming; it reached its peak in her heart like water in a full bucket spilling over. Placing one hand over her heart, looking dazed in her eyes at everyone, Amelia darts as fast as she can down the hallway.

Chapter Thirteen

Stopping right in front of the elevators after running so fast down the hallway, Amelia quickly pushes the UP button. Beep. An elevator appears as the light to go up turns green. Rushing inside, she pushes the number 4 button several times, hoping the elevator will close fast. Still crying, she reaches in her purse to pull out a tissue. The elevator beeps going past the first floor.

"God, *please* forgive me! *Forgive me,* Lord!"

The elevator beeps again, going past the second floor. In a frenzy, she wipes her eyes, almost shaking, looking at the numbers of each floor as the elevator passes them. Beep. The elevator passes the third floor. Anxiously, Amelia waits for the elevator to beep at the arrival of the fourth floor. The elevator doors open. Dashing off the elevator, Amelia runs down the hallway. A nurse walking toward her from the other end yells, "Miss! Miss! There's no running in the hallways!" Hearing the nurse up ahead, Amelia stops running right in front of one of the patient's room.

"Please! I'm looking for Lynn Braxton's room?"

"Well, you're standing right in front of her room."

Shaking, Amelia nods her head and slowly turns to her left. The nurse proceeds to the nurses station.

Amelia looks into the room. Lynn is lying peacefully on the bed. Different kinds of machines surround her. Monitors are everywhere and lots of tubes are connected to her body. Slowly, Amelia walks toward Lynn's bed. The room's cold. Lynn is covered with lots of white blankets folded neatly over her body. There's one pillow in back of her, slightly propping up her head. Amelia's surprised to see so many machines and computers in the room. She's never visited anyone in the intensive care unit before.

Getting down on her knees, Amelia raises her arms up to place her elbows on top of the bed. For a second, she lowers her head some, then puts her hands in prayer position and glances to the right. There's Lynn's hand lying close to her. The nurses laid Lynn's arms along the side of her body over the covers. She looks at the IV attached to the top of Lynn's left hand and the clear bandage covering the needle. Still crying, Amelia gently grabs Lynn's fingers.

Thinking about everything, Amelia sobs with her head held down over the covers, praying.

"God, I repent for what I did to Lynn. Please forgive me, Father. I sinned badly. Giving Rihanna that note was wrong, God. It was evil. And now, because of what I did, Lynn is here fighting for her life. Please, God let Lynn live! She didn't deserve any of this. Jesus, help her! I regret, Lord, with all my heart, what I've done and how I hurt Lynn and her mother and my family and friends. I wasn't thinking about Lynn, Lord! I was thinking about myself!" She cries loudly, *"I was only thinking of myself, Lord! I was selfish! I know now…"* She pauses, shaking her head. *"I know now, Lord, that all of the things I did were wrong and for all of the wrong reasons. From cyberbullying Lynn on Twitter, setting her up for Mrs. Stephens' stolen purse, to the endless nasty comments…Lynn, never did anything wrong to me, Lord…even to the note I gave to Rihanna, Lord. It was all wrong! All Lynn ever did was try to be nice to me. When I spoke in a nastAmey way to her, she never spoke back to me that way, Lord! I was the*

evil one, Lord. Everything I did was wrong! I never knew it all could come to this! God, please forgive me!" She pauses again, weeping uncontrollably with her head still down on Lynn's bed.

Amelia doesn't know that everyone downstairs saw her walk into Lynn's room when they got off the elevator at the other end of the hallway. She was dazed and in a rush to find Lynn's room. They ran behind her to try follow her, but couldn't catch her and ended up going in a different direction. Even, Mr. Smith, Mr. Manning, and Connie's parents saw Amelia enter Lynn's room from the family waiting area.

There everyone stands quietly in the doorway in utter amazement, hearing Amelia pray out loud. They were all at the door, because Mr. Smith, Mr. Manning and Connie's parents saw Cheryl, her parents, Margaret, Bruce, Robert and Connie walking down the hallway fast to get to Lynn's room. They wanted to be sure everything was alright.

Amelia kneeling beside the bed, holding Lynn's hand, weeps out loud. *"Lord, I repent. Please forgive me! Please, God! Please! I will never do evil things like I did before! Forgive me! I give my heart to You, Jesus! Please help me! Come into my heart, Jesus! I'm Yours! I believe You're the Son of God and that God rose You from the dead! Lord, come into my heart and have Your way in my life! Be my Lord, Jesus! I'm so sorry for what I did to Lynn, Lord!"* She pauses, crying. *"Please, let her live! Please, Lord!"*

In the doorway, Cheryl and Margaret stand with everyone else, astonished, hearing Amelia pour her heart out to God. Margaret is overwhelmed inside, seeing her daughter for the first time truly repent.

Feeling Amelia's agony, Margaret begins to walk toward her when Cheryl touches her, whispering, "let me."

Margaret stops, looking at Cheryl's face soften now, having heard Amelia pray from her heart. Cheryl whispers again, "if God can extend me mercy, I wouldn't be His, If I can't do the same thing."

Margaret smiles with tears in her eyes and nods. Everybody looks on as Cheryl quietly walks over to Amelia.

"Lord God!" Amelia pauses again, wiping her eyes. "My Mom always says that You will forgive us, if we forgive others, and that You will *never* leave us, nor forsake us. *Help me,* Lord God! I *need* You, Jesus in my life, right now! I *need* You, Jesus! I realize now, I *can't*...I just *can't* live without You, Lord! I see You in Lynn all those times she treated me so kind! I want you to be my Savior too! Lord, don't let her stay like this! Make Lynn come out of this coma, and I *promise* You, Lord, to serve forever!"

Quickly glancing back at Margaret, Cheryl puts her hands up to her mouth, almost crying out loud. She doesn't want to interrupt this endearing, heartfelt moment between Amelia and the Lord. They all could hear the conviction in Amelia's heart. She can't believe what she's hearing almost...*total regret* and *sorrow* from Amelia. All of the anger she was holding in her heart toward Amelia for hurting Lynn has faded away like a distant memory.

Margaret's standing in the doorway with the others, holding her hands together under her chin in prayer form. Tears of joy are streaming down her face. This is the moment she and Nana have been praying for. Not only did she witness her daughter truly repent, but she watched her give her life to Christ.

Just as Cheryl is about to place her hand on Amelia's shoulder, she sees Lynn's hand in Amelia's. Then, the miraculous happens...Lynn slightly squeezes Amelia's hand. Feeling Lynn move her hand, Amelia quickly lifts her head and looks in astonishment at Lynn's hand and then, at Lynn.

Cheryl's mouth drops. She's so shocked that she waits a second to see if what she saw was real moment.

Amelia shouts with tears running down her face still. "Lord! You did it! You did it! *Thank You, Jesus! Thank You, Jesus!*" Looking at Lynn's hand in hers, she's amazed by the power of prayer. God answered her.

Lynn tightens her grip in Amelia's hand. Amelia shouts again. "Thank You, Lord! Thank You, Lord!"

Seeing this miracle take place before her eyes, Cheryl shouts as she touches Amelia's shoulder at the same time…"Lord, thank You! Thank You for waking my Lynn up!"

Shocked, Amelia turns quickly around, not knowing everyone was at the door watching her. Margaret rushes over to her. Amelia gets up and runs into her Mom's arms. They embrace tightly, rocking slowly from side to side.

"It's OK, baby! It's OK, baby! God is so Good! God is so Good!" Margaret's repeating herself, holding Amelia tight in her arms, rubbing her hair. Amelia hugs her back, feeling relieved.

Still crying, Amelia's so glad to be in her mother's arms.

"Yes, Ma! He *is*, Ma!" Amelia cries.

Cheryl yells excitedly, "call the nurse! Call the nurse, Mr. Smith! Thank You, Jesus! Thank You, Jesus!" Cheryl's standing on the side of Lynn's bed.

"Mom," Lynn whispers, opening her eyes.

"Oh, baaaaaby! Yes!"

Cheryl's leaning over stroking, gently the side of Lynn's face, careful of all of the machines around her.

"I'm right here, baby! I'm right here! You're going to be just fine! The *Holy Spirit* is here, baby!"

Bruce and Robert walk over to Amelia and Margaret, placing their hand on Amelia's back.

"It's going to be alright, Sis." Bruce looks at his Mom, smiles, and puts his arms around both of them. Bruce and his Mom both know something changed in Amelia for the good.

Feeling the warmth of the Presence of the Holy Spirit in Lynn's room, Amelia looks at her Mom. "Ma, forgive me."

Margaret looks directly in her eyes, smiling. "I already have, baby. I already have."

"No, Ma. Forgive me for not being the daughter you raised me to be, for all of the horrible things I did, and for putting our home in danger. I'm sorry, Ma, for disappointing you and hurting you."

Smiling wider now, Margaret says, "I have, baby…over and over again."

Remembering the talk they had that special day about the king and the unforgiving servant and forgiveness before basketball practice, Amelia smiles with her eyes puffing from crying. "I get it, Ma. I get it."

"Thank You, Jesus!" Bruce says and smiles, still hugging them. And, they all chuckle.

Chapter Fourteen

Three and a half months after Lynn's accident...

"Are you ready?" In the back of the stage, Amelia's smiling at Lynn and Connie.

"Ready as I'll ever be!" Lynn's smiling, waving her crutches up in the air.

"Praise God!" Connie looks, smiling back.

"Then, let's go!" Amelia leads the way onto the stage.

Today is a *big* day. They look so beautiful and radiant.

Standing, everybody in the school auditorium is cheering loudly, as Amelia, Lynn, and Connie walk across the stage together. The place is packed. People are clapping and chanting.

"Lynn! Lynn! Lynn! Lynn! Lynn! Lynn! Lynn!"

The cheers are so overwhelming, Lynn almost cries. Reaching the podium where Mr. Smith's standing, Amelia looks in amazement at how many people gathered today for the event. "Wow! God is *so* good!" Amelia says.

Lynn's smiling, looking at all of the people in the audience.

Connie's eyes are wide open. "He *sure* is!"

Smiling at the girls, Mr. Smith turns to look to the audience, pausing before he speaks. "Today…is a *very* special day! First, we'd like to thank God for Lynn's speedy recovery!"

Some people are shouting all sorts of things in excitement, "Yeaaaaah! Praise God! Glory! We love you, Lynn!"

Mr. Smith continues. "And, thank you all for celebrating this momentous day with us. Myself and the faculty at Lake High would like to thank a *very* special, young lady, Lynn Braxton, for all of her hard work and dedication in helping fellow students. Lynn has a big heart. She loves to help people and we appreciate that about her so much. Lynn's given hours of her time to help not only students at Lake High, but faculty also. She's a smart, beautiful, selfless young woman who loves Jesus. And, she represents what the core values of Lake High are all about." Mr. Smith pauses. The crowd cheers.

"Thank you, Lynn. Your hard work is much appreciated by all of us at Lake High. We all will certainly miss you around here." The crowd applauds.

"This past May, as many of you know, Lynn was unable to attend graduation, due to a major accident she was involved in. But, we thank *God*, because He brought her out of the coma she was in and is healing her! God made a way out of no way! Only God could do it and He did!"

"Yeeeeeessss! Yes, He did! Thank You, Lord!" Cheryl shouts from the audience.

"And, yes! I said it! God! I said *God*…made a way and is healing her! Glory to God! Hallelujah!" Mr. Smith's standing proudly, giving God glory for Lynn's miraculous healing.

"Amen! Amen, Mr. Smith! That's right!" Margaret shouts.

A woman behind Cheryl and Margaret yells, "I *know* that's right, Mr. Smith! Preach!"

Picking up the diploma laying on top of the podium, Mr. Smith pulls the microphone inward a bit more.

"So, without no further ado, I would like to hereby declare this day, Lynn Braxton, a senior graduate of Lake High!"

The audience goes wild. All of Lynn's family, friends, and people from the community who came to support her are shouting.

"Yeeees!! Go, Lynn!! Wooooooo hoooooo!!"

Cheryl looks over at her parents, smiling, clapping her hands. "My baby *made* it!!"

Margaret's clapping, because she's so happy to be able to share this moment with Cheryl and her parents. "Congratulations, Lynn!!" Margarets shouts.

Putting her arm around Cheryl's shoulder, Margaret squeezes it and smiles at her. They look at each other for a brief moment, remembering the night God brought Lynn out of the coma.

Clapping and smiling, Amelia and Connie take a step back some for the photographers to take photos as Mr. Smith hands Lynn her diploma. Several reporters from local news stations are standing at the base of the stage, recording. New specials on Lynn's story are being aired live. Cameras are flashing and people are still cheering loudly.

Stepping back to the podium, Mr. Smith grabs the microphone. "Now, we're not done! Can I get everyone to quiet down for just a moment, please? We're not done." Mr. Smith smiles. We have another very special announcement to make!" He says.

Mr. Smith looks at Amelia. "You can get the box from Mr. Manning now."

Mr. Manning quickly walks on the stage holding a beautiful gold box. Taking it, Amelia smiles. Mr. Manning winks at her and says "you got this," then walks to the side of the stage. Lynn looks at Amelia with a slight smile and a surprised look on her face whispering to Connie, "What's she doing?"

Amelia smiles wider, looking at Lynn, but doesn't say anything yet.

In the audience, Cheryl and Margaret look at each other, wondering what's in the gold box. They're surprised too.

Connie stands on the other side of Lynn, just smiling, because she knows what's in the gold box.

Mr. Smith looks at Amelia. "Amelia, you can take the mic now," he says.

Lynn's squeezing her eyebrows a little, looking at Mr. Smith and back at Amelia, really curious.

Taking a deep breath, Amelia steps towards the podium. "Yes, sir." You can hear a pin drop in the audience. Everyone's wondering what's in the gold box.

Adjusting the microphone, Amelia stands looking at everyone. The camera men from the local news stations zoom in on her face as she begins to speak.

"During our senior year here, I wanted to be Lake High's Queen, so bad that I decided I would do anything for it, even if it cost more than what I could imagine. Well…" She pauses. "It almost did. My actions almost cost someone's life and that person is Lynn. When I knelt down beside the hospital bed to pray the night Lynn was taken into intensive care, something changed inside of me. I was desparate for God to help me at this point. I glanced, and saw her hand lying next to me with a needle tapped in it. I prayed like I never prayed before. I couldn't bare seeing her almost lifeless." Remembering again, tears form in Amelia's eyes.

"You know…we do selfish things sometimes, thinking more about ourselves than others. We don't realize in our pursuit for greed…" Amelia looks at the audience with sincerity…"what the impact of our actions will be on someone else's life until its to late. This isn't good. I like many others needed to know that the consequences for evilness are grave. The "stakes" for competing against one another are high as the truth of what's really the cause inside people who do things like I did is hidden. I was a master almost at what I did, like many others who play wicked games with people." She pauses again, sustaining the courage to speak the truth.

"In some aspects it's okay to compete, but for good reasons, not bad ones. To think that one bad act can alter the life of another or even take it away forever…is terrifying. It was for me as I knelt down on my knees that night. When you do evil things to others…you're so consumed with it that you don't have the capacity in your heart to consider another; evil in the heart doesn't allow you to. The feelings and well-being of the other person you're trying so hard to hurt is the last thing you even think of, because you're the only person evil makes you think about." Amelia clears her throat.

"The sight of Lynn on that bed, made me realize I wasn't who I thought I was trying to become…which is someone I wouldn't want to associate with today. God caused me to see myself in a way I probably never would have. He allowed me to come to the end of myself to realize how much I needed Him and that I couldn't have a real life without His Son, Jesus. So, only God could help me that night and He did." Taking a deep breathe, Amelia's glancing at Mr.

Smith. Mr Smith nods with an encouraging look to continue. He
knows this is a big moment for her, as well as, Lynn. Mr. Smith has
become her Pastor, giving counsel in the spiritual things of God, so
she can grow in the Lord.

"I gave my life to Christ that night and it felt right in me." She
clears her throat again. Anyone who knew Amelia before could see
an amazing change in her; she even looked different.

"I never believed in miracles, because I was so full of myself
that there was no room for the Lord. But, that night I witnessed one
when I gave my heart to Jesus. I plead for God to *forgive* me and to
keep Lynn alive. The pain was unbearable. And, I knew God
answered my prayer when Lynn squeezed my hand. That was the
first sign that she was waking up and moments later she did."

"Praise the Lord!!" Someone shouts from the audience who
cheers. Lynn is loved by so many.

Looking at Lynn with a slight smile and tears in her eyes,
Amelia looks back at the audience again. She's preparing now for the
big moment of unveiling what's in the gold box.

"Lynn laid on that hospital bed with lots of monitors hooked
up to her body. She was in a coma." Amelia cries a little. Looking
downward for a second, Lynn's crying a little more, remembering
what God did for her…she's full of gratitude…but, also for the
beautiful witness of what she knows that only the Holy Spirit can
do…change the heart of a sinner.

With tears rolling down their faces, Cheryl and Margaret look
at one another and hug each other tightly. Connie looks at Amelia,
slightly smiling with tears in her eyes as if to say, "thank You, Jesus."
Mr. Smith just smiles with great joy in his heart seeing the
redemptive Power of God's Love at work.

Amelia looks down for a minute to gather herself again. *"Through Lynn,* God taught me what I didn't know…what love and forgiveness are really about, and I'm *so* grateful. Thank You, Lord. I didn't know what I was missing out on. I thought I was okay, not *understanding* what I was missing…God's love. God is love and I experienced that in Lynn. This *whole* situation has taught me *a lot,* but more than anything that I'm *somebody* in Christ. God can take anything bad and turn it around for His Good. Look at me." Amelia pauses again, fighting back tears, so she can continue to speak clearly.

"Like I said, I wanted to be Queen of Lake High badly, but for all the wrong reasons. But, thank God that's all changed. When I think"…Amelia pauses again, more tears are flowing now. This is the moment of revealing what's in the gold box. But, it's also the expression of God's Love in a heart that was once compelled by the pursuit of evil that brought about so much pain…"when I think of being Queen of Lake High…I think of Lynn, she's an example of one in every way."

People in the audience are crying and cheering. Cameras are flashing and news reporters continue recording this precious moment live. Mr. Smith's standing next to Lynn and Connie, watching, so proudly.

With tears in her eyes, Lynn takes two steps with her crutches towards Amelia, giving her a big hug. Amelia hugs her back tightly as they weep with their heads laying on each other's shoulders. God's Love is so intense; they hug for a few moments.

Then, wiping her eyes and gently smiling at Lynn, Amelia's reaching inside the gold box to pull out the beautiful gold crown with emeralds and diamonds Mr. Smith had custom made, especially for Lynn. Lynn's mouth drops as her eyes get wide. She is so surprised.

Connie's clapping and crying for her best friend. The audience gasps at the beauty of the crown. No one knew what was in the gold box, except Connie, Mr. Manning, and Amelia and now everyone else. Mr. Smith smiles lovingly. Lynn deserves it.

Then smiling, with tears in her eyes, Amelia places the crown on Lynn's head. "I love you, Lynn."

Lynn hugs her again crying, "I love you too, sister."

Moved by the Holy Spirit in her heart, Lynn takes Amelia's hand in hers and holds it up high in the air above their heads! The whole auditorium stands and cheers, clapping loudly.

"Yaaaaah! Alright! Praise God! Thank You, Jesus! Yeeeeah!"

The rest of the faculty comes on stage, joining Mr. Smith, Mr. Manning and the girls. Everyone's clapping. Margaret and Cheryl look at each other, smiling, barely able to see one another through their tears.

In the midst of all of the excitement, from the stage, Amelia spots Robert standing in the front row. He blows her a kiss and smiles, clapping his hands. Bruce standing right next to him, winks at her, clapping his hands. Uncle Joe holds up five tickets for L.A. and smiles. Faith smiles, giving her two thumbs up. And, Nana and Aunt Mable just smile, pointing up to Heaven, nodding their heads.

Still smiling and clapping, Connie leans over, putting her arm around Lynn's shoulder. "Look at what God did!"

Looking at Connie, Lynn smiles. "Yup!" Then, looking at Amelia, Lynn smiles saying, "we can do all things...through Christ."

Two months after Lynn's graduation...

It is evening. Nana and Mable just finished eating dinner at Nana's place. Nana cooked black-eyed peas with rice, cabbage, turkey wings, and homemade cranberry sauce. Mable brought homemade bread pudding with chantilly cream. They decided to leave the dishes on the table and take their dessert out back on the porch.

Rocking in her favorite chair, eating her dessert, Nana smiles, looking out into the garden. "So much has changed since everybody last saw each other at that graduation event for Lynn."

Mable grins, sitting across from Nana on the sofa, nodding her head. "Amelia sure has come a long way, hasn't she?"

"Yes, she has. You know, sometimes we don't see the fruit of our labor right away in our children or that what we preach even *matters*, 'cause they might get off track in the process. But, if we raise them up in the ways of the Lord, there's *always* room to come home."

"So true, and that's exactly what Amelia did."

"Thank God. Everyone's doing well now. Amelia finally decided to take the full scholarship to play ball at Spelman College, 'cause she wants to be near home. She's so excited. Margaret is so proud of her, and glad that she and Bruce are in Atlanta. And, I'm so happy that Margaret hasn't had any problems with high blood pressure for months now. Bruce is still at Morehouse, but quit his part-time job to start his own computer business. Margaret's not sure that's not going to get in the way of his studies, but these days kids think they can do it all. Margaret's worried, but he's a smart young man. With both kids in college now, I sure would love to see Margaret marry again soon. But, this time…the right man. Who knows, maybe Margaret's conversations with Mr. Smith might turn into something more. I *think* they might have potential."

"Whaaat? Mr. Smith and Margaret talk?" Mable stops eating her bread pudding for a moment. "You know, I *thought* I saw him looking at her when we were at that event."

Nana chuckles. "At least we'll have *one* family wedding to go to soon, 'cause Joe popped the question after he finished his last CD."

"Yes! We can do the Electric Slide!"

Nana takes a quick look at Mable. "Mable, they don't do the Electric Slide anymore, Hun."

Mable frowns, finishing up the bread pudding.

"Anyway, Charlie's still working on Wall Street, but he's learned the importance of family now. I was so glad he came home for my birthday, and he'll be back for Christmas too. And, that Blake is still locked up. Glad he can't see my grandbaby no more! She wouldn't give him the time of day anyway, even if he tried."

"Praise the Lord for that!" Mable says.

"And, Robert...I like Robert for Amelia, Mable. He's such a nice guy and he loves the Lord. He goes to Morehouse like Bruce. He and Amelia are still talking. And, Lynn made the decision to start UCLA in January, instead of September to give her leg a little more time to heal. The world sure could use a few more young women like Lynn. And, Cheryl, she decided to move to California to be with Lynn. It was hard for her to bring charges against her brother. She did the right thing though by moving."

Finishing her delicious bread pudding, Mable looks over at Nana, smiling now, happy to hear all of the good news. "My, my, my! So much good news. Thank You, Lord Jesus!"

Nana takes another bite of her dessert and puts it down on the small table next to the rocking chair.

"Yeees, Mable. Looking back on everything, Amelia had to learn what we all have to learn…people *think* they forgive, but *real* forgiveness comes from real love in our hearts. Having real love is having the Presence of Christ in us, and it's *His Presence* that establishes real love. We can be mad for a minute, but madness can't stay in us, *not* if we have Christ, 'cause forgiveness flows from real love. We have to love first to forgive."

THE END

About the Author

Apostle Sabrina Maria Evans, a highly spiritual, anointed and gifted woman of God, is the founder and chief operating officer of Hearts, LLC, which is a global movement. She is also the founder and president of Passion for Purpose, LLC, which is a media, coaching and mentoring company. Apostle Evans is a new breed of warrior on the scene—she wars for the nations and particularly women who are seeking peace, freedom, healing, authenticity and most of all intimacy with the Holy Spirit, Jesus and the Father.

The Biblical Training Workshops that Apostle Evans writes with the Holy Spirit for partnering churches experience spontaneous, life-changing, creative miracles of all kinds! Apostle Evans is gifted in the areas of art (she was born an artistic savant), ministers deliverance and healing to those that are emotionally, physically, and sexually abused. As a seasoned prophet and seer, Apostle Evans often sees maladies inside of people's bodies in exact detail. To date, Hearts, LLC has witnessed hundreds of miracles and deliverances. However, the major message of Apostle Evans' focus remains the heart!

Apostle Evans knows how to touch the heart of Father God through praise and worship, and change atmospheres by ushering in the Glory of the Lord through pure worship from the heart. She has had numerous heavenly visitations, meetings with angels, and best of all, meetings and many personal visitations with Jesus Christ! Over the years her worship has intensified as has the visitations from our Lord Jesus.

An accomplished writer, Apostle Evans, is the author of "Love First to Forgive" an awesome Christian fiction novel that was downloaded in her spirit by the Holy Spirit who is the true author.

She authored two children books, "The New Covenant for Kids," "God's Salvation, Jesus the Mediator" (audio only) and co-authored "Words from the Low Place," (a short story about her life and experience with abuse). "Peace and Freedom" is her most recent book on identifying and defeating deception from false witnesses in personal relationships that damage and destroy.

Prayer of Salvation

Lord God,
I believe Jesus Christ is the Son of God.
I believe Jesus Christ died to save my soul.
I believe You, God, raised Jesus Christ from the dead.
I confess that Jesus Christ is the Lord of my Life.
I declare, from this day on, Jesus Christ, reigns in my heart.
I believe this by faith.
I believe that I have a new life in Christ now.
My old life is gone.
As of this moment, I'm living my new life in Christ.
I am one with, Jesus Christ, forever and have eternal life.

If you prayed this prayer and meant it with your heart, you are now born again and a new person in Christ. Welcome to God's family!

Made in the USA
Columbia, SC
12 July 2020